EVERYTHING I KNEW TO BE TRUE

RAYNA YORK

Published by Toad Tree Press.

167 Terrace View NE

Medicine Hat Alberta TIC-OA4

Publishers Note

This book is a work of fiction. Names, characters, places, and incidents are either the product of the author's imagination or used fictionally, and any resemblance to actual persons, living or dead, business establishments, events or locales is entirely coincidental.

ISBN 978-1-9990951-0-9 (paperback)

ISBN 978-1-9990951-1-6 (ebook)

Cover design by Rocio Martin Osuna

For the real Tony and Anna, who emigrated from Trieste, Italy in 1957 and have been married for sixty-two years. You are loved by your family beyond measure.

1

I STARE in numb silence at my mother's casket, waiting to be lowered into its final resting place. Everything happened so fast, I've hardly had a chance to process it all.

A spilt second image of Mom sitting at our tiny kitchen table flashes through my mind—that's where we'd catch up on the daily grind. She had so many outrageous customers, Maria's antics, her daily goof-ups, but I guess that comes with being a waitress for thirteen years.

I know she tried hard to hide it from me—I can see that now. It started with her being tired all the time and then throwing up constantly—the weight loss was staggering. When she finally went to the doctor, they diagnosed her with stage IV pancreatic cancer. They gave her three to six weeks to live. Her name was Allora, and I still can't believe she's gone.

"Cassie?" Roxanne gently places a hand on my shoulder. "Are you ready?"

I look around, momentarily confused. There were so many people here. Where did they go?

I guess I've been pretty out of it the last couple of days, which is understandable considering. I swallow hard against the emotional lump that's jammed in my throat and tell her I need another minute.

"Okay," she replies solemnly. "I'll wait for you by the car. Take your time."

There's only a marker now. I guess the headstone comes later; at least that's what they tell me.

I leave for California tonight. Mom made arrangements for me to live with her closest friend—a person I never even knew existed until two weeks ago. I'd always assumed that Mom had grown up in New York—it's where her parents lived before they died. Apparently, I was wrong.

I begged her to let me stay here with Luigi and Maria—they're like family. At least then *some* things would have remained the same. Instead, she insisted I live with Roxanne and her family.

We drive back to the apartment so I can get my stuff. "I won't be long," I tell Roxanne, leaving her at the door looking bewildered. I feel bad being thrust on her like this. She doesn't even *know* me, and now I'm going to live with her. She seems fine with it, but still.

I can't believe how empty the place seems. Yeah, all our stuff's gone, but it's more than that. Mom was my best friend—my *only* friend. She made this dinky little hole-in-the-wall a home, made every day special no matter how hard things got—and there were some pretty tough times. How am I going to start over without her?

I step in to the tiny sunroom and stare out one of the many windows with my arms wrapped tightly around me. Mom surprised me on my thirteenth birthday when she turned it into an art studio. She built shelves and lined them with jars of paintbrushes, pens, and pencils. She even placed an easel in the corner next to the wall of windows, with blank canvases stacked next to it. I know it cost her a lot of money—money we didn't have to spare—but it was an amazing gift. Art was everything to me.

Now the walls are bare, the colorful murals painted over with coats of white paint, easily erasing all that I was—all that we were.

"Cassie, honey. I'm sorry, but we really have to go if we're going to make our flight."

I look over my shoulder at Roxanne, holding my small suitcase in her hands. "Yeah. Okay." I cross the room and pick up the backpack sitting at her feet, sling it over my shoulder, and take one last look around before closing the door on the only life I've ever known.

We got to Roxanne's house around one in the morning. I slept on and off through the flight, but I'm still wiped out.

As we pull into a garage, the inner door opens, and a man stands waiting. "Cassie, this is Jeff, my husband," Roxanne says as we step out of the vehicle.

"Hi. Um . . . thanks for letting me stay with you." The words sound lame, but it's the best I've got.

"We're so glad to have you with us." He walks down the few steps from the doorway and takes the suitcase from Roxanne, giving her a look like, *is everything okay?* She nods her head. "I'll go put this in your room," he says. "It's right across from

Cody's. He's asleep now. We'll introduce you two in the morning."

"Sure, no problem." We used to play together as kids—not that I remember, but I also don't remember living in California. Apparently, I was four when we left—one of the many tidbits of information I've received recently.

"Let me give you a quick tour," Roxanne says, motioning for me to follow her.

From the garage we walk through a laundry room, which opens up into a large kitchen, dining slash family room with the biggest TV I've ever seen.

"The refrigerator is always stocked—Cody eats like a horse. There are snacks in the cupboards. Please help yourself to whatever you want." I follow her past the family room down a hallway. "The bathroom's here." She flips the light on and off, before continuing down the hall. "Cody has an en suite, so you don't have to feel uncomfortable about sharing a bathroom—although, it does double as a guest bathroom, so you might not want to leave your stuff lying about," she jokes awkwardly.

Yeah, okay, I reply in my head.

"And here's your room. I hope you like it," she says, her voice tinged with a cautious enthusiasm. "There's lots of closet space and a dresser for your things." She demonstrates by opening and closing some of the drawers, then steps into a walk-in closet, turning on the light.

I wait by the door, feeling like an intruder in somebody else's life. She turns to look at me. I see the mournful pity in her eyes, but I'm too dazed to care. "Look," she says brightly, pointing to a desk with a laptop on it, "we picked up a MacBook Pro for you. We figured you would need it for school."

I nod my head indifferently. Seeing her smile drop a little makes me feel guilty. I know her kindness is an attempt at normalcy, but there's nothing normal about this situation, so it's hard to know how to respond appropriately. I mean, it's not like this is some exciting new experience that's only temporary. This is the rest of my life.

"I'll show you the rest of the house in the morning, okay?" She walks toward me. "You must be exhausted."

"Yeah. I'm pretty wiped out."

"Okay, then. If there's nothing else you need . . . I'll head off to bed and let you get some sleep."

"Sure. No, I'm good."

She steps in and hugs me. I'm slow to respond, making it awkward. "It is so wonderful to finally meet you," she says, moving toward the door, then turns to face me. "I wish it wasn't under these circumstances, and I know you must have lots of questions, but it can wait till you're ready. In the meantime, we'll try to get you settled into your new life as best we can."

"Sure. Sounds good."

She shuts the door behind her, giving me privacy and a small sense of relief for the first time today. I've reached my destination. I have a room with a door to shut everything out—a safe haven when I need one.

I am so tired. My eyes drift toward my suitcase. Eventually, my feet take the necessary steps toward it. It's hard to believe my entire life is in there. It's not like I have much for clothes, never have, and I threw out all my art supplies.

I pull out a big T-shirt and change. Grabbing my toothbrush, I head to the bathroom, passing Cody's door on the way. It's going to be weird living with men in the house. Well, Cody isn't exactly a man, I guess . . . I don't know, but still

. . . his room is across the hall from mine, and he's my age. My dad died when I was little and there's never been a man in my mom's life or mine. It's going to be weird.

2

I WAKE up to sunlight blasting me in the eyes. For a moment, I'm confused where I am. I shield my eyes and look around. It all comes back.

I stumble toward the window, stubbing my toe on the desk before finally lowering the blinds. As the shade falls, my brain briefly registers a kaleidoscope of colors—a complete contrast to the blackness I feel in my heart. Man, this sucks.

With the blinding light diffused, I take it all in—the large room that's half the size of our old apartment, the light smoky-blue walls, white furniture, and fluffy white duvet with fine blue stitching, rumpled on the enormous bed.

It's so rich looking.

I really have to pee. Rubbing the sleep out of my eyes, I open the door and walk into something hard.

What the hell?

Realizing I've braced my hands against a *naked* male chest, I jump back, mortified. "Oh . . . *Aaaa* . . . I—I'm so sorry," I sputter. "I didn't see you."

"Cassie? Hey, sorry." He runs his hand through a tangled mess of dark hair while appraising me. "You sure look different from when I used to pull your braids. I'm Cody."

As I look up into his dark-lashed blue eyes, I feel a sudden punch in the gut as memories and faces—some familiar, some not—rush through my mind, making me feel lightheaded. My knees suddenly go weak, and I take a step back to balance myself.

Cody takes hold of my arm. "You okay?" He stares at me, looking concerned.

How could I have forgotten him?

"Cassie?" He gives me a little shake. "Are you okay? Should I go get Mom?"

"No. I'm fine . . . just a little out of it."

I find myself fixating on his eyes again. Realizing I'm gawking, I quickly drop my gaze to a pair of black briefs and the bulge within.

Oh my god! He's practically naked!

I instantly direct my focus to the floor. That's when I notice the only thing covering *me* is a baggy T-shirt. My cheeks turn flaming red. "Uh . . . nice to meet you," I say, backing up toward the bathroom, pulling my T-shirt down as far as it will go. "Um . . . I need to go, and . . . uh, get some clothes on." I smile sheepishly at him. "Well, I have clothes on," I giggle nervously, "but I mean, more clothes . . . 'cause I . . . uh, don't have much on." Cody looks at my bare legs and grins while I babble. "Maybe you should do the same, since you don't have anything on either, well you do, but . . . oh hell." I turn and move quickly to the bathroom, shutting the door behind me. Leaning against it, I drop my head into my hands and give it a shake. What the *hell* was that?

I giggled.

I don't giggle. And I don't do the whole timid, shy, girly thing either. I involuntarily shudder at the repulsiveness of my actions.

I stare at my reflection. *Uck!* I look like crap. My eyes are bloodshot and hollow with dark circles underneath.

I strip down and get into the steaming shower, doing my best to forget the encounter-of-the-worst-kind. By the time I dry off, brush my teeth, and put my clothes back on, the distraction by mortification is gone and the emptiness returns. I sigh loudly and slump my shoulders.

I open the door and peek out. No Cody. I run to my room, shutting myself in.

Safe.

After throwing on a pair of baggy gym shorts and a clean Yankees T-shirt, I reach into the outside pocket of my backpack to fish out a hair tie. I take it to the full-length mirror that's on the wall next to my dresser and begin the mindless process of pulling my hair into a ponytail. When I'm done, I stare past my reflection into the unfamiliar room behind me.

Full-scale reality hits me like a wrecking ball, putting me to the floor. On hands and knees, I force air in and out in tiny gasps as tears stream down my face. I curl into a ball over my knees and try for a full breath. The position helps, and after several more attempts, I'm able to fill my lungs completely.

Mom, I can't do this.

"Cassie?" Roxanne's voice wakes me from outside my door. I lift my head from a tear-soaked pillow and look around. "Can I come in?" She sounds concerned.

I must have crawled into bed and fallen asleep. I sit up and attempt to smooth back a snarled mass of hair that came loose from the elastic. "Yeah, sure." My voice sounds hoarse. I cough to try and clear it.

"I was starting to worry," she says, entering. "Cody said he saw you this morning, but it's twelve and we haven't seen you. Are you okay? He said you two ran into each other in the hall. He might have scared you."

"Startled is all. I'm okay, just not feeling like being around anyone."

"I understand," she says, looking sympathetic. "But you must be starving?"

"Not really." I should be. I can't remember the last time I ate.

"Why don't you come to the kitchen anyway? Cody left for basketball and Jeff had some work to do. It's just you and me."

"Okay. I'll be there in a minute." She nods and smiles before leaving.

I slide off the bed to stand. My body feels like it weighs a ton. I take my hair out of the hair tie and smooth it back, trying to fix it as I find my way to the kitchen. I notice a large set of glass doors leading out to a big screened-in porch and beyond that . . . an enormous pool. "Is it okay if I go out?"

"Of course," Roxanne says from the kitchen.

I navigate my way through the family room and then outside. The sun feels good on my skin, so does the warm breeze. The dazzling colors I saw before dropping the blinds this morning are spread out in before me—trees and flowers of every height and color, coming together in perfectly organized chaos, all surrounding a kidney-shaped pool.

So, *this* is how the other half live.

I make my way back inside and sit on one of the barstools that line a large island with a built-in sink. "It's pretty out there."

Roxanne turns from the refrigerator, briefly looking outside before turning back to me. "Oh, that's *all* Jeff. He's the green thumb around here. It's his Zen garden."

"His what?"

"His Zen garden—you know—where he goes to relax."

"Oh, yeah . . . right. What does he do? I mean, for a living and all."

"He's a contractor. He builds houses."

"Nice."

"I'm an interior designer, which is great because I can work from home."

"I guess that's why your house looks like something out of a magazine."

Did that sound snarky?

She looks around. "Thank you. I tried to make it homey, but still keep it stylish." We stare at each other for a moment. "So, what sounds good? A sandwich okay?"

The thought of food makes my stomach queasy, but I know I should put something in it. "Sure. Whatever you've got. I'm not picky."

I watch as Roxanne pulls meats and cheeses, mayonnaise, and mustard from the refrigerator, then opens the pantry and pulls out a loaf of bread. She arranges it all on the counter, then looks up at me. "Is there anything here you don't like?"

"No. It's all good."

"Lettuce and tomato?"

"Yes, please." She layers a monster of a sandwich, which I know will be impossible to finish. "Can I ask you something?"

"Of course."

"If you and Mom were so tight, why didn't you stay in touch with each other?"

She fumbles the knife in her hand before cutting the sandwich in half. "Huh . . . well, your mom moved away after your dad died. I think you were about four. After that, we kind of lost track of each other."

"Weren't you mad?"

She drops a handful of chips next to the sandwich and sets the plate in front of me. "No. I knew she was in a rough place and did what she needed to do."

"Yeah, but wouldn't it have been easier if she stayed near the people she was closest to? Have some kind of support system? Things were hard."

"I can't say. I'm sure she had her reasons."

I consider her response with the brain equivalency of a melon.

After lunch, Roxanne shows me the rest of the house. It's one story but really spread out and ridiculously large for three people—well, ridiculously large regardless.

The central part of the house is a massive space with vaulted ceilings and lots of windows overlooking the backyard. An enormous sectional couch sits around a fireplace, with the formal dining room off to the side. To the left there is a hallway leading to the master bedroom, an office, another guest room, and bathroom. To the right is the kitchen, family room and the hall that leads to my bedroom, bathroom, and Cody's room.

"Feel free to use the pool anytime," she says once we've returned to the kitchen. "There are towels in the bin." She points to a large wicker basket just inside the sun porch. "Your mom told me what an amazing artist you are. I thought for sure you'd have come with boxes of art supplies. Maybe we could set up a small studio for you out there on the porch."

For a brief moment, I visualize an easel in the corner—the light is amazing, just like my little sunroom—then my heart sinks. It's not the same. Nothing will ever be the same again. "No. I threw it all away. It was just kids' stuff. I'm not into it anymore."

Roxanne looks astonished. "Oh. But your mom said it was your dream to go to Pratt and study art."

"Yeah, well that's not gonna happen now, is it? Oh." I cover my mouth. "I'm so sorry. I didn't mean it to come out like that."

She waves it off. "Don't give it another thought. I *am* sorry to hear that you've given up on your art, though. I hope you change your mind."

I shrug my shoulders, for lack of a better response.

"So, school starts in a week. Do you need anything?"

"Maybe just some notebooks, pens, and pencils."

"No problem. We always have extras. Cody will be able to drive you to and from school."

"That's okay. I can just take the school bus." *I doubt he's going to want me tagging along.*

"Don't be silly. You two are going to the same place. We'll have to come up with a different plan when basketball season starts, but other than that . . . he most *definitely* can give you a ride."

"Sure. Sounds good." It doesn't feel right to argue—although, I'm sure *he* will. "If it's okay, I'm going to go unpack." I'm done being social.

"You bet. I was thinking that maybe tomorrow I could drive

you to see the school. You know, get a look before the first day. If they're open, we could walk around and you could get a sense of the general layout."

"Okay, sure."

"Oh, and we usually eat dinner around six."

"Thanks." I turn to leave.

"Cassie?"

I look back at her. "*Hmm?*"

"Please don't feel like you have to be socially responsible right now. We all know how hard this is for you. If you need me, I'm here. If you want to be alone, that's fine too. Okay?"

My heart sinks again and I fight back the tears. "I'm sorry. I just—"

"No, baby. Don't be." She takes the necessary steps and pulls me into an embrace. "It's going to take time." She pats my back, then holds me out at arm's length. "All I ask is that you don't close up completely, okay? I want you to feel like you can talk to me if you need to. You don't need to be alone through all this."

"Okay," I say, but really . . . How can I turn to a complete stranger for something so personal? It's just me now and I need to accept it.

3

ALMOST EVERYTHING I have fits into two drawers. The rest of my limited wardrobe hangs pitifully in the mammoth-sized closet. I place Mom's picture on the nightstand and sit on the bed, staring at it. You hear people talk about how their lives are surreal after traumatic events—it always seemed like such a cliché. But really? After going through this? There's no better way to describe it. And it doesn't help that my mind is whirling like a computer pinwheel, trying to process everything that's happened.

I walk to the window and lift the blinds. It still amazes me that people actually live like this.

Now what do I do?

I sigh deeply as I survey the room, hoping for inspiration. I'm so used to being busy. With no art, no job, and no school, I also have *no* purpose. I should probably look for a place that's hiring. Problem is, I have no way of getting there. This doesn't seem like the kind of neighborhood that would have public transportation.

Thinking of work makes me miss Luigi and Maria. They own Luigi's, an Italian restaurant about five blocks from where I used to live. They gave Mom her first job and insisted I stay at the restaurant while she worked, so I was either upstairs in their apartment, or in everyone's way trying to help out.

Eventually, Mom had to look for another job—one with higher tips. She was hired on at an upscale restaurant in Lower Manhattan, but the commute took an hour, sometimes longer, because of subway delays and shutdowns.

Maria and Luigi didn't want her to leave and felt the job was too far away, so they insisted on paying her more money. But Mom refused, knowing it would put them in a financial bind.

Apparently, I became the compromise. Maria would *allow* Mom to go, but only if she could care for me until she got home. Maria had a funny way of showing she cared—it came out in the form of demands.

I don't know how we would have survived without them.

Starting at age twelve, I begged them to let me work at the restaurant. It wasn't until I turned fourteen that I got my wish. But it came with strict stipulations. Every day after school, I had to eat, do my homework, and *then* they'd let me work. They had strict ideas when it came to priorities.

When Mom got sick, Maria helped me take care of her and always made sure we had enough food to eat. When Mom died, she helped with all the funeral arrangements and insisted I stay with them until I had to leave.

Leaving them behind was almost as hard as leaving my mom. They were such a big part of my life—they were family.

I should get some fresh air. Maybe I'll go for a walk and check things out, see if there are any job prospects within walking distance.

I slip my feet into a pair of flip-flops and leave through the front door. I walk down four steps to a beautifully laid brick path lined with a large variety of flowers—an obvious extension of Jeff's Zenness.

How he can spend this much time gardening and still make the kind of money he does, is beyond me. I turn around and look at the gargantuan residence that is now my home. I shake my head. *Unbelievable*.

I make my way down the path to the sidewalk. I look both directions and decide to go to the right. Cement, extremely tall buildings, people rushing everywhere—*that's* normal to me. Kids playing outside while parents do yard work? Not so much. And it doesn't take long for me to realize I don't belong. People are staring at me like I just escaped from the hood.

I laugh to myself. I guess, in a way, I did.

It's a weird feeling. I've never stood out before—there were so many people, no one cared. And at my school, no one had money unless they were in a gang, selling drugs, or both. I wonder what this new school will be like. If the neighbors are any indication, I can only imagine the hell waiting for me.

The farther up the street I go, the larger the houses, to the point where two houses make up an entire block—most with gated entrances. *Ridiculous*.

I seriously doubt there will be any job options in this direction. It's not the kind of neighborhood you'd find a mini-mart or fast-food place. I turn around and head back the way I came.

I pass our house and walk several more blocks, but with each one I feel more and more self-conscious. I should have stayed in my room. Needing the safety of my refuge, I hurry back to the house.

I open the front door and hear everyone talking and laughing. This is someone else's family—I feel like I'm intruding. I don't belong here.

If I could just get to my room without being seen. But with the layout of the house, I know it's impossible.

"Oh, Cassie . . . you're back," Roxanne says from the kitchen when she sees me. "Where did you go? I got a bit worried when I couldn't find you."

Jeff and Cody are seated at the table for dinner, watching me.

"Sorry. I just went for a walk around the neighborhood." I point in the direction of my room. "I—"

"Good for you," Roxanne cuts me off. "Fresh air does a body good. Now come sit down and have something to eat. It's hot and ready."

I look toward my room—my sanctuary, then back to the table where Cody is now busy texting.

"Come on everyone, let's eat. Cody, put your phone away," Roxanne says, placing a large bowl of salad on the table and sits down. "Cassie, you can sit here." She pats the seat next to her.

I pause for a moment, debating the necessity of food versus my safe zone—my empty stomach wins. The sense of hunger feels foreign—it's been a long time.

Cody slides his phone into his lap as I sit across from him—he smiles briefly, acknowledging me, before loading his plate with food.

I'm still embarrassed by my reaction to him this morning. Why can't he be some dorky-looking nerd?

Roxanne slides a hand up and down my back affectionately before taking the bowl of mashed potatoes Jeff has just handed her.

"So, Cody," Jeff says, "how was basketball?"

He gives an indifferent shrug. "Lots of the guys came out. It was okay."

Roxanne plops a scoop of potatoes on her plate, then passes the bowl to me. I take a small amount, then set the bowl on the table in front of Cody.

Jeff looks at me. "Cody is on the varsity basketball team. They get together and scrimmage over the summer."

A plate of BBQ chicken comes my way. I take a breast and set the plate next to the potatoes. "Nice," I say.

Cody directs his attention to me. "Do you play any sports, Cassie?"

"No"

"That's too bad." He says with an almost condescending expression.

"Why is that too bad?" As much as I want to remain invisible at the table, I hate when people act like sports are the answer to all adolescent deficiencies. They aren't the end all be all—there *are* other avenues.

He looks at me curiously. "It's good exercise and a great way to meet people."

Oh, because that's what I need right now.

"Well, I'm not the sporty type, and I'd rather be alone."

"Yeah, but you need friends, right?"

"Not really."

Roxanne interjects, "Says our Mr. Social. Don't listen to him, Cassie. There's nothing wrong with alone time. I actually quite like it myself." She shoots Cody a look that says, *shut your yap, you insensitive jackass.*

He looks at her like, *what did I do?*

Which is true, he was just being polite and asking a random question. I don't know, it just struck me the wrong way, I guess.

Roxanne and Jeff ask me lots of questions over dinner. Cody basically texted the entire time. After his few words to me, I ceased to exist. I guess I don't blame him. I was a total bitch.

I continue to be polite, but feel miserable and on the spot. When everyone is done eating, I ask if it's okay to go to my room? I tell them I'm tired and promise to help with the dishes tomorrow. Jeff tells me not to worry about the dishes, that generally Roxanne cooks, he cleans, and Cody does homework. It's nice to know Jeff isn't a deadbeat.

I breathe a sigh of relief as soon as my door is closed. My natural reaction is to reach for my journal, but I don't have it anymore. It got chucked in the garbage with all my other art stuff. It wasn't a writing journal, like a diary or anything, it was more like a sketchpad of daily events.

Mom loved seeing the daily additions. She was always going on and on about how talented I was—she was my biggest fan. *God, I miss her.* The stabbing pain hits me again. I turn off the light, climb into bed, and bury my face in the pillow as the tears come pouring out.

There's a knock at my door. "Are you okay?" Cody asks.

I try to normalize my voice. "I'm fine."

"I don't believe you."

I roll over onto my back and wipe my eyes as I stare at the ceiling. "No, I'm good."

I startle as the door opens and Cody fills the doorway, his head almost reaching the top of the doorframe.

Sitting up quickly, I wipe the remainder of my tears off my face. "Oh my god! Ever hear of privacy?" I snap, hating that I feel exposed and vulnerable in front of a complete stranger.

He ignores my distress. "Yes. I like it myself, but this is an exception." A smooth, easy smile spreads across his ridiculously handsome face.

My mind sputters with swear words as I lean against the headboard, hugging my knees tightly to my chest.

"You know," he says casually as he sits on the side of my bed, "I remember you from when we were kids."

"I don't," I grumble. Well, I didn't until I saw him this morning. That was crazy. How did I suppress all those memories?

"Come on. You don't remember chasing me around, trying to kiss me?"

I snort.

"I had to practically beat you off with a stick."

I feel a tug at the corner of my mouth. "Well . . ." he says, standing up. "I'll let you have your space." He pauses when he reaches the door. "I'm really sorry about your mom. I can't imagine how hard all this must be . . . being without her, moving to the opposite coast to live with a family of strangers. If there is anything I can do, or if you need anything, just come knock on my door, okay?"

"Okay . . . Thanks." Maybe the guy isn't so bad. "Night."

"Night."

4

I OPEN my bedroom door a crack, making sure the coast is clear. I don't need a repeat of yesterday morning. I sprint to the bathroom for a long hot shower.

Feeling more than just alive, I pull my hair into a ponytail, then survey my reflection. I could never figure out where my looks came from. Mom had blond hair and icy-blue eyes. The fact that I ended up with reddish-brown hair and muddy-green eyes always made me wonder if she found me in an alley and adopted me.

I look a lot better today. My face doesn't look as pale and some of the darkness under my eyes has faded. Last night was the first decent sleep I've had in weeks.

I smell bacon when I open the bathroom door—my stomach growls in response. Maybe I could wait until everyone clears out, then find some leftovers. I'd rather avoid everyone if possible, but my stomach growls louder. I cover it with my hand. *Traitor*.

I force myself to walk down the hall and resist the urge to turn around when I see the family enjoying their breakfast.

A bare-chested Cody is already at the table eating. *Put some clothes on!*

"Have a seat," Roxanne says, smiling when she sees me. "There is lots of food. Sunday breakfasts are a big deal in our family."

Jeff walks in and sets a large stack of pancakes in front of me. He kisses Roxanne on the top of her head, then takes his place at the end of the table.

"Smells amazing, honey," she says.

"*Mmm-hmm*. I'm starved," he says as he loads his plate. "How did you sleep, Cassie?"

I tentatively take a piece of bacon. "Good."

"Cody!" Roxanne yells suddenly, making me jump. "Go put some clothes on! You *can't* walk around half-naked anymore!"

Thank you! It's *totally* unnerving.

Cody shrugs his shoulders, gets up while continuing to text, and leaves. He's only wearing underwear. I thought he would have at *least* had shorts on at the table.

Watching him walk away, I find myself noticing his backside is just as impressive as his finely chiseled front side. I feel my cheeks burning at the thought.

"Sorry about that," Roxanne says with an embarrassed smile. "It's going to be nice not being the only female in the house." She leans over with a conspiratorial smile. "They can't gang up on me anymore." She bumps her shoulder to mine and winks.

Cody comes back in a tight T-shirt, but still no shorts. He walks over to Roxanne and kisses her on the cheek before returning to his chair. Roxanne rolls her eyes. "He's a work in progress," she says, laughing.

Jeff looks at Roxanne, and then at Cody. He shrugs a shoulder, as if to say, *what's the big deal?*

Roxanne lets out a sigh of defeat.

Jeff focuses his attention on me. "Roxanne tells me she's going to drive you around today so you can see your new school."

"Yeah. That's the plan."

"I can take her," Cody says, not looking up from his phone.

Roxanne turns to me. "If it's okay with Cassie?"

"Um, sure . . . I guess."

"Cody, when do you want to take her?"

He glances up and stares at us. "What?"

"Cassie, said she'd go with you—*you nob*."

He shrugs his shoulders, then starts texting again. "Where are we going?" he asks.

Ohmygod! Seriously?

"Cody!" Roxanne exclaims.

He gives her a mischievous grin. "Just kidding, Mom. Chill."

I hate people who make jokes at other people's expense. And I've never had a cell phone before. But I'm pretty sure if I did, I wouldn't be glued to it 24/7 like he is.

Even though my appetite was still a little iffy, breakfast was amazing. I've never had an enormous, home-cooked meal like that before. For a special treat, Mom and I would go around the corner to Bert's diner, but that was it.

I help clear the table along with everyone else, then stay to help Roxanne with the dishes, seeing as Jeff and Cody have disappeared.

I load a plate into the dishwasher. "So, Mom mentioned she knew you since kindergarten?"

"Oh," she says, looking startled. "That's true. My first memory of her was when she stole my crayons and made me cry."

A half laugh escapes me as I try to picture my mother as a little girl. "Were you always friends?"

"Yep. Pretty much. We had our ups and downs, but she made the world brighter and I loved being around her."

"Yeah," I say, my heart aching, "that's what I always thought too."

A freshly showered and *totally* dressed Cody walks in and asks, "Do you want to change before we go?"

"Into what?" I look at him, confused.

"Well . . . into something other than bumming around clothes?"

"Cody!" Roxanne says, looking dismayed.

"This is how I dress." I realize my cheeks are hot again, which pisses me off. I nail him to the wall with a *you're-a-piece-of-shit* glare.

I don't think I've *ever* blushed. And then there was the stupid thing running into him yesterday morning.

"Oh. Sorry. I just don't see many girls . . . who, um . . . dress like that."

"Cody Stanton! Have you lost your mind!" Roxanne looks at me apologetically. "*See* what I've been dealing with? No manners, *what-so-ever*!" She shoots Cody a dirty look.

"Sorry," he says, looking sheepish. "I'll . . . go, uh . . . take out the trash." He walks around the counter and pulls the bag from the bin. "Come outside when you're ready."

"He's a great kid—really, he is," she says ruefully.

He seems like a total dick to me. "It's okay," I lie.

I know I need some new clothes. The old me doesn't fit into my new life—not that it's a big deal, but I think I'm ready for a change anyway. I've got some money from Mom's insurance policy. She wanted me to use it for Pratt. But since I'm not going there anymore, why not use it for what I need now?

I find Cody in the garage vacuuming out a black Jeep Wrangler. His shirt is off . . . *again*. "Do you have a problem with wearing clothes?" I blurt out, disturbed once again, by how the sight of him makes me feel.

He's like a Calvin Klein billboard ad come to life. You would have to be a brain-dead to not be affected.

"What?" he yells over the vacuum before shutting it off.

"Nothing," I mumble.

"Are you ready to go?"

"Is that yours?" I nod my head in the direction of the shiny, new-looking vehicle.

"Yes."

Of course it is.

The top is off the jeep, so my ponytail keeps smacking me in the face. At the first stoplight, I wipe the tears from my irritated eyes and manage to pull my tangled mop of hair into a messy bun.

"Much better," Cody says, looking over with obvious approval.

I return it with a sideways glance of, *I-don't-give-a-shit-what-you-think*. But really? I'm flattered, which irritates the hell out of me even more.

Ignoring my prickly attitude, he continues. "So, what did

you do for fun when you lived in New York? There must have been tons to do."

"I wouldn't know. I worked all the time to help pay for food and rent."

"Sorry," he says with a hint of guilt in his voice. "You must think I'm a spoiled brat?"

"I can't comment on the brat part, the other . . .?" I shrug my shoulder. "I haven't known you long enough."

"You know," he says, sounding irritated. "I'm not a complete waste of space."

He looks at me sideways when I don't respond, which has me shrugging my shoulders again. "What the hell do I know?" I return, still pissed off.

I wish I could stick a bag over his head so I don't have to look at how beautiful he is. I glance over at him anyway. He looks more like Roxanne than Jeff with the dark hair and blue eyes—Jeff's hair is more a sandy color and I think his eyes are brown. He's probably got every girl at school falling over him. I know I shouldn't judge, but guys like that bug the hell out of me. They think the world revolves around them, and everyone in it, especially females, should bow to their every whim.

I shake my head. "So, are you one of those guys that everyone either wants to be or be with?"

"I like being around people, if that's what you mean," he snaps, sounding just as surly as I do. "What's *your* social dilemma?"

Seriously? My what? "I don't have one." I glare at him. "I've never had the time or inclination to deal with the educational, social hierarchy."

"Social hierarchy has *nothing* to do with having friends."

"What can I say? I had more important priorities," I bite back.

He's quiet for a moment. "Fair enough." His tone is softer. "About that . . . Mom mentioned that art was a big part of your life, but you threw all your supplies away?"

"It was a big part of mine and *Mom's* life, so . . ." I trail off, not wanting to discuss personal matters with someone who probably has the emotional depth of a peanut.

"What would she say about you quitting?"

I watch the scenery pass by, letting the question sink in. Lush green foliage and colorful flowers blur together in shades I've never experienced in the cement jungle I came from. The artist in me is thrilled, making my heart twist with a slight sense of guilt. "She would probably tell me I'm being an idiot," I respond without thinking.

"Sounds about right."

"How the *hell* would you know?" I snap.

"Just stories Mom told me."

This is so messed up. He knows more about my mother than I do.

"Here it is," he says, stopping.

His declaration of pride pulls me from my black thoughts. The sight takes me by surprise. "It's huge." Football field, running track, tennis courts—it's even got a massive outdoor pool. I didn't realize a public school could be this nice. It's all about being in the right zip code, I guess.

"Really? What was your school like?"

"Small, dirty—basically a shithole."

"Oh." He slides his hands up and over his steering wheel. "You know . . . being with you really makes me feel shitty about myself."

"It's not your fault you're rich, spoiled, and self-centered," I lash out.

"As opposed to an indignant teenager with a chip on her shoulder?" he counters.

"*Pfff*. At least my attitude is justifiable."

"You mean certifiable."

My eyebrows shoot up in surprise. He's sparring with me—totally unexpected. "At this point, probably." I'm not usually this bitchy.

"Seen enough?"

I exhale loudly. "Yeeup."

"Don't worry. You'll be fine."

Not that I give a crap, but senior year isn't exactly the best time for starting over.

On the drive back, I spot a pizza place not far from the school. Seeing it, makes me long for home. "Hey, have you ever been to that restaurant we just passed, Antonio's?"

"Yeah. A lot of kids go there for lunch and sometimes after school, why?"

"It reminds me of the place I used to work."

"Nice."

"Maybe I'll apply."

"You know you don't have to work, right?" He looks over at me briefly, his expression thoughtful. "We're family. You don't need to stress about money or help pay to live."

"Thanks. But I'm not the type to accept handouts. Besides, it will help me stay busy—you know, keep my mind off things."

"Sure. Okay."

He pulls into one of the four garage doors. "How does a movie and some popcorn sound?"

"Actually? Not bad." I could use a diversion.

"You're not the chick-flick type, are you?"

"I don't know."

"Right. They didn't let your kind into the movie theater."

"Asshole."

"Bitch."

Nice. I appreciate the joking. It's a reprieve from the emotional suck-hole that is my life.

5

"Cody! Hurry up," Roxanne yells. "Cassie needs to get to school early to get her class schedule."

He comes from the hall with his hair wet and shooting in all different directions. "*I'm coming*, all ready. Frick!"

Grumbling something as he walks into the kitchen, he stops when he sees me. He looks me up and down, and then, shaking his head, scrunches his face into a frown.

"What?" I say, looking down at my clothes then back up in time to see Roxanne shoot Cody a hard look.

"Nothing," he says, heading toward the garage.

I look at my clothes again. What's so weird about spandex capris, flip-flops, and a baggy T-shirt? I even pulled my hair up into a messy bun because shit-for-brains seemed to like it.

"You look fine," Roxanne says, reading my mind. "You'd better hurry up, though. Cody is a grump this early in the morning and won't want to wait. I have to view a house for a prospective client. Wants a total redesign. Wish me luck."

"Good luck."

"I'll be home in time to cook dinner. We'll eat around six, okay?"

"I usually fend for myself. You don't have to cook for me."

She nudges me toward the door as a loud horn sounds. "Comes with being part of the family. Have a great day."

I groan inwardly.

He doesn't talk on the way to school, which is fine with me, I'm really nervous anyway. Cody parks his jeep in the full—I mean, totally full—student parking lot.

Rich kids suck.

He's out of his vehicle and halfway to the school before I climb out of his stupid jeep. I don't bother to catch up. He obviously doesn't want to be seen with me.

Students holler to him in greeting—many of them girls—pretty ones. He waves in return with a smile plastered on his face. Stopping abruptly, he turns, looking irritated. "Come on, will you?" he hollers, causing everyone to stop and stare. "I've got to get to class, and Mom wants me to show you where the office is."

"Screw you!" I say, approaching him. "I don't need you babysitting me. I can find my own way."

"Fine. Whatever," he says, leaving me and continuing toward the school.

"Cassie Roads," I tell the secretary when she asks for my name.

She hands me an information packet and my schedule with a kind smile. "Have a nice day, dear."

I want to roll my eyes at her, but I stop myself. It's not her fault that my life sucks.

Walking to my first class is fun—not. Oh my god! I'm not that freakish. *Seriously, get over it, people.*

My schedule's pretty easy, nothing I can't handle. Cody ends up being in my history class. *Figures.* So far, he hasn't seen me. I got here before he did and I'm in the corner of the last row. When class is over, I wait for him to leave before I head out. I am *not* in the mood to deal with him right now.

I lean against Cody's jeep with my arms crossed in front my chest, wishing I was invisible, when a ridiculously beautiful, dark-haired girl walks toward me, all attitude. Just what I need . . . lip service from the leader of Mean Girls-R-Us.

She eyes me up and down. "Are you waiting for Cody?"

I return the gesture with some added hostility. "Yeah."

She responds with an expression of distaste. "You're not Cody's new girlfriend, are you?"

Bitch. "No. We're just fuck-buddies," I say, stone-faced.

"I doubt that," she sneers. "Cody and I are *very* close. I'm pretty sure he would have told me if he was . . . that desperate."

I shrug my shoulders indifferently.

Her facial expression changes from disdain to a fake-best-friend smile. "So, anyway, tell him Shandler says hi. 'Kay?"

I imitate her sing-song voice with a matching phoney smile. "'Kay."

Man, if looks could kill. She turns on her spiky heels and walks away. Each step looking calculated to elicit a desired response from any male in visual range. But in this case, it's probably more for my benefit.

Whatever. I'm sure most females would be envious of her perfectly shaped rear end, molded into high waisted skinny jeans. Me? I'd just like to put my foot up her ass.

The obnoxious stares continue as students pass by me. Where the *hell* is he? This is getting old.

Finally, I see him weaving through the parked cars.

"Why are you scowling at me?" he asks when he gets close enough. Someone calls out his name. He looks over and acknowledging them, before turning back to me.

I shake my head, still not wanting to talk to him.

It's slow going out of the parking lot. I plant my feet on his dash just to piss him off. Of all the crap I had to deal with today, him acting the way he did earlier bothered me the most. Every time I think he might be a decent person, he proves me wrong. And for some reason, it's really disappointing.

"Look, I'm sorry for being such a prick this morning. I *really* hate the first day of school, and me and early mornings don't mix. Now, will you get your feet off my dash?"

Yeah, it's probably more that he and I don't mix. I make a show of my reluctance as I remove them. "By the way . . . Shandler says 'Hi'."

"*Does* she? How did you meet her?"

"She was *kind* enough to introduce herself when she saw me waiting next to your stud-mobile."

He looks over, glaring.

I can see him out of the corner of my eye, but I continue facing forward, unaffected.

"She can be pretty nasty," he says after a bit.

"Who is she? She made it sound like you two have a thing."

"*Had*. I got sick of her self-centered, controlling, viciously mean attitude."

"And demented," I mutter.

He laughs. "And then there's that. So? How was your first day?"

"*Pfff*. Awesome. Yours?"

"Same. I'm glad it's my last year."

"Really? I would think Mr. Popular would never want to leave."

"Enough with the type-casting shit, okay?" he growls.

"Okay. Fine." *Jeez. Sensitive.*

He's quiet for a minute, then continues. "It's not who I am, okay? It's just how things turned out." He looks over at me.

I give him a look like, *Aw, sucks to be you.*

He shakes his head and rolls his eyes. "Anyway, I've been with these kids since Kindergarten. I'm ready to meet some new people. New York must have been interesting—the diverse culture. There must be an infinite number of things to do . . . to explore."

"I suppose there is if you have the money and time for it."

He ignores the barb. "I'm hoping to get scholarship offers from some east coast schools."

"You think schools might be interested in you?"

"Don't look so surprised. It's a possibility."

"You don't have to go all the way to the other coast to meet interesting people. Your family's here."

"I know. I'll apply to schools in Cali as well. But I've heard it's a whole different culture on the east coast—I'm interested."

Cody drops his books on the kitchen island and goes straight to the fridge. I go to my room, flop on the bed, and stare up at the ceiling. What an effed-up day.

"So what classes do you have?"

"*Aah!*" I scream and bolt upright. "What the hell!"

"Sorry." He leans against the doorframe, casually taking a bite of an apple.

"Frick! Give me a warning or at least make a sound or something." I huff out a breath while Cody continues to chew, patiently waiting for his answer. "Fine! Whatever. Calculus, English Literature, Computers, and History."

"No art?" The corner of his mouth edges up into a grin.

"No."

"You should at least draw."

"No."

"Chicken."

"Seriously? Why do *you* care?"

"You can't just stop doing what you love."

I pause, not really knowing how to respond, so I change the subject. "We have history together," I grumble.

"I didn't see you in class."

"I was avoiding you—being that you were such a shithead this morning, I didn't want to deal with a repeat."

"Ouch!" He takes another bite of apple and chews slowly. Meanwhile, I'm like, *you can leave now*! He swallows and says, "So . . . got any brains in that head of yours? We could study together if you did."

"Why would I want to help you?"

"Who says I need help?"

"Good looking Jock . . . I didn't expect there to be intelligence in the mix."

"Stereotyping again, are we?"

I shrug my shoulders.

"You think I'm good looking?"

Shit! Why did I say that? "Mildly," I retort.

He laughs. "Anyway, back to the idea of studying together. I've never had a live-in study-buddy before. It could be useful."

I chuckle. "You are a *strange* person."

He smiles. Still, not moving.

"Do you mind? I'd like to get back to . . . " I motion with my hand, indicating my room.

"Yeah . . . I don't think so."

"Excuse me?" I half laugh. "*Get out*."

"Somebody's got to help you out of this funk."

"You say it like I've got a choice?"

"There's always a choice."

"Don't you have someone to go text?" I bite out.

"I know there's no way to comprehend what you're going through—and let's hope I never have to—but at some point, you're going to have to find some *good* moments to balance out the bad ones. Otherwise, you're going to shrivel up and die inside that head of yours. Why don't you get your bathing suit on and meet me out by the pool? It's super nice out."

"As if *that's* gonna fix this shit-show that is my life."

"You'd be amazed at what a little vitamin D can do."

I stare at him a moment, debating. "Okay, fine," I scowl.

"Really?" He sounds surprised.

"Jackass."

"Ass-tard." I notice a dimple of his left cheek as he smiles.

"See you out there?" he asks, as he turns to leave.

I nod. "And shut the door. I need to change."

"What? It's nothing I haven't seen before."

"How would you know?"

"Unless you have scales and four boobs . . . it's nothing new."

I laugh.

"I like the sound of that." He winks at me before shutting the door behind him.

The action sets off butterflies in my stomach.

Oh, hell no.

I dig out my bathing suit from my underwear drawer. Mom and I didn't get to the beach much, being that we were both so busy, but I loved it when we did. The sound of the waves, the sun, the feel of the sand under my feet—it was definitely a cure-all.

Pushing away the emptiness threatening to swallow me, I grab a towel and wrap it tightly around me before heading out.

Cody shields his eyes as he looks up. "Hey."

"Hey." I take the towel off, lay it on the lounge chair next to him, and quickly lie on my stomach. I turn my head to face him. He's grinning. "What now?" I snap at him.

"I *knew* you had a nice body under all those baggy clothes."

"Oh my god! Seriously?" I quickly stand up. Fumbling with my towel, I rewrap myself.

He releases an exaggerated sigh, showing his disappointment. "Why you choose to hide it is beyond me."

I lift up the back of the chair and sit down, pulling my knees up. "I like to be comfortable."

"Comfortable is one thing, dressing like a slob is another."

"I do *not* . . . dress, like a slob!" I laugh, but only because I can't believe we're having this discussion.

"You do too."

"What's it to you?"

"I don't know. I guess I like seeing people live up to their potential."

"*What* potential? Like trying to rise to some bogus level of popularity by wearing itty-bitty-strips-of-nothing that cling to my essentials?"

"Interpret however you want, but you have pretty nice essentials." I open my mouth to slam him, but he cuts me off. "I'm just saying . . . there's more to you than your sloppy exterior, and I think it blocks people's interest in finding out what your valuables are."

"Are you seriously listening to yourself right now?" My voice sounds shrill. I swing my legs around so I'm facing him. "I don't give a rat's ass what people think of my . . . 'valuables'. The only 'value' the rich brats around here understand . . . is the monetary kind."

"Don't get so defensive."

I hate when people tell me to not get defensive when I'm angry, it pisses me off even more. "You are such a dick!" I stand up and leave his bronzed, nakedness behind me laughing.

I almost slam my bedroom door. Self-righteous, conceited, shit-for-brains, spoiled brat! Live up to my potential . . . *Asshole.* What does he know about potential? He's had a silver spoon shoved so far up his ass, he's clueless to what's happening in the real world.

I take my bathing suit off and change back into my *unfashionable clothes*. The prick was probably born Mr. Amazingly Cute, then grew to Mr. Adorable, then into Mr. Downright Hot, all while having an amazing family and shit tons of money. He's never had to work at anything in his life! *Potential, my ass!* Who do I need to impress? *Nobody!*

I lay on my bed and stare angrily at the ceiling with my arms crossed over my chest, continuing the rant inside my head until the rage tapers off.

I process the conversation again. Shit! I might have overreacted.

No way! He was way out of line! Then I get to the part where he said he liked my essentials. I realize I'm smiling. "*Grrr!*"

Get a grip!

6

Cody and his friends are blocking my entrance into history class. I sort of smile and say a reluctant "Hi" as I weave my way through them. Cody returns my greeting with a mumbled "Hey."

Halfway to my seat, I hear one of his friends make some comment about how it must suck having to drive me to school every day, *and Cody agrees!*

I'm so angry I can barely concentrate during class. I didn't want to friggin' drive with him anyway! Roxanne set it up.

When school's done, I decide to blow Cody off and walk home. It's a long way, but whatever. It's better than being near *his* sorry ass. Besides, I can check out that pizza place . . . see if they're hiring.

The canopy over the restaurant reads 'Antonio's'. It's in a small shopping plaza, with a café on one side and a flower shop on the other. I open the door to the familiar sound of bells hanging over the entrance and the scent of Italian cooking. It reminds me of the place I worked at in New York—the round tables covered in red and white checkered tablecloths and the high countertop with its glass partition, enclosing the prep-station and pizza ovens. I close my eyes and inhale deeply.

"Hello there, young lady. What can I get you?" A dark-haired man with a strong Italian accent asks from behind the counter.

"I just moved here from New York," I say, feeling apprehensive. "I worked at a pizza place in The Bronx for three years, and I was wondering if you were hiring."

"The Bronx in New York?"

I chuckle. *Is there another one?* "Yeah, in New York."

He throws his hands in the air. "My wife's cousin's husband's brother has a pizza place in The Bronx—in Little Italy. Anna," he yells. "Come out here."

A short, robust women with graying hair pulled back into a tight bun comes through a swinging back door. "Tony, what do you want? Why you yelling?"

He comes from behind the counter to stand beside her. "Wa's the name of Georgina's husband's brother's place called?"

She looks annoyed. "How am I supposed to remember that?"

"Wa's your name?" Tony asks me. "I forgot to ask."

"Cassie."

"Cassie might have worked there. I'm going to call your cousin?"

"You don't have to call," I start to say, but he's already behind the counter picking up the phone. "I can give you their number. They'll give me a good reference."

Anna looks at me. "Wa's this all about?"

I shrug my shoulders. "I'm looking for a job. I worked at a pizza place since I was fourteen, but I pretty much grew up in the restaurant, so I have lots of experience."

"Luigi's," Tony yells as he hangs up the phone.

Hearing the name feels like a stab to the heart. I miss them *so* much.

"I know you," she says, pointing a finger at me. "My cousin told me about a little girl and her Mama that came and she worked there, yes?" Tony comes to stand with us.

"Yes," I say, flabbergasted.

"You and your Mama move here?"

"No," I say, feeling the loss. "She passed away, and I came here to live with my Mom's friend and her family."

Anna looks up at Tony, then back to me. "You want a job, you got a job!"

"Thanks. That's great."

"Wait." Tony holds up a finger. "Wa's the phone number at Luigi's?"

"Huh?"

"Tony! What are you doing?" Anna demands.

"Hush woman."

I rattle off the number as Tony walks to the phone behind the counter.

"Is this Luigi?" Tony yells into the phone. "You know a Cassie?" Tony nods his head listening, says several things in Italian, then holds the phone out to me.

I stare at him a moment before walking over and taking it from him. "Hello?" I say into the receiver and hear the voice I have known forever. "Nono," I choke out. It means grandfather in Italian. They always insisted I call them Nona and Nono.

His sentences are broken by all the emotion. It's so good to hear his voice. Nona got on the phone as well. I explained all about the school and the family I'm living with. They cried. I cried. I should have called sooner, but I'd been avoiding it. I didn't think I could handle it. I was wrong. It was exactly what I needed.

I hang up the phone and wipe my eyes just as Tony hands me some napkins and pulls me in for a big bear hug. He's taller than Luigi, but has the same big-barrelled chest.

"Thank you," I say.

"You needed them, yes?" he asks. I nod my head in return. "That's what I thought."

"You will start tomorrow," Anna says firmly, ignoring the exchange.

"Thank you. I really appreciate it." And I do. I need this place desperately.

Maria waves off my comment. "You come here tomorrow after school. And you better not be late!" She wags her finger at me, but there is humor in her eyes. "You will eat, help make pizzas, and wait on customers. I'm gettin' *too* old." She wipes her forehead with a rag, indicating her exhaustion. "I could use some help around here." She gives Tony a pointed look. He shakes his head at her in return.

"Okay. I should get going then." I turn to leave. "See you tomorrow."

"Hey!" Anna yells. "Are you forgetting something?" She taps her cheek.

I laugh and plant a loud kiss on each cheek, then go to Tony and do the same. I feel like I've been gifted with a little piece of home.

"That's better," she says. Holding the door open for me, she looks around outside. "How are you going home? I don't see a bike. Do you have a car?"

"No. I'll just walk."

She puts her hands on her hips, narrowing her eyes at me.

"Today you can walk—it's light out. Tomorrow, our grandson will drive you home. He delivers pizzas in the evening. *No way* will you walk home in the dark!"

"Okay, okay." I smile to myself as I leave the restaurant.

Lost in thought, I'm startled when Cody's jeep screeches to a stop in a driveway in front of me. He jumps out. "Where have you been?" he hollers at me.

"Whoa there, big boy. Didn't realize I had to report to you."

"I waited *forever* after school. When you didn't show up, I drove all over the place looking for you."

I brace a hand on my hip and glare at him. "Well, sorry, but I didn't want to *burden* you any longer."

"What the hell are you talking about?"

"I *heard* what you said!" He gives me a blank stare. "You told your friends that it sucked having to drive me to school."

He shakes his head at me, looking confused. I'm just about to enlighten him further, when the corner of his mouth inches toward a grin. "You are such an idiot! And I didn't say that —*they* did. I agreed that it sucked at first, but then I got to know you."

"Well . . . still, you looked at me like I had no right being near you."

"I did not!" he says, looking indignant.

"You totally did!"

He turns his head away and stares down the street. "I didn't mean to, but you throw me off sometimes."

"What's *that* supposed to mean?"

"I don't know. You just do."

The moment suddenly shifted into something awkward. "Oh."

"*Oh*? That's all you have to say?" he half-heartedly lashes out. "After I've spent the last hour stressing myself out?"

"Sorry, but you were being a *dick*, and I wasn't in the mood to be stared at like some kind of street rat while *waiting* for your sorry ass."

He shrugs his shoulders and smirks. "One word . . . Po-ten-tial."

I bark out a laugh. "*Screw you.*"

"Sure . . . maybe if you smiled more."

His words take me by surprise, so does the snapshot image of his body intertwined with mine. *Oh, hell!* "In your dreams."

He laughs and point to the jeep. "Come on. Get in."

I pull the seatbelt across my shoulder, buckling it at my waist and stifle the urge to put my feet on his dash again.

"You were wearing an ear-to-ear smile when I pulled up. What was that all about?"

"You call that pulling up? You just about ran me over!"

"Well, I was pissed—don't change the subject."

"I got a job."

"You were smiling because you got a job?"

I fill him in on the drive home. He tells me he's happy for me, and comments on what a small world it is, then tells me some funny stories about his friends and apologizes for how they acted toward me. Things feel settled between us, and I'm relieved. I like him when he's not being a turd-nugget.

7

I'M GOING clothes shopping with Roxanne today, which in the past would have been torture on *so* many levels. Since I've decided that looking nice isn't a crime against humanity, I thought I'd give it a go.

I find Roxanne in the laundry room pulling clothes out of the dryer.

I lean against the door. "Are you almost ready to go?"

She jumps. "Holy hell!" Her hand flies to her heart. "You scared the bajeezus out of me!"

"What's a bajeezus?"

"*Whoo!*" Air whooshes out of her mouth as she fans herself. "I have no idea. What did you ask?"

"I was wondering if you still had lots to do, or can we get going soon?"

"Yes. Just about. I need to fold these clothes and then I'll be ready. I'm excited. This should be fun. Being that Cody is my only child, I missed out on the whole mother-daughter shopping experience."

Aah. That hurt.

She places a hand on my arm. "Oh, honey. I'm so sorry. I know I don't come *close* to replacing your mother. I just meant . . . well, you've seen what I've had to deal with."

"It's okay." I smile to relieve her of her guilt. "I get what you mean."

"Maybe we could have lunch after?"

"Sure. Sounds good. I'll just wait outside by the pool."

She nods her head, lost in thought, as she continues to fold. I pass through the porch and sit on one of the loungers. The warmth of the breeze feels nice against my skin. I breathe deep, enjoying the barrage of fresh scents—cut grass, trees, flowers. I actually feel above miserable today—an improvement—even with Roxanne's absentminded comment.

"So . . . how are things going at school?" Roxanne asks as she shoulder-checks before merging onto the highway.

"It's okay." No sense in going into the crappy details.

"And your new job?"

"Really good. Tony and Anna are hilarious. They're always yelling—not in a mad way or anything—it's just the way they talk to each other. Sometimes when Anna gets going, I call her out on it and she'll start laughing at herself. She's just like Maria."

"I'm glad I got a chance to meet Maria. She's such a kind woman. And you got to talk to her and Luigi?"

"Yeah, it was so nice to hear their voices."

"I bet. You said Tony and Anna's grandson gives you a ride home?"

"Yes, Marco. We go to the same school. He's in my grade—

he's quiet, but super nice. I don't have any classes with him, so I only see him at the restaurant."

She turns to me. "Nice, huh?" Her eyebrows pumping up and down, suggestively.

I roll my eyes. "Not like that."

"You know . . . your mom had all the guys chasing after her."

"Then I must take after my father, 'cause no one's ever chased me."

"I doubt that. You actually look a lot like both of them. He was a very handsome man."

"You knew my father?" I ask, confused.

"Well, yeah, uh . . . remember? You were here till you were four. Sometimes we would all hang out, but usually your dad was too busy, so it was just you and Allora—you know . . . before he died."

"Right. I guess I haven't gotten around to putting all the pieces together."

"That's understandable. You've been overwhelmed by a lot of things."

"She never wanted to talk about him. Was he a total loser?"

"She never told you anything?"

"No."

"Oh . . . well, he had his moments, and they didn't get along that well. Plus, like I said, he was gone a lot."

"*Huh*."

"I bet you didn't know your mom was a wild child when she was your age."

"My mom? That's hard to believe." I really don't know anything about her, other than what I grew up with. The thought makes me angry. Everybody else seems to know more about her than I do.

"Oh, yeah . . . total free spirit. She did whatever she wanted, whenever she wanted, and was *always* getting into trouble—me along with her. But I didn't care. I was like a moth to a flame, and she always burned bright. I wasn't the only one drawn to her. And even though she had this massive presence, she never made you feel small." She briefly turns to me. "Sorry if I've said too much. I was going to let you ask me the questions, but I thought maybe you'd like to hear a little bit about the Allora *I* knew."

"No, it's okay. Why didn't she tell me about any of this?"

"I wish I could give you an answer, but I can't. We're here," she announces, pulling into a parking space. "Are you ready?"

I take a deep breath. "I guess."

"Do you want me to stay with you while you shop or go at it alone?" she asks casually, but I can see the hopefulness in her eyes.

"You should stay with me. You probably have a better eye for fashion anyway."

"How do you figure?"

"You're a successful interior designer. Doesn't style come with the territory?"

She laughs. "I don't know. I guess we'll see. I'll follow you."

Roxanne ended up being a huge help. She brought me to several amazing stores, and surprisingly, I found lots of stuff I liked. She even talked me into a salon so we could get a medi pedi. I had no idea what that was, but ended up really enjoying it. Afterwards, she suckered me into letting a stylist cut my hair. It was getting long and stringy anyhow, so I went for it. They took off about six inches. I just about jumped out of the chair after the first cut. But it all went well. It feels a lot lighter and healthier. Turns out my hair is wavy. I had so much weight on it, I didn't know.

Successful shopping accomplished; we sit down to lunch. I've never been a salad person, but this was the best I've ever eaten—roasted chicken with caramelized onions and red peppers, roasted pecans coated in brown sugar and coarse salt, and sliced apples with a sweet but tangy poppy-seed dressing.

Wow! Who knew food could taste like this?

Roxanne is a very interesting person. She was a gymnast, part of student council at her high school, and was involved with several charitable organizations—still is. On her parents' advice, she got a business degree from California State, but ended up hating her options after she graduated. So, after a long search, she found a job as an assistant to a very exclusive interior designer. She fell in love with the industry and pursued it further. With the experience and some extra schooling, she went out on her own and, to her parents' delight, was able to use her business degree.

Throughout our time together, questions concerning my mother continued to nag at me. "So, Mom takes off to New York, doesn't talk to you for thirteen years, then she asks you to take me in. And you just say 'okay'?"

She pauses before responding. "When you're as close as we were, you accept things unconditionally. She needed me to take care of what was most precious to her, so of course I said yes. She would have done the same for me."

"I guess. But I still think it's strange."

"Your mom was an amazing surfer," she interjects suddenly.

"Really?"

She smiles wistfully. "Really. She competed and did quite well."

I try to imagine her as the person Roxanne described, but all I see is a woman worn out by life—no flame or hint of the spontaneous wild child, no powerful presence or outstanding beauty—just Mom, working hard to make life bearable for us.

The aching sense of loss mixed with the hurt of Mom keeping so much from me is suddenly unbearable. "Can we go please? I'm not feeling good." We are done eating anyway.

"Absolutely." Roxanne looks worried as we stand. "I have some work I need to do anyway." She pauses when we get outside. "Honey, I'm sorry. I didn't mean to make you feel like this. Try not to be too angry with Allora. Her life was complicated. Focus on how much she loved you, okay?"

"I guess. I do want to hear about her. It's just hard realizing that you know absolutely nothing about the person you lived with for seventeen years."

"I understand. All I can say is, give it time."

What other choice do I have? I just don't understand. Why did she keep all this from me?

8

I WAKE up for school with the sun blinding me as usual. I groan and pull the pillow over my head. Another day of endless scrutiny . . . perfect.

I do my thing, getting ready, and just as I finish my breakfast, Cody stumbles in, texting someone.

"Hey," he mumbles.

"Hey."

I rinse my cereal bowl and place it in the dishwasher.

"Are you wearing a dress?" Cody asks, eyes wide open and suddenly alert.

"Yeah. So?" It's a cute floral-print sundress—super comfortable. And since I'm all about comfort, I was okay buying it.

"So? You look hot!" He shakes his head, looking stunned. "I mean . . . uh, well . . . um."

I tuck a rogue wave of hair behind my ear. "*Pfff,*" I respond, disregarding his comment, but secretly my heart's doing a crazy little dance. *Grrr!*

"Well, that's a first," Roxanne says, walking into the kitchen. She must have overheard our conversation. "Cody's at a loss for words, will wonders never cease?"

He narrows his eyes at her before turning back at me, all smiles. "I just meant to say, you look really nice."

"Thanks. Your mom helped me shop."

"Way to go, Mom. See, Cassie? Potential."

"Oh my god!" I storm. "If I hear that word come out of your mouth *one more time*, I'm going to take your head off."

"Am I missing something?" Roxanne eyes the two of us.

"It's all good, Mom."

No, it's not. He's driving me crazy!

"You two better get going. You're going to be late for school."

Cody shakes his head. "This could be an interesting day."

Cody keeps glancing sideways at me as he drives.

"What!" I snap.

"Nothing! Sorry." He returns his focus to the road.

It's quiet for the rest of the drive—mornings on the way to school usually are. He parks and I climb out of the jeep—which is tough to do without flashing everyone—and follow Cody toward the school.

"What did you do to your hair?"

"Nothing." I sound defensive. I don't mean to. He just has me all twisted up. "I got it cut."

A guy comes out of nowhere and side checks Cody. "Hey," he says, looking me over. "Who's this?"

He's stunningly good-looking—sun-bleached hair, bright

blue eyes—total California hottie. Regardless, I don't like being stared at like I'm a mouth-watering dessert.

"It's Cassie, you ass!"

"No effin' way!" He turns, walking backwards as he speaks. "Well, aren't you going to introduce me?"

"Do I have to?" Cody sounds bored or annoyed. I can't tell.

"Yes." He grins at me with obvious intent.

This guy knows how to reel them in—a total player—probably doesn't even have to try. Well, he can try all he wants—no way *I'm* interested.

"Cassie, Josh—Josh, Cassie," Cody's says, his voice flat.

"So, are you two hangin'?" Josh pumps his eyebrows suggestively.

Cody shoves him, making him stumble backward. "We live together."

"So?"

"You're a sick bastard—you know that?" Cody says.

"Cassie, if you're not into this jackass, maybe you might wanna go out with me sometime."

I notice Cody's wary expression. "Sorry. Not interested."

"Oh, I see. You're not into guys," he says. "That's cool."

"Maybe I'm just not into you," I say and walk off, hearing Cody roar with laughter behind me.

Arrogant asshole!

"You show too much leg!" Anna yells at me as soon as I walk in. "You'll never see *me* wearin' a dress that short!"

"Anna, you're like, sixty. You're not supposed to wear short dresses." She whips my leg with her towel. "Ow!" I laugh, surprised by the attack as well as her aim. "Besides, girls at school wear them *a lot* shorter than this."

"You never you mind. They're not my Cassie!"

I roll my eyes at her before walking behind the counter to kiss Tony on the cheek.

"Leave her alone, Anna! She looks bellissmo!" He winks at me.

I make a face at Anna who, in turn, throws her hands in the air. "*Aah!* Kids today!"

We are super busy. I don't mind. It makes the time go by fast—keeps me from thinking about things I shouldn't be thinking about. I drop off an order and rush to the next table. "Can I take"—it's Shandler and Josh—"your order?"

Oh, eff! The last two people I want to see. And what the hell? He asks me out, then shows up with the psycho bitch?

"Oh, you work here?" Shandler says, all syrupy sweet. "That's so cool!"

"I know, right?" I mimic her tone. "So, did you want to order pizza or what?" I ask, sounding snarky.

"Oh, me?" Shandler places her hand on her chest. "No way . . . too much fat. Can I just get the antipasto salad with the dressing on the side?"

"Sure." I look at Josh impatiently. I find myself wanting to hurt her and need to get away.

"I'll just have a slice of pepperoni pizza, please . . . and a Coke."

"Sure thing." I tear their order off my pad and slam it down on the counter in front of Tony. I turn just as Shandler leans forward to whisper something to Josh.

"Whatsamatter with you?" Tony asks.

I turn back. "Nothing!" I snap.

"Ho'kay." He raises his hands in surrender before turning around.

I busy myself and take their food out as soon as it's ready. The sooner they eat and get out of here, the better. They both smile politely and say thank you. I restrain myself from rolling my eyes.

I go back to taking orders, serving, and clearing tables, but keep a constant eye on them. As soon as I notice they're done eating, I'm there. "Can I get you anything else?" I ask as politely as possible while removing their plates.

Shandler smiles sweetly at me again. "You know"—she sits back in her chair, assessing me—"we really should hang out sometime."

I furrow my brows. "*Yeah*, no."

There is a split second of confusion, then rage, before a kicked puppy look takes over. "Wow. Just thought you might want a friend," she pouts.

Josh leans back in his chair and laughs. "Give it up, Shandler. She's already got you figured out."

She huffs at him then turns to me, the real Shandler back in play. "Watch yourself," she warns.

"Please," I say with a tilt of my head. "I grew up in The Bronx. You think I'm scared of your skinny ass?"

Josh starts laughing hysterically. I look at him. *It's not that funny*. Shandler's expression turns lethal. She opens her mouth to say something but Josh cuts her off. "Back off, Shandler," he warns.

"She—"

Josh gives her an icy look. She closes her mouth instantly.

"Well, we should get going," he says, standing. Shandler follows his lead, refusing to look at me. Does he have her on a leash or what? Totally weird dynamic.

Balancing their plates in one hand, I fish their bill out of my apron and hand it to him. He looks at it, then hands it back to me with a twenty. "Keep it."

"Thanks," I say, stuffing it in my front pocket before quickly walking to the back.

I rinse off the plates and stack them in the dishwasher. And after what seems like a fair amount of time for them to have left, I walk out. Josh is waiting for me.

Shit!

I look past him to Shandler, who is waiting by the front door, watching.

"Sorry about that. She can be difficult?"

I can think of a lot of better words to describe her. "No big deal."

"Look, I know you said you aren't into the whole dating thing, but it doesn't have to be like that. We could just hang as friends."

"That's okay. I'm good."

He looks stunned by my response, but recovers quickly. "You don't know many people at school, right? I could introduce you around."

I start to give him another excuse, but he cuts me off. "Look, I didn't mean to come across like a jerk earlier. I'm actually a really nice guy."

"I'm sure you are, but I'm super busy with school and work. I don't have a lot of extra time." He opens his mouth to reply. "Ah . . . so anyway," I say, making a thumb gesture in Tony's direction. "I should get back to work. It's kinda busy." Which is a total lie—the rush is over.

"Can I at least text you?"

"I don't have a cell phone."

"No way!"

"Yeah, well. I'm one of the lucky few."

He looks perplexed by my statement. "Well, I guess I'll see you at school?"

"Yeah. Sure." *Anything to get you out of here.*

He starts to walk away, but turns. "Look," he says, shifting from one foot to the other, looking embarrassed, "I'm sure Cody will tell you I have a bad reputation. He may have already. I just want you to know that none of it's true—I swear. If you give me a chance, you can decide for yourself. Okay?"

"Okay." *Leave!*

"I don't like that one." Anna says from behind me after Josh leaves through the door with Shandler. "He's no good for you!"

"Don't worry, Anna. I'm not interested."

"Good! Marco!" Anna yells right next to my ear.

I instinctively cover it. "Anna, are you trying to make me deaf?"

She grins and says she has no idea what I'm talking about.

"I'm here!" Marco comes from the back drying his hand on a rag. "You don't have to yell, Nona. Cassie, you ready?"

I look at her like, *see?*

Marco's head barely clears the back door as we leave, making me wonder if he ever played basketball with Cody. In the truck, I notice how his lashes are thick and long, and fan over his eyes as he blinks. Women pay big money to have lashes like that.

"What?" he says, looking self-conscious.

"Sorry. I was just wondering if you played basketball?" I

hope he doesn't think I was checking him out. I just never really noticed him before. That sounds awful. He drives me home every day from work—just too many other things clogging my brain.

"Why?"

"Just wondering—mostly because of your height, I guess."

"Sometimes, but mostly I'm too busy working. I need money for college."

"Where do you want to go?"

"The International Culinary Center. It's just north of here, outside of San Jose."

"How come you never do any cooking at Antonio's?"

"I do. All the time. I come in before school for an hour to do prep work and make the sauces. Then on the weekends I prepare all the entrees, like lasagna, manicotti—stuff like that."

"Sorry. I guess I should know that. I've only ever seen you deliver pizzas. Your food is amazing."

"Thanks."

"Wait. Anna let you into her kitchen?"

"They are all her recipes, I just tweaked them a little. She's never said anything, but I know she knows—just little off-handed comments she's made."

He pulls up in front of the house. I open the door and climb down from the truck. "Thanks for the ride."

"Sure, no problem. See you tomorrow. Oh, and Cassie—"

"Hmm?"

"That Josh kid is a total dick. I would watch out for him if I were you."

"Don't worry, I will."

I shut the truck door and watch him drive away, then look up toward the house. I still can't believe I live here.

"Cassie, is that you?" Roxanne calls when I'm inside.

"Yeah, it's me." I head in the direction of her voice.

I've never been in her office before. It's a complete mess. There are samples of her industry everywhere.

She looks up from her computer. "How was school? Did everyone like your new outfit?"

"I guess . . . didn't really pay attention, but no dirty looks, so I suppose so . . . well, except for Anna. She yelled at me, said my dress was too short."

She laughs. "I really should meet her, and Tony of course."

"I'm sure they'd like that."

"Your birthday is coming up soon. Would you like to do anything special?"

"I don't know. I kinda forgot about it." I case the room, looking at all the different color and textures. I open one of the textile books and look through it.

"Well, you let me know."

I put the book back. I'm glad she isn't going to pressure me. It's too depressing to think about.

"I need to get started on my homework, so I'm"—I point in the direction of my room—"going to get going."

"Okay. Happy studying."

I start to turn into my room, but pause, looking into Cody's. I've never been in there before. Curious, I flip on the light. You can tell Roxanne's been in here. It has a professional's touch. The walls are a similar color to mine, only maybe a shade darker. The furniture is a charcoal gray and very masculine. His bed is messy, and clothes are spread out all over the floor—I kick a few out of my way as I move toward his trophies that sit on top of his dresser—surprisingly, they're from track. There are also framed family photos from the beach and other vacations. My memories are one thing, but seeing a little Cody in the photos makes it even more real.

I check out the bathroom next. I smell his cologne by the sink. Yep, definitely Cody. I like it; it's on the musky side and not overpowering.

I'd better go. I don't know how he would feel about me snooping.

I sit down at my desk and pull my books and notes from my backpack and spread them out, then flip open my computer.

After a while, I find myself staring out into the backyard. It's almost dark, but there are little lights dotting the flowerbeds. It's pretty. I wonder what Mom would have thought about this place.

I can't believe I forgot my birthday. Mom always made such a big deal about it. One time, I woke up to our entire apartment filled with balloons. There were only three rooms—the combined living room, kitchen, and bedroom, the bathroom, and my sunroom. The whole apartment was maybe four hundred square feet, but still . . . it must have taken her all night to blow them up. I think I was about nine.

I can still see the proud-of-her-sneakiness expression. I hope I don't ever lose those images. The thought of them fading is terrifying. Damn. I didn't want to think about this.

"Can I come in?"

I jump. "Frick! You scared me." Cody stands in the doorway, school books in hand. "Sure. I guess." Actually, the diversion would be good. He can help keep my mind out of the suck-hole of sadness.

"I thought maybe we could study for that quiz tomorrow."

"Okay. Sure. Do you want to go to the kitchen table? There's more room."

"No, this is okay." He sprawls out on his stomach diagonally across the bed.

Sure. Make yourself comfortable. I open my history book and look at him, waiting for guidance on how he wants to proceed. He opens his book and flips through some notes. His phone makes a noise. He looks at it but sets it aside.

"*Um* . . . Josh and Shandler came in to Antonio's today."

He raises a quizzical eyebrow. "That's a scary thought—the two of them together."

"He asked if he could text me. I told him I didn't have a phone."

His expression turns hard. "You should avoid him, Cassie."

"He said you would say that." I tap my book with my pen. "Where do you want to start?"

"I'm serious. He's a total prick when it comes to girls."

"I thought he was your friend."

His phone makes a noise again. He grabs it and flips a switch on the side.

"We play basketball together, and he's part of the group I hang out with, but we're not friends."

"Fair enough." He frowns at me. "*Okay*," I say. "Don't worry. I'm not interested anyway."

I move over to the bed with my stuff and lean against the headboard. He shifts his body to a more vertical position, leaving me more room to stretch out. I cross my legs as I extend them—and pull my dress down to length. The back of his hand touches the side of my knee as he opens his book, making my skin tingle.

He looks up at me and smiles, before going back to reading.

Ugh. I should have stayed at my desk.

I don't know what my deal is. He's not even my type! Well . . . I'm not even sure what my type is, but he's supposed to be like a brother or something—we live together. And although he has his good moments, he's basically a twit. I'm only being drawn in by whatever pheromonal force grips every other female at our school, not to mention the easy-going attitude, lighthearted humor, and that damn dimple on his cheek that just, *bam*! knocks you over when he smiles.

I groan inwardly as I desperately try to force unwanted thoughts out of my head.

Cody looks up. "Did you say something?"

"Nope." *Stop reading my mind!*

"Oh. Okay." He looks back at his book. He flips the page and touches me again.

"I think I'm done for now," I say abruptly, scooting off the bed and placing my books back on the desk. Is he doing that on purpose?

"We just started."

"You're jamming my frequency," I say without thinking.

He gives me a panty-dropping smile. "*Really*," he draws out, teasing.

"Oh, get over yourself. I'm not used to studying with anyone, and I can't focus."

"Fair enough." He pushes himself off the bed. When he gets to the door, he turns. "I thought you looked really pretty today."

I can feel my cheeks heat up. "Thanks." He shuts the door as he leaves. I fan myself with my notebook. This is not good.

9

Josh Trainer turns out to be the most popular guy in school next to Cody, and for some reason, decides he wants to be my new best friend—it's irritating.

I'm *not* interested in him and he can't possibly be into me, so I'm not sure what his deal is. And we get so many strange looks when we're together—like they can't figure out why Mr. Man is hanging out with me. Surprisingly, he's nice, and somehow, we have a lot to talk about—he's not what I expected. Regardless, it's weird.

Shandler's been a total bitch ever since that day at Antonio's. If she's not giving me the stink eye, she's slinging her horseshit comments whenever she can. I'm sure she's not used to people standing up to her. Whatever, she's irritating but irrelevant.

Deciding to take advantage of the amazingly warm day, and the fact that Cody isn't home, I change into my bathing suit and head out to the pool. As I adjust my towel on the lounger, I hear Jeff and another man in a heated conversation coming from the side of the house. Hearing my mother's name, I freeze.

"It's not up to you," Jeff says. "You can't see her."

"We'll see about that!" The man says in return.

Jeff comes around the corner and startles when he sees me. "Ah . . . hey, Cassie. Are you going to sit out in the sun? It sure is a beautiful day."

"Why were you arguing with a man? I heard my mother's name."

He looks anxious. "Sorry about that, just an old friend of hers. He's not a stable person, so I've asked him not to come around here." He pauses. "Hey, why don't you get comfortable and I'll bring you out one of my famous smoothies, okay?" His smile seems forced.

"Sure. Okay. Thanks." I adjust myself comfortably on my back after he disappears inside. The sun feels amazing, but I'm weirded out by the confrontation. Hearing my mother's name from a complete stranger—I don't know, something's not right.

"As promised." Jeff returns after a bit and hands me a large plastic glass with and enormous straw. "The best smoothie ever made."

I take a sip. "*Mmm!* That *is* good!"

He smiles. "It's my version of Hunkie Monkey . . . or is it Chunky's Monkey?" He scratches his head. "Whatever it's called. You know . . . from Ben and Jerry's."

"I think you mean Chunky Monkey." I smile up at him. "And it's amazing."

There's an uncomfortable silence.

"Okay," Jeff says. "Well, I'm going to go back in and leave you in peace."

"Jeff?"

He stops, holding the screen door open. "Yeah?"

"Is everything okay?"

"Don't give it another thought. He was just some guy from your mother's past who heard she passed away and wanted to meet you. I told him that it wouldn't be a good idea. Like I said, he's not an overly stable person, so I don't want him around you."

"All right," I say, but I'm not convinced he's telling the truth. How would the guy have heard about my mother's death?

10

TODAY, Anna is on fire. First, she's yelling at Tony because his apron is dirty, then she doesn't like his shoes. She yells at Marco because his hair is too long, then turns on me, saying I shouldn't wear flip-flops to work and that my skirt is too short.

"Anna," I finally say. "Why are you picking on everybody?"

"I'm not picking on nobody!" She throws an arm in the air dramatically. "Everyone is driving me crazy! Nobody knows how to take care of themselves."

"Really?" I laugh.

"Really!" she says, smiling a little. "If it wasn't for me, you'd all be a bunch of bums!" I stifle a laugh. "*Bah!*" she says, throwing her hands forward in dismissal before walking to the back. I look over at Tony, who shrugs his shoulders.

"Hey," Marco says to me. "Do you want to come on a delivery with me? It's dead here anyway, and it's a big order. I could use the help carrying it in. Tony? It's okay if Cassie comes and helps me with this big delivery, right?"

"Ya. You two go. I got it here." He wipes down the counter.

"Go get the warmers, will ya," he says to me. "I'll gather the pizzas."

I do as Marco asks and hold them while he loads them in. "Why are they so light?"

"I don't know? Thin crust pizzas?"

"What! Now you leaving?" Anna yells as we walk through the back kitchen toward the door.

"Nona," he yells in frustration. "She's just coming with me to help with this huge delivery, remember?"

"You kids with all your comings and goings. Who can keep up?" She scowls.

Marco walks over to her and kisses her on the cheek. "I deliver pizzas, Nona. I come and I go. That's what you pay me to do."

She tries to hide her smile. "Don't get *smart* with me, Marciano," she says, gently patting the side of his face.

"Come on, Cassie," Marco says.

"You drive carefully with my Cassie," Anna yells from inside. "You hear me?"

"Okay," we holler back in unison.

"Marciano?" I tease, getting into the truck.

"Yeah. What of it?"

"It's cute."

He groans.

I stare out the side window as we drive, watching but not really seeing. Today is my birthday. If Mom was around, I'd already be wishing she'd stop making such a fuss, but she's not, and I'd give anything to hear her get all goofy about it. I wring my hands in my lap, holding back the tears. Damn. I was doing so well.

I do my best to snap out of my private pity-party and

realize we've been driving around for a long time. "Are we lost?"

"Yeah, I can't find the address. The GPS isn't working, so I'm going off of Tony's directions."

"Oh, boy. This could be bad."

"I think I better head back and check those directions again."

"Why don't you just call him? Wouldn't that save time?"

He pats his pants pockets, then quickly looks around him, before turning his attention back to the road. "I must have left my phone back at the restaurant."

"Those people are going to be *so* pissed."

"No, it's all good."

Marco returns the truck to its parking space behind the restaurant. "You'd better come in with me to make sure I get the directions right this time."

I follow Marco inside, thinking we're going to catch some serious hell from Tony.

"Surprise!"

Marco stands looking at me expectantly—so do Tony, Jeff, Anna, Roxanne, and Cody. It takes a couple of seconds to take in the balloons, and Anna holding a flaming birthday cake, for me to realize what's happening.

"Okay everybody," Anna says. "One, two, three . . ."

Next comes the painfully awkward moment when all eyes fixate on you during the horribly butchered, but lovingly sung, rendition of *Happy Birthday*.

I hate this part the most, but Maria insisted on it every year, only it would be Mom and Luigi and whoever the dish washer was at the time, singing.

I count to fifty really fast, trying to drown out the heart-wrenching thoughts. I don't want to break down and cry in front of everyone.

Finally, the song is over and I blow out the candles.

"I'm gonna put this cake down and cut the slices," Anna says.

Roxanne leans in for a hug. "I hope it's okay. I know you said you didn't want to celebrate your birthday, but when Luigi called the other day to talk to you, he reminded Jeff about your birthday and said he was going to call Tony, and once Anna found out . . . there was no stopping her."

I give a weak smile. "No . . . not when she sets her mind to something."

Marco gives me a quick squeeze. "Pretty good acting, huh?"

"Had *me* fooled. You should get those pizzas inside before they get cold."

"The boxes were empty."

"Pretty sneaky."

Marco smiles proudly.

Anna is handing out slices of cake as Cody weaves his way in my direction. I start to thank him for being here, but he pulls me against him, crushing me in a hug.

"Happy Birthday," he says softly against my ear, sending goosebumps everywhere.

Luckily, he let's go right before I shiver. That would have been embarrassing.

"Hold on. I got you something." He steps away, returning a second later holding a gift bag out to me.

"Thank you. Should I open it now?"

"Sure. I guess."

We walk over to the high counter. I pull out the tissue paper. Pretty sure this part was all Roxanne. "Oh, I—"

"I know what you said . . ." He looks concerned as I stare at the small sketchbook in my hand. "Even if it's kids' stuff, or whatever other excuse you can come up with, I know it was something special to you."

Holding it in my hand feels so familiar, like a singular missing piece of my being was just returned to me.

He nods his head in the direction of the bag. "There's one more."

I reach down, pull out a long box, and lift the lid.

"I wasn't sure what you liked to work with, so I got you every kind of pencil they had."

I stare at the items in my hand. They symbolize the precious connection I had with my mother that I threw away out of grief, not realizing it was and would always be a link to her. And Cody was the one who gave it back to me.

"Ah, crap! I knew I was taking a risk getting this stuff, but I felt I needed to do it. It was stupid of me. I'm sorry." He tries to take the gifts from me, but I turn my body, keeping them out of his reach.

"It's okay." I finally find my words. "I'm just overwhelmed—the surprise party, my mom not being here, you knowing what I needed when I didn't."

He looks pleased with himself, but shrugs it off with a lopsided smile.

I set the items on the counter and can't resist throwing my arms around his neck, hugging him hard. "Thanks, this means a lot."

"So do you," he says into the side of my neck, squeezing me back. I'm surprised by the sentiment and glance up at him as we separate. "And don't you forget it," he adds awkwardly.

"Cassie, Cody." We both look over at Anna, who looks like she's scowling. "Come get your cake," she commands.

"Is she always so . . ."

"Angry, loud, bossy, and demanding?"

"Yeah."

"That's how she shows her love."

Cody snorts.

Homemade chocolate cake, just like Maria used to make it. At the first bite, I close my eyes and sigh as the cake melts in my mouth. "*Mmm*. Anna, this is beyond good. Thank you."

"You're welcome," she says, looking pleased. "But it was my Marco that made it."

I look around for Marco, who's seated at one of the tables talking to Jeff. "Marco," I shout. When he looks at me, I raise my fork. "You *do* have a gift."

He nods his head in appreciation, then continues his conversation with Jeff.

I put my paper plate in the garbage can. "You are so beautiful," Anna says, walking toward me, "and dear to us." She pats my cheek.

"Thank you. That means a lot when you don't have a family."

"What do you mean you don't have a family!" she says, looking suddenly cross. "You gotta *big* family, and they're all here wishing you the happy birthday! What are you talking about—no family! Are you *stupid*?"

"Okay, I'm sorry," I laugh. "Calm down before you give yourself a heart attack."

"*Bah!* I'm too busy to have a heart attack."

"You should have been an actress, Anna. You had me fooled today."

"I don't know what you are talking about," she says with a sly grin. "Tony!" she yells, even though he's two feet away. "You tell her what we all did for her birthday!"

"*Okay!* Quit yelling at me. I'm not deaf."

Anna smiles mischievously and smacks him on the arm.

"Cassie," he says to me, putting his arm around Anna. "Me and my Anna, Luigi and Maria, Roxanne and Jeff started a savings account for you to go to that fancy art school of yours in New York." I start to object but he cuts me off. "*And* . . . you will stay with Luigi and Maria while you go there." I start to open my mouth again. "*And* don't try to say no!" He squints at me out of one eye and wags a finger at me. "Luigi and Maria told me about you and your art, and Jeff and Roxanne told me why you won't do it no more. But I say you will go and that's that!"

"But, Tony."

He lifts his chin in defiance. "Don't you argue with me, young lady! I'll not have it."

"I wasn't! I was just going to say thank you."

"Oh," he says, looking surprised by his victory as everyone laughs.

I'll let them think what they want for now. I'll pick another University and get a degree in . . . I don't know, something, and who knows.

I stare out the window on the drive home—the excitement of the night is wearing off and deep sadness settles in.

"I hope you had fun tonight," Roxanne says, turning on the

light in the kitchen when we get home. "Birthdays are special. They're for celebrating life and every year is like a new chapter with endless possibilities." She laughs. "At least that's what your mother always used to say."

I smile, but it's weak. "I got that speech every year for as long as I can remember."

She takes my hand in hers. "You are such a gift. I know you probably still feel like a stranger here, but I want you to know how honored I am to have you with us. Not just because I loved Allora like a sister, but because I've always wanted a daughter." Tears brim, threatening to spill over. "Oh, look at me," she says wiping them away. "I've always been a bit on the mushy side."

"How come you never had any more children?" I ask gently.

She takes a deep shuddering breath. "Oh . . . well . . . it wasn't for lack of trying." A strained laugh escapes her. "I had two miscarriages. And after that . . . I—we knew we couldn't handle another heartbreak like that and still stay sane."

Jeff steps into the kitchen with Cody right behind him. They stop when they see us. "Is everything okay?" Jeff asks with concern.

Roxanne wipes both of her eyes with the back of her hand as she composes herself. "Just girl talk."

Cody rolls his eyes and walks around us, heading down the hall to our rooms.

"Well, I'm ready for bed," Jeff declares. "How about you, hon?"

"Definitely." She gives me another hug. "Goodnight, sweetie."

I watch as Jeff puts his arm around her, leading her in the direction of their room. The endearment makes my heart ache even worse.

I'm so sick of feeling sad. I shut my bedroom door behind me, then stretch out on my stomach on the big comfy bed. Grabbing my pillow, I scrunch it up and bury my face in. I try to keep my mind clear, but too many memories seep past the wall I've carefully constructed, and the tears fall, despite all my efforts to build it.

Damn!

I'm unaware of a knock, or of Cody entering my room, just the bed compression of the bed as he sits next to me. I want to yell at him to get out—to leave me alone—but as he starts stroking my hair rhythmically down my back and I can't. It feels too good.

When I have nothing left, I roll over and look up at him.

The room is dark except for the hallway light casting a halo around him. Gazing through puffy eyes, I wonder who this guy really is. Every time I think I've got him figured out, he surprises me.

"Hold on," he says, running out of my room and returning with a box of tissues.

"Thanks," I say, pushing myself up. I imagine how horrible I look, then realize I'm too drained to care.

"No problem. I'm sorry this is so hard, but I'm sure your mom wouldn't want you being so sad."

I blow my nose—and blow, and blow.

He laughs. "Man. How can so much gross snot come out of someone so pretty?"

I snort. "Dickhead!"

"Psycho."

An un-energized chuckle escapes me.

"Feel better?"

"Yeah, thanks."

He gets up to go.

"Cody?"

He turns around. "Yeah?"

"Thanks again for the gift."

"You're welcome."

I change into my T-shirt when he leaves and crawl under the covers. As I drift off to sleep, all I can think about is Cody's touch, and how much I want to feel it again.

Aw, man. This sucks.

11

I WATCH as this really pretty girl with long, blond hair, perfect figure, and full pouty lips, hangs on Cody's arm, giggling at something he must have said.

I shake my head as I walk by.

Disgusting.

"What's wrong?" Josh appears by my side.

"Nothing."

"Hey. You're not falling for Cody like every other girl, are you?"

"No! It's just ridiculous how they act around him." I look at him poignantly. "The same way they act around you, actually."

"Jealous?"

"Hardly."

"You really know how to get a guy right where it hurts?"

"Well, considering your heart is probably in your pants along with your other junk . . . good."

"Cold, Cassie—very cold." He smiles, feigning hurt.

"Yeah, well." I can't help laughing. He's not so bad. I'm even starting to enjoy his company.

I'm close to Antonio's when I hear someone say, "Cassandra?" I turn and see a man, who looks kind of familiar, looking at me with a nervous, hopeful expression on his face.

I stare at him, trying to register where I know him from—maybe the restaurant? Whatever . . . it's creepy. "Sorry, you've got the wrong person." I continue to the door.

"You're Allora's daughter, aren't you?"

The hairs on the back of my neck stand on end as I recognize the voice. It's the guy I heard fighting with Jeff.

"Look," I say calmly, remembering Jeff said he was unstable. "I'm not sure who Cassandra is or how you know my mother, but I'd like you to leave me alone." I reach for the door.

"I'm sorry, but I can't do that."

Planning on ignoring him, I pull the door open. I'm almost inside when I hear: "Cassandra! I'm your father."

I freeze for a moment, anger bubbling up to an explosive level, then step back outside, letting the door close. I turn to him. "How *dare* you! My father's been dead since I was four."

"Just give me a minute. I'll explain."

"Explain? There's nothing to explain." *You're obviously some crazed psycho*. "And stay away from me!" I turn and walk into the restaurant again—it's what I should have done originally.

Tony meets me just inside the door. "Wa's wrong. I heard you yelling." He looks out the door behind me. "Who was that man?"

"Nobody."

"Was he bad to you? Maybe I should call the police." He walks quickly away, heading toward the phone.

"No! Don't." Tony stops. "It's okay. He's just a little confused. He thought I was someone else."

"You're white as a sheet." He comes to my side. "Come sit down." He pulls out a chair for me. "Anna!" he yells. "Come bring Cassie some cold water."

I sit down. "No, it's okay. I'm fine." I've never been good at handling people with mental problems. They're unpredictable. You don't know what they're capable of. And to have my mother involved—it just makes me feel sick inside.

Anna comes running from the back. "Wa's wrong?" She sets the water in front of me, then places the back of her hand on my forehead. "Are you sick?"

"No. I'm fine." I take a sip of water.

"You don't look fine!" she yells at me.

"Some man was bothering her," Tony says with a dramatic wave of his hand.

"Who would bother our Cassie?" Anna demands, looking outraged.

"What's all the commotion about?" Marco asks, coming from the kitchen.

"Some man was bothering Cassie. You need to walk her from school!" Tony yells angrily at him.

"What did I do?" he hollers back.

"No. It's fine, you guys. I just got a little overheated."

"You should wear a hat!" Anna declares. "That way you don't get so hot!"

"Okay, Anna. Thanks." *That'll solve everything*. Everyone is still looking at me. "I'm fine. You don't all need to hover."

. . .

After, working through the dinner rush, Anna suddenly comes from the back kitchen, insisting that I don't look good and tells me I am going home. On the way, I realize I'm glad she insisted. I need to talk to Jeff. I find him outside working in the flowerbed. Roxanne is relaxing in a lawn chair near him with a tall drink in her hand.

"Jeff?"

He looks up at me, shielding his eyes from the setting sun. "What's up, kiddo? You're home early?"

"Um . . . you know that guy you were talking to the other day—the one you were kind of fighting with?"

Roxanne looks over at him. "You were fighting with someone here at the house?"

Jeff raises his hand to halt her questioning as he stands up. "What about him?" He sounds apprehensive.

"But who—"

"Roxanne!" he says firmly, cutting her off. "Cassie, what about him? Has he confronted you?"

"Yes . . . on my way to work. He said he was my father."

Roxanne places a hand over her mouth. "No. He couldn't have. Jeff?"

Jeff looks at Roxanne. Taking his gloves off, he runs his fingers through his hair before answering her. "He came by the other day."

"Why didn't you tell me?" she stands, visibly distressed.

"I didn't want to worry you. I know how you feel about him."

"How would he know?" she says, wringing her hands together.

"What's going on?" I shout.

"Oh, Cassie, honey," she says, looking at Jeff.

Jeff nods his head, as if to say, *okay*.

"Come on. Let's all go sit down." Roxanne puts an arm around my shoulder and leads me into the porch.

After we get settled, she continues. "That man you heard talking to Jeff . . . his name is Brent Carson, and he *is* your father."

Adrenalin kicks me in the stomach, making me feel nauseous. "What? That's not possible. He died when I was little. Mom *told* me so." This can't be right. Roxanne must not know my mother as well as she thought she did.

Roxanne takes a deep breath, letting it out slowly. "Your father was starring in a movie that your mother had a small part in—that's where they met."

"My mother was an *actress*?" *Wait, what?* I grip the edge of my seat to steady myself. I feel lightheaded.

"She was just starting out. They fell in love on the set. It began like a fairytale romance, but then his career took a nosedive, your mom became pregnant, and he started drinking heavily.

"Are you serious? Why didn't she tell me any of this?"

"I'm sorry, baby. I don't know. To protect you?"

"My father is alive?"

"Yes."

"But . . . I don't understand."

"I'll try to explain, okay?" I nod my head yes, but I can barely breathe. "After you were born, the drinking escalated and the affairs began. At first, he had the decency to hide them, but when she found out and confronted him, he started flaunting them in her face and became verbally abusive as well—even blaming her for his failing career. Jeff and I tried to talk to him, but he didn't think he had a problem.

"The verbal abuse eventually turned physical, putting Allora in the hospital after one of his tirades. After that, he said he'd get help and swore he would never touch another drop. It lasted six months before it started all over again. One night, he knocked her down the stairs. She said it was an accident, that he was just too drunk to realize where they were when he pushed her. Luckily, she only suffered small cuts and had some really big bruises, but it was enough for her to finally leave him.

"We offered to have her stay with us, but she knew that was the first place he'd look and she didn't want us involved. So, while he was still passed out, we packed her car with as much stuff as we could, and watched her drive away. We never heard from her after that . . . well, other than a postcard she picked up from some small town somewhere, telling us she was safe."

I don't understand. "So, my father has been alive all this time, and she never told me? Are you freaking kidding me right now!" My voice sounds shrill. "This isn't right. Are you sure?"

"I'm sorry, Cassie, I'm sure."

"I can't believe this. Why didn't she tell me when I was older?"

"She probably still felt the need to protect you," Roxanne says. "Maybe if you knew he was alive and decided to find him? She probably didn't want to take the risk of you getting hurt."

"That wasn't her choice to make!" I holler at them. "So, my name isn't even Cassie Roads? I'm like, what . . . Cassandra Carson?"

Roxanne looks over at Jeff with such a helpless expression. I take a deep breath, trying to calm myself. "I'm sorry. I know none of this is your fault."

"We understand what a shock this is," Jeff says.

"How did he even know she died?"

Jeff regarded me thoughtfully. "He had detectives looking for you for years. They must have come across a death certificate that somehow linked her to her real last name, and that's what brought him here the other day. He must have hoped that Allora would send you to us. He's a famous movie director now."

"And that matters, why?"

"It doesn't. Sorry. I'm just thinking, he probably has lots of connections. That could be another way he found out. I don't know . . . I'm grasping for answers."

"I can't believe this is happening. Does Cody know anything about this?"

"No. He was so little when you two left." Her eyes turn sad. "He kept asking why you couldn't come over to play—it just about broke my heart. You two loved playing together."

I stand up and pace. "She was supposed to be my best friend!" I yell.

They stare at me, looking lost.

"Shit." Why am I yelling at them? This isn't their fault. "I need to go."

Roxanne starts to say something, but Jeff touches her arm, stopping her. "We understand," Jeff says softly.

Reaching to open the door, I turn back. "Why didn't *you* tell me? I lost the only family member I had left. It would have helped to know I wasn't alone." I bite out, feeling betrayed by everyone.

"Cassie," Roxanne says, standing. She looks at Jeff as he takes her hand and shakes his head, *no*.

"Whatever," I snap and walk into the house. Even on her deathbed, she kept me in the dark—kept her past hidden from me.

My shoulder bumps Cody's arm in the hallway. "Hey," he says startled. "Are you okay?"

"Yeah! Effing great!" I slam my door behind me, this time remembering to lock it.

It's close to dark out when I hear Cody calling my name from the door. "Come on, let me in." The doorknob jiggles.

"Go away," I yell.

"Not until you let me in."

I don't answer him.

"You are my sunshine," he sings horribly off-key, "my only sunshine. You make me happy, when skies are gray."

I pull the pillow over my head, trying to drown him out.

"I'll stand out here and sing till you let me in." I pull the pillow tighter against my ear. "You'll never know, dear, how much I love you. Please don't take my sunshine away."

Finally, there's silence. He must have given up. I lift the pillow off and turn onto my back, but then he starts again, singing it louder, at an even higher, more irritating pitch.

I tolerate it for another three repetitive rounds of pure torture. "*Ahhh!*" I scream, throwing the pillow at the door. "Why won't you leave me alone?"

He doesn't answer, just keeps singing.

"You're such an ass!" I yell. Jumping up, I unlock the door and yank it open. "Will you please stop!"

"Yeah, sure," he says calmly as he brushes past me to sit on the side of my bed.

I stand with feet braced apart and hands on my hips. "Oh my god! Didn't anyone ever teach you about personal space or *boundaries?*"

He ignores my question. "Mom explained everything to me, and I wanted to make sure you were okay."

"Oh, great," I say, crossing my arms over my chest. "So what? You'll tell all your friends how my father's some famous director and spin it into some juicy gossip so everyone at school can start whispering behind my back?"

"No." He looks at me like I'm stupid. "I'll continue to tell them what I've *been* telling them . . . that I'm living with a certifiable nutcase, and I only tolerate her 'cause she's kind of cute in a lost, bulldog sort of way."

I glare down at him. "I'd like to see how *you'd* react."

"Probably worse than you." He stands up and steps in front of me. He slides his hands up and down my upper arms gently. His touch is soothing. "There'd probably be lots of holes in the walls."

I snort. "Damn you! I want to be mad!" I drop my hands to my side.

"Cassie? Can we come in?" Roxanne says from the door. Jeff is behind her, peering over her shoulder.

"It's your house," I grumble. "Privacy doesn't seem to count for much around here." I glare at Cody, who throws his hands up in defeat and leaves.

Roxanne is the first to respond. "We're so sorry, baby. We know you wanted to be alone, but we were worried."

She's twisting her hands again nervously. I feel like a shit for making her feel that way. "Sorry," I say, my anger deflating.

"No . . . don't apologize," Roxanne says. "I know this is overwhelming. We were *hoping* we'd never have to tell you, but maybe that wasn't the best idea."

I look from Roxanne to Jeff, their expressions thoughtful. "I know you were only following Mom's wishes, but no one had the right to keep the fact that he's alive from me."

"I know," Jeff says. "But understand, looking out for your safety is our number one priority. We didn't know how he would react, what he might do, or his mental state. From what the media says, he's successful, a philanthropist even—but still, we don't know a lot about him."

I stare at the floor. Roxanne puts an arm around my shoulder and squeezes. "We're so sorry, honey—for this whole mess."

"I shouldn't have reacted like that toward you." I look between the two of them. "All you've done is try to help—you didn't ask for any of this drama to be hoisted on you."

She squeezes me again. "You didn't ask for it either. We will all just make the best of it and help each other through, okay?"

"Okay. Thanks . . . for telling me."

She smiles and pats my shoulder. "Are you hungry?"

"Yeah," Jeff says. "I could make you some of my famous chocolate chip banana pancakes."

"*We* just ate," Roxanne says. "I was asking Cassie."

"Dessert!" he clarifies, looking hopeful.

I feel the corners of my mouth lift a little. "Yeah, sure. That sounds really good."

I hear Cody yell from his room. "I'm in!"

Jeff claps his hands together. "All right! That's what we'll do." He says it like pancakes are the cure-all. Who knows? Maybe they are.

As they leave, I sit on my bed, drained. Cody comes back in, sitting next to me.

I drop my head in my hands and groan. "I was such a shit to your parents."

"Don't worry about it." With my head still resting in my hands, I crank my neck to look at him. "Cassie, you didn't do anything wrong. That kind of news would shock the hell out of anyone. Besides, you did what any normal teenager would do when they were pissed. They're used to it. They raised *me*."

I straighten. "I'm not usually this emotional. You must be getting sick of it by now?"

"*Naw*, you're a girl. It's expected."

I lean away from him, insulted. "*Excuse* me*?*" As I glare at him, I get a mental image of my expression, adding in the bloodshot eyes and Rudolf-red nose, and laughter bubbles up.

"Feeling better?"

"No, just losing it."

Cody's phone makes a noise from his pocket.

"Do you want to answer that?"

"No. Aren't you curious who this guy is? You must be dying to Google him."

"I'm not an avid Googler, being that I've never had a smartphone or my own computer."

He looks at me like, *and?*

"Yeah. I guess I'm curious."

He whips out his phone and types in Brent Carson Movies and a whole bunch I've seen with Mom pop up.

"Wow. He's had a lot of blockbusters," Cody ogles.

"So what? He's still an abusive asshole! I wonder what the media would think if they found out about his long-lost daughter or why she had to be kept hidden from him."

"Cassie." He looks displeased by my train of thought.

"I'm just talkin' out of my ass. The last thing I want is attention."

"Good to hear."

"Cassie. Cody," Roxanne yells from the kitchen. "The first batch of pancakes are just about ready."

He jumps up, shoves me backward onto the bed, then bolts out of the room like his ass is on fire. He is such a dork. I wonder if anyone at school sees this side of him or if it's just me. The idea that I might be the only one makes me feel special.

Aah, hell.

When I walk in, Jeff is setting an enormous stack of pancakes on the table. "Ta-da!" he exclaims proudly. "*I am good*—darn good!"

I look at everybody around me as they fight with their forks for the first pancake. It's crazy, my life, and how it brought me to this place with these people. I was so angry when Mom said I had to move here, especially when I had a family where I was, but right now . . . in this moment, I'm grateful. She knew what was best for me. I'm still super pissed at her, but she got this right.

I make a vow. I'm done being sad and feeling sorry for myself. It's time to let go—as best I can—and move on. I have to. I've got an abusive, asshole for a father in my life now. I need to have my head on straight to deal with it.

12

I HAVEN'T SEEN or heard any more from Brent, AKA, Dad. Hopefully, I scared him off. And if I didn't, I can use the time to process.

It's so weird—I have a father. Well, I knew I had a father, obviously, but a living one? It's been tough to grasp.

I Googled him on my own. He's won some academy awards for directing. He's a huge benefactor—supporting charities involved with domestic abuse—which I found hypocritical, to say the least. Maybe he did it out of guilt—either way, I wasn't impressed.

And now I know why I don't have blue eyes and blond hair like my mom. So nice to see I resemble my scumbag father—makes me feel really good about myself.

I still can't believe she didn't tell me—she didn't tell me a lot of things. How do I even begin to process this? It's bad enough dealing with the loss of her, but add in anger and disappointment? It's painful.

"Are you ready?" Roxanne yells from down the hall.

I take one last look in the mirror—cute, ankle length skinny jeans, an off the shoulder sweatshirt, and a black pair of sparkly Bob's flats. I even did my makeup—which took me forever, mostly because I never wear it and partially because I wanted it to look good.

I hear Cody's words in my head, "Potential."

I shake my head at my reflection. "Coming."

Jeff is holding the garage door open for me. "Hey," I say, slightly out of breath.

"You look beautiful," he says thoughtfully.

I'm embarrassed for even trying.

Cody is in the alumni game at his school. They're raising money for their upcoming year. I can see why scouts would be interested in him—he's the leading scorer, not a ball hog, a skilled playmaker, and tough around the basket. Josh, on the other hand, is the asshole that gets in everyone's face: elbows, jabs, fouls constantly, and continually complains to the refs. But to Josh's credit, he does open up some room for his players.

I may not play sports, but I know a lot about them; although, I'd never tell Cody that. Luigi was a big fan, so I grew up with it on the radio and hearing him discuss games with customers and friends that stopped by. He loved the Knicks. Eventually he got a little TV and when it was dead at the restaurant, we would watch. I learned a lot.

Watching Jeff and Roxanne get worked up is fun. They're involved, crazed fans. Not in a bad way—just parents totally invested in their kid's passion. I like it.

The game is packed. I watch all the students assembled in their little cliques—they're all there—the popular kids, the wannabes, the geeks to the stoners and everything else in-between. Regardless, they're all laughing, cheering, and having a great time.

Fitting in has never been a big deal to me, but for some reason . . . tonight it is. My comment to Cody about not wanting friends due to social hierarchy was such a load of crap. Having some like-minded people to chill with would be great. It just never worked out for me.

We walk down the steps of the bleachers to the court where Cody is waiting for us after the game. He hugs his mom, his dad gives him a small shove and comments what a great game he played—as for me? I get the no-big-deal, who-cares-that-you-spent-an-hour-getting-ready-because-you-look-like-you-always-do greeting.

Yep, I feel stupid.

Why did I bother? To impress him?

Frick!

"Okay, well, see ya," Cody says to us as a whole. A pretty brunette is waiting for him by the exit. I watch him walk the distance, then throw his arm around her slender shoulders, squeezing her into him. She giggles as they leave the gym.

Disgusting. And he says he doesn't do the whole Mr. Popular thing—bullshit—he lives, eats, and breathes it.

I helplessly sigh to myself. But he's more than that, and I really like the more.

"Hey," a male voice says from behind me. I startle and turn to see Josh giving me his panty-dropping smile. "What are you staring at?"

"Oh. Hey. Nothing." I sound disgruntled, which I am, even though technically Cody didn't do anything wrong.

"It's nice to see you too," he jokes. "Hey, there's a party tonight. Do you want to go with me?"

"No, thanks."

A flash of astonishment crosses his face like, *you're seriously turning me down, again*? He laughs regardless. "I like you."

"Well, thank you."

"No, really. I know it sounds like a cliché, but you're not like the other girls."

"You mean I don't fall and kiss your feet."

"Pretty much sums it up. Come on. Go with me. I can introduce you around, give you a chance to meet some nice people."

"You mean those social leeches that constantly suck up to you? No thanks."

He tilts his head. "*Hmm*. Okay. Never thought of it that way. But you're probably right."

"Probably?"

"You're right. But do you want to go with me anyway?"

"Look, why are you wasting your time with me? I doubt it's because of my spunky personality . . . and you can get any girl you want . . . so did someone challenge you with some kind of perverse dare?"

"No," he laughs. "Look, I know you're not the type of girl that needs her ego stroked—I doubt you have one. But honestly? I *do* like your personality—you don't take any of my bullshit, you're beautiful, and I like being around you."

I snort. "Okay, anyway, I'm not interested in doing the whole dating thing."

"I get the feeling you're just not interested in *me*."

"Well . . ." I stumble, trying to think of a response.

"*Ouch.*"

"I barely know you."

"Well, I guess there's still hope then. This doesn't have to be a date. And they can't all be leeches. There have to be *some* people at the party worth knowing."

I guess I'll never find anyone to hang with if I don't put myself out there.

He looks at me intently. "Just as friends, okay? I promise." He holds his hands up. "Hands off. Unless you beg me." He pumps his eyebrows suggestively.

I roll my eyes, making him laugh. I'm glad he finds me so amusing. Maybe I'm like a pet monkey. He likes to keep me around to see what weird and funny things I'll do.

"Okay. Sure," I relent.

"Great."

I walk over to Roxanne and Jeff. "Is it okay if I go to a party for a while? Josh is going to give me a ride."

Jeff gives Josh a stern look. "Cody's probably going to the same one, so he can give you a ride after."

Yay. I can watch girls fall over him all night—*so* fun.

"Oh, it's okay. I can give her a ride." He places a hand on my lower back. "I'll see you in a bit?" he asks, looking hopeful.

"Yeah."

"Just wait for me outside the locker room."

Oh, goody.

This is ridiculous. I feel like a groupie.

I nervously shift my weight side to side as players assess me on their way out of the locker room. *Ugh.*

I hope Cody doesn't see me standing here.

Oh, who gives a crap what he thinks?

Josh is taking forever.

Why the hell did I agree to this, anyway? I can't even bail now. Jeff and Roxanne are long gone.

"You ready to go?" Josh says, coming out with several teammates. Some of them look me up and down knowingly. One of them pats Josh on the back in approval.

I want to scream, *I'm not a groupie, you friggin' jerkoff's*!

This is such a bad idea.

The party is packed. "Can I get you a beer?" Josh asks, motioning for me to follow him.

"Sure."

He opens a cooler, pulls out two bottles, twists off the caps, and hands me one. I really don't want it, but it will give me something to hold on to.

Josh grabs my free hand and leads me out the back door to a pool area. The house is enormous, and the backyard makes Jeff's look like a dumpy patch of weeds.

Immediately, I'm intimidated by the scene in front of me—half-naked girls in the pool, couples grinding or making out to a strong beat, people yelling over the noise, trying to be heard. And everyone staring at me as we pass like, *what the hell are you doing here?*

Josh seems totally oblivious as he leads me to a place that's less crowded but is front and center to all the insanity—see and be seen, I guess.

"Hey." He squeezes my hand. "Don't worry. I'll introduce you around, you'll be fine."

I don't care about fine. I want out of here, and I want my hand back.

"Come on," he says pulling me with him.

"It's okay," I say, holding my ground. "I'd rather stay here." Ignoring me, he tugs gently, pulling me forward.

I consider using the crush of people as an opportunity to pull free, ditching him to find another way home.

But I don't lose him and he spends the evening finding clever ways to touch me *everywhere*, while introducing me to *everyone*—most of whom politely acknowledge me but generally ignore me. He does his best to include me in all the conversations, which is nice, but still very awkward. I have to give him credit, though. He hasn't dumped me in a corner to be with his friends—he's been engaging, quick-witted, funny, and surprisingly interesting.

He places his hand on the small of my back and leans into me. "I'm sorry for the way some of my friends are treating you. I don't know what their deal is."

Cody appears out of nowhere, grabbing me by the arm and pulling me away.

I stumble a little as he pulls me to the side of the room. "Ow! What's *your* problem?"

"Are you here with him?" He scowls at Josh over my shoulder before turning his attention back to me

"He asked me to come," I say casually, yanking my arm from his grasp. "What's it to you?"

"I told you he treats girls like shit."

"Well, he's been nothing but nice. And I can take care of myself!"

"Hey." Josh appears at my side. "Everything okay?" Cody glares at him, which Josh ignores. "If this is some protective brother thing, you don't have to worry . . . we're just hanging out. And I'm helping her meet some people, which is what you should be doing, but as per usual you're, uh . . . busy." He nods his head in the direction of a group of girls; one being the one he left the gym with.

I cross my arms over my chest with a look that says, *mmm-hmm*!

Cody gets in his face and in a low, barely controlled voice says, "Don't even *think* about playing her. She'll see right through you. And just so we're clear . . . if you lay a hand on her in any way she doesn't find acceptable, I will end you."

Is he drunk? What the hell!

"Well, you can try," Josh says, an icy gleam in his eyes.

Cody growls and shoulder checks him as he passes, forcing Josh to take a step to the side.

I look around. People are staring at us.

"Do you know what that was all about?" Josh asks me.

"I have *no* idea," I say, completely mortified.

"If I didn't know better, I'd think he was jealous."

"What do you mean . . . if you didn't know better?"

"Well, him and Shandler have this on again, off again thing." He nods his head toward the front door.

I look over. Sure enough, he's talking to her. She's got a hand on the side of his face, like she's trying to console him. My heart involuntarily sinks.

"See what I mean?"

"Yeah . . . whatever," I say bitterly. "I just live with the guy. I don't care who he's on and off of."

Josh's friends crowd us, wanting the scoop on the confrontation. Josh responds like it was all in fun—just two teammates messing around, giving each other a hard time.

Some of the girls question me. I mostly shrug my shoulders, wanting to crawl under a rock and die.

There are tons of people throughout the house. Cody could be anywhere, but he seems set on being in my line of sight. I'm just *loving* watching him work the crowd. It's not just girls, guys too. "Mr. Social" loves his element.

I stifle a yawn. Will this night ever end? The meaningless babble is starting to drive me crazy.

I'm about to ask Josh if we can leave when I feel a hand grasp my shoulder. "Come on, Cassie," Cody says. "It's getting late. We should go."

I'm still pissed off from him losing his shit earlier, as well as him getting cozy with the Bitch Queen, so I get snarky. "Well, *I'm* not ready. Can't you see I'm enjoying myself?" I know I'm stirring up shit, but for some reason, I can't help myself.

Josh confronts Cody again. "Dude! Seriously . . . what *is* your deal?"

"I'm Cassie's ride." He squares off with him. "It's time to go."

"I already told her I'd take her home," Josh says, unaffected. "Besides, I'm sure you'd rather hang with Shandler . . . right?"

Cody takes a step toward Josh.

"It's okay." I raise a hand, stopping him. Then turn to Josh. "It's fine. We're going to the same place. It will be easier." And I am *sooo* ready to go.

"Yeah, sure. No problem." Josh's eyes are still fixed on Cody's in a stare-down.

I touch Josh's arm. He returns his focus back to me. "Thanks for keeping me company tonight."

His eyes brighten. "Hey. Hanging out with the prettiest girl here isn't a hardship."

Cody snorts.

I glare at him. *Asshole!*

"I'll see you at school?" I ask Josh.

"Sounds good."

I whirl on Cody as soon as we're outside. "What the hell is your problem? You were *so* out of line!"

"You shouldn't encourage him. He's not what you think."

"It's none of your damn business." I bite back.

"Cassie . . ." he starts, running his hand through his hair, looking frustrated, but doesn't continue.

"And how *dare* you say I'm ugly to Josh! I know I'm not much to look at, but that was full on mean!"

He looks at me like I've lost my mind. "What are you talking about? I never said you were ugly!"

"You totally implied it!"

"How?"

"You snorted when Josh said he was hanging out with the prettiest girl at the party."

"That's because Josh is a lying sack of shit!"

"Screw you!" I turn away, frantically looking around for Cody's jeep. "Where the hell is your car? I want to go home!"

"I didn't mean it like that," he softens.

I double back, stopping in front of him, seething as I glare up at him. "You know what? Never mind. I'd rather catch a ride with Josh." I turn in the direction of the house.

"Cassie. Don't be mad. It's just . . ."

I stop abruptly, rounding on him. "It's just what?"

"You know."

"No. Tell me, Cody! What do I know? That you're nice to me at home and out in public I cease to exist? You're embarrassed to be seen with me? What?"

"No." He shakes his head, suddenly looking confused. "Nothing like that. What are you talking about? I just don't like you hanging out with him. I don't want to see you get hurt."

"I can take care of myself! You had no right to freak out like that. Do you know how embarrassing that was?"

He stares at me.

I don't wait for a reply. I turn my back on him and run toward the house.

Dick!

I push my way through the crowd, looking for Josh and find him with Shandler. He has a hand on the wall next to her head, leaning in, his mouth right next to her ear. They looked strangely intimate.

What the hell?

She giggles right before our eyes meet, then elbows Josh before nodding in my direction. The moment he sees me, he steps away from her and waves me over.

"Hi, Cassie," Shandler says, looking sheepish. "Sorry I've been giving you a hard time lately. Josh was just giving me crap and saying how I need to apologize—so perfect timing." She beams.

You are so full of shit.

"What are you still doing here?" Josh asks me.

"Changed my mind. Can I still catch a ride?"

Shandler intervenes. "Cody can be a bit dramatic at times. I wouldn't worry about it." She places a hand on my arm, looking at me like we share a common strife. "I totally know how you feel." She tilts her head and sighs dramatically.

I have a sudden urge to clap at the outstanding performance. The girl is mental.

Josh gives Shandler a you're-an-idiot look then says, "I'd be happy to take you home. Did you want to hang out some more or go now?"

"If it's okay, I'd like to go now."

"Sure. I'll see you later?" he asks Shandler.

"Most definitely," she purrs.

The exchange makes me weary once again. Something's not right. Whatever, I'm just getting a ride.

"Cody's never liked me," Josh admits as he pulls away from the curb. "I'm not exactly sure why. It might have to do with those rumors I told you about. It was a couple of girls that started them. It's total bullshit."

"Don't worry. I tend to make my *own* judgments on people. Gossip is usually a bunch of crap anyway."

"I'm glad to hear you say that."

The ride doesn't take long. He stops in front of my house, then turns to me as I reach for the door handle. "I meant what I said . . . about you being the prettiest girl at the party."

I hold myself back from rolling my eyes. "I bet you say that to all the girls," I say, mocking the phrase.

He leans in close to me. "No . . . I don't."

"Well . . ." I back away, putting space between us and killing his big move.

"Sorry," he says, sitting back. "Habit."

"I bet."

He laughs "*Hey*. I'm new to this female friendship thing."

"Thing?"

"You know what I mean. Girls like to *be with me*, so I'm used to giving them what they want."

"*Hmm*. Not sure what to say to that."

"I like being friends with you, but I'll be honest, I wish it could be more." I start to say something but he continues. "But it's okay. It's kind of nice having a female like me for something other than my body." He grins.

"I should go in," I say, opening the door. I glance up at the house and see Cody's standing in the open doorway.

"I guess your babysitter is waiting for you."

I ignore the comment. "Thanks for inviting me to the party and for the ride. It was fun," I say, not really meaning it.

"Me too. I'll see you at school."

"Yeah, sure." I shut the car door and walk toward the house.

"Did he try anything?" Cody snarls as I pass him in the doorway.

"Why would he try anything? I'm ugly remember?" I walk quickly to my room, trying to get some distance, but he follows close behind anyway.

"I didn't *say* that!"

"Whatever."

"I just don't want you falling for his bullshit. He's such a scammer—he'll say anything to get with a girl."

I stop suddenly, turning to facing him. "Oh my god, Cody! Really? Am I that hideous? That the only way he'd admit to being attracted to me was so he could hook up?"

"No! That's not what I meant! Stop turning my words around! You're totally attractive . . . uniquely beautiful, actually."

What a stupid description. I roll my eyes at him and walk away. "Stop being so defensive. I just don't want him taking advantage of you."

I stop and turn again. "Yeah, right. You know what? If anyone's a scammer, it's you. I've seen you work your entourage."

"They're just friends."

"You are such a hypocrite!" I walk into my room, throwing the door closed behind me, but Cody blocks it and follows me in.

"Cassie, why are you so angry with me?"

I round on him, "Because *you*"—I jab an accusing finger at him—"are a blind . . . stupid excuse for a human being."

He grabs me by the arms and pulls me up against him. My breath catches. "I'm neither. Now, what's going on?"

His heated blue eyes have my anger back peddling, leaving the sensation of our closeness. "Nothing," I say, reaching up between us, giving a half-hearted push. I feel his heart, it's pounding as fast as mine. He doesn't release me, but drops his forehead to mine.

"Cassie? Cody?" It's Roxanne. "What's going on? It's late. Why are you yelling?" Cody and I separate, seconds before she shows up at my door in her bathrobe.

"Sorry, Mom. Cassie was hanging out with a guy I don't like. I guess I was being overprotective and she didn't like it."

"Sorry we woke you up," I say, my heart still pounding from the confrontation.

"Fine," she says, sounding perturbed. "It's late. You should both get to bed."

He places an arm around her shoulder walking her out. "Night, Mom." He kisses her cheek.

"Night," she says, leaving us.

A minute passes and he's back. "Doesn't *seem* like nothing," he says.

I had to think back to where our conversation ended. "I'm just PMS'ing and I'm exhausted. It's been a long night." He stares at me, scrutinizing. "I'm sorry, okay? I'm super sensitive right now."

He runs his fingers through his hair, looking frustrated. "Okay, fine." He looks toward the door. "I guess I'll go."

I have nothing else I want to say . . . *out loud*, so I don't say anything at all. He looks at me one last time, like he's trying to solve a puzzle, then shakes his head and leaves, shutting the door behind him.

I change into a tank and boxers and crawl into bed. Everything . . . it's too much. I bury my face deep in my pillow and scream.

I need my mother. I want to ask her what to do with my feelings. How do I handle this with him? We've never had the opportunity to have a guy talk, *because* there was never a guy I was interested in. Now I need her. I need to ask her and I can't. I feel the sinking feeling again.

No! I'm not going there!

I break down anyway.

Eff!

13

I HATE MONDAYS. I hate school. And I hate Cody. That's my mantra for the day. We basically ignored each other the rest of the weekend and barely talked on the way to school. If I knew where the damn school bus stop was, I'd have taken it.

Who am I kidding? There probably isn't one, just a limo service—lifestyles of the too damn rich.

I know it's not his fault I have feelings for him, and I can't freak out and be a total bitch because of it, but that shit he pulled at the party was unforgivable.

So where do we go from here? Do we keep ignoring each other? I guess, maybe in time, things will lighten up. I don't know. This sucks.

I was expecting whispering or stares when I got to school, but so far there haven't been any. It might be the expression I've been wearing that says, *I'll kick the shit out of anyone who looks at me wrong*. I'm not *that* tough. I'm just so sick of everybody having an issue with me.

Josh has been annoyingly attentive—hanging around me like some lovesick puppy. It's got to be about the challenge. I doubt anyone's ever turned him down before.

I reach for the door to Antonio's.

"Cassandra."

I turn. Eff! It's the Jackass—my long-lost daddy. *Man*, did *he* pick the wrong time to confront me.

"My name is *Cassie*!" I whip around facing him. "I know who you are! Jeff and Roxanne told me all about you and how you abused my mother." He steps back, looking like I physically assaulted him. "*You're* the reason we had to run and live like we did! She didn't have anybody. She was alone. Did you know that?"

"She had you."

There are so many words I want to scream at him right now, it's choking me. I reach for the door again, opening it part way. I need to get away from him.

"*Cassie*, I'm sorry."

"Well, it's a little late for that, don't ya think . . . *Daddy*?" I say, mocking the endearment.

"Cassie, you okay?" Tony peaks his head out. I turn to him and see the butcher knife he's holding as he glares at my father.

I do my best to stay calm. I don't want Tony doing something stupid and getting into trouble. "Yeah, I'm okay."

"You come inside, yes?"

"I'll be right there. Just give me one more minute."

"Okay." He lets the door close but stands where he can see me.

I turn back to Brent. "You lost your chance of any

relationship with me the moment you hit my mother. Now leave me the hell alone!"

"I'm sorry, but I can't do that."

"You can't? Or you won't!"

"I won't. Whether you like it or not, I'm all you have left."

"Well, *that's* a real comfort." Once again, *bam*! The pain in his eyes says it all. But I don't care. I open the door and leave him standing there.

"Cassie, who wa's that man?" Tony asks as I march past him. "Wait. I seen him before."

I stop. "Yeah, some nut job that says he's my father."

"*What* you say! How can you have a father? You said he died." He starts to go back out with the knife, but I grab his arm to stop him.

"Don't," I say. "He's gone."

I pull out a chair and drop into it, exhaling loudly.

"Anna!" Tony yells. "Get out here!"

She comes from the back hurrying toward us. "What?" she snaps. "Why are you yelling at me?"

"Sit down, Anna." Tony's voice takes on a softer more serious tone. "Cassie has something to tell us."

She looks at him and does what she's told. Never thought I'd see that. I tell them everything Roxanne and Jeff told me—who he was, his accomplishments—not that it means anything. I just wanted them to know that he has something to lose if he gets out of line.

"Santa Cello!" Tony exclaims. "What a mess. What will you do?"

Anna pats my hand. "She will do nothing but stay away from that *man*!"

Suddenly, I'm exhausted. I slump in my chair. "I'm not sure if I can. I have to face him sometime."

"No, you don't!" Anna points a finger at me. "He's a bad man and you need to stay away from him!"

"I'll try."

Marco walks up. "What's going on? Is everyone okay?"

"Yes," Anna says standing. She puts an arm around Marco's waist, leading him toward the kitchen. "Come into the back and I will explain."

Marco looks over his shoulder at me with a worried expression. I give him a weak smile before he turns around and disappears into the back.

I guess it's okay if he knows, probably a good thing if Brent turns out to be a problem.

I look across at Tony. There's so much concern in his eyes. "It's okay. I'm fine." I do my best to reassure him. I attempt a smile. "Let's just get back to work and try to forget the whole thing."

"You don't fool me, young lady. I know you're in pain."

"Yes. I am. But it will help me to stay busy."

"Okay, but I could get Marco to drive you home."

The bells over the door jingle. My eyes dart to the door, fearful that it's Brent, but it's only Josh.

I don't want to deal with him right now either.

"Hey, Cassie," he says walking up.

Tony looks him up and down and grunts before getting up and leaving.

"Hey," I return.

He sits down as I stand up. "What can I get you?"

"Are you okay? You look like you want to rip someone's face off. It's not mine, I hope."

"Not at the moment," I say, feeling raw. "Do you want a slice of pizza? Pepperoni, right?"

"You remembered, and a Coke, please. Are you sure you're okay?"

I sigh, remembering he's a nice guy. "Yeah. Just a ghost from my past."

"Do you want to talk about it?"

"Thanks, but no. I'll go get your food."

Tony pushes a slice of pizza on a paper plate toward me. "Cassie, you know I don't like that boy."

"I know. But he's okay."

"*Bah!*" He waves a hand in dismissal and turns away.

I set the pizza in front of Josh.

"Sit with me." He looks around. "You're not busy."

"Yeah. Sure. Okay." I don't have the energy to argue.

"There's a bonfire beach party next weekend? Do you want to go with me? It's Saturday."

Once again, I wonder what his deal is, then I think of Cody and just get pissed off. "Sure. Sounds like fun. Who's going to be there?"

"Pretty much the whole school, I guess."

Great. Not too sure I want to deal with those self-centered pea brains again.

"Don't worry, we don't have to hang out with them, okay? We could just walk the beach or something."

I look up quickly as the door opens again, still feeling skittish. But it's only a couple of kids from school. They wave at Josh and sit at another table.

"Wow. You're really on edge. Did something happen with Cody? Did he hurt you?" He sits up at attention.

"Oh my god! No."

"Well, something is going on."

"It's involved, and I don't want to talk about it right now."

"Fair enough. But I'm here for you when you do."

"Okay. I should get back to work." I stand up. "See you at school?"

"Definitely," he says, all smiles.

Another group of kids come in and come to our table. I say "Hi," remembering some of them from the party and take orders. It gets crazy busy after that, and I'm grateful.

"Cassie . . . dinner," Roxanne calls to me.

I close my laptop and walk into the kitchen. Tony insisted I go home anyway. He said I was being too grumpy with the customers. Marco dropped me off on his first delivery, so I made it home in time for dinner.

"Can you go get Cody?" Roxanne asks when I enter the kitchen. "He's in the garage."

Do I have to?

I grudgingly open the door expecting to see him polishing his precious jeep, but instead, he's half-naked, bench-pressing a lot of weight.

I wish they'd fall on his big fat head. I'm about to verbalize my thought, when I'm silenced by the look of him—long, lean body stretched out, his muscles flexing and relaxing with each rep, the striations in his muscles.

His ear buds are in and he's deeply focused on his task, so he hasn't noticed me. Watching him unobserved gives me an odd thrill. I've never been one for big muscles, but the human form is an amazing thing to draw.

Who the hell am I kidding . . . I'd like to run my hands over every inch of him.

"This is ridiculous!" The words accidentally escape me.

"What's that?" Cody asks, sitting up, pulling the ear buds out.

My cheeks burn at being caught. "I . . . uh, um . . ." Frick sakes, I'm stammering like an idiot. "Your mom sent me out here to tell you dinner is ready!" I snap.

He looks down and flexes his pecks, making them jump independently, then looks up at me, grinning.

"You conceited asshole!" I whirl around, gripping the doorknob.

"Cassie. Wait."

I huff out a breath before reluctantly turning around. "*What?*"

"I'm just teasing. And I'm sorry about the other night—at the party. I'm not sure why I acted like that. I don't want things to be like this anymore—you know . . . between us."

I'm glad he said something. "Me either."

He holds out his hand. "Friends?"

I step down to him and take his hand. "Friends."

He leans in and kisses my cheek, then walks around me into the house.

Why does he *do* stuff like that! I scream in my head. He probably doesn't know how to turn it off. *Ahhh!* And I hate that I can relate to the mass-majority of girls at our school.

I crawl into bed and get the sketchpad out Cody gave me. I've been working in it quite a bit. There are sketches of everybody, even my father, but his portrait has a more demonic portrayal. I start sketching Cody, the way he looked working out—the contours of his biceps, the definition of his six-pack abs—every curve, angle, and texture.

I wonder what he's doing. I put the sketchpad down and creep to my door to listen. His door opens suddenly. I'm tempted to run back to my bed, but I hold my breath instead.

He stops in front of my room.

Shit! Shit! Shit!

He doesn't move. It's so quiet. Then I hear him walk down the hall.

I exhale loudly as I lean against the door with my hand over my heart as it hammers against my chest. I can't keep doing this to myself.

I go back to my computer and try to get some schoolwork done, but it's useless—all I can do is think of Cody. I close my laptop and drop my forehead on top of my folded arms. I'm such an idiot.

14

I HAVE no idea what to wear to this beach thing. It's going to be dark out, so do I wear my bathing suit or what? It gets cool by the water at night, so I doubt I'll be swimming. I opt out of the swimsuit and decide on high-waisted skinny jeans rolled past my ankle and a loose, off-white tank. You can see a bit of my stomach, but not much—hopefully, I'm not sending the wrong message by wearing it.

I pull my hair into a messy bun and add a touch of makeup. Roxanne calls me from the other room, and I know it's because Josh is here. I grab my jean jacket and turn off the light. Cody's room is dark. I haven't seen him since dinner. *Good.* I don't want him making a scene.

Josh is waiting just inside the door.

"Hey," I say as I slide my feet into my flip-flops.

His eyes take me in slowly from bottom to top, making me feel exposed. "Don't *you* look . . . amazing." His grin is not the buddy-buddy friendship type, but predatory.

I chuckle nervously wondering if this is a mistake? He

places a hand on my lower back as we step out. He caresses an exposed area of skin with his thumb.

Yep . . . definitely a mistake.

I'm going to have to set him straight again real soon.

Josh talks about all kinds of random stuff on the way. I comment when I need to, but have trouble concentrating. He's different, I'm not exactly sure how . . . just a vibe, I guess. Something just seems off.

We park near the beach. I slide my arms into my jean jacket and button up the front as I walk to the rear of the car. He opens the trunk and hands me a large blanket, then takes out a cooler.

"You ready?" he asks.

I give him a forced smile.

"It'll be fine. Remember, we can leave the group anytime, maybe do our own thing." His eyebrows pump up and down suggestively.

"Hey! You said we were just hanging as friends," I joke to keep it light.

He grins. "A guy can hope, can't he?"

I let out a nervous laugh. I don't like how this is feeling.

"Oh, come on," he says pulling on my arm. "I'm just kidding. Chill!"

Josh makes his grand entrance with lots of cheers, high fives, and pats on the back—I'm pretty much ignored.

Nice.

He lays out a blanket near the fire and sits on it. "Have a seat." He pats the spot next to him.

I sit down, purposely keeping a respectable distance for the image I'm trying to convey—friends.

People are up, then down. Groups interchange with new faces appearing, familiar ones disappearing. I watch all the interaction that doesn't involve me and wish I hadn't agreed to come.

I pull my knees tightly against my chest, wishing I could tap my heels together and be anyplace but here.

Why did I come?

Oh, right . . . because I was pissed off at Cody—a stupid, dumb-ass reason.

Josh looks over at me. "Are you cold?"

"Yeah, a bit," I lie.

"Here." He takes my arm and pulls me toward him.

"No, I'm good." I resist, but he continues, coaxing me between his legs. I relent, not wanting to make a scene. I returned to my balled-up position. He wraps his arms around me, pulling me tightly against him. "There. That's better," he says, sounding satisfied.

I sit quietly for what seems like eons. Josh begins to gently caresses my wrists with his thumb. *Uck*. Okay. Time to go. "Um," I say, straining against his arm bar. "I'm going to walk around a bit. My legs are cramping up."

He doesn't release me at first, but let's go when I lean forward to stand up. "I'll go with you," he says, beside me now.

"*No*." I put a hand up, motioning him to stop. "That's okay. I won't be gone long."

"Now what kind of date would I be if I let you walk around all by yourself?"

"No really. It's okay. I'm sure you'd rather hang with your friends."

"Not at all."

Eff!

He picks up our blanket and follows me down to the water. I listen to the waves as they roll in from the dark and crash on the beach, then watch as they glide up the sand, foaming at the edges, before sliding back into the darkness once more.

I stay on dry sand, not wanting to get wet. Josh takes my hand. "Josh," I say, shaking it off. He looks at me surprised. "Like I said before . . . *No*. I'm pretty sure I've made it clear."

His eyes go hot, making me tense, but then immediately turn thoughtful. "I'm sorry," he says wistfully. "I've gotten so used to girls throwing themselves at me. It never occurred to me that you *really* might not be interested. I guess I keep expecting you to change your mind. But it's okay. I like that you're not after my looks or popularity." He makes a goofy expression. "Smile. It's all good."

I give a half-hearted chuckle. I'm not sure what to make of the situation.

"No. I'm serious. I'm sorry if I made you feel uncomfortable." His smile seems genuine, not put on like sometimes.

"It's okay. Thanks for being cool about it."

"Not a problem. Here . . . follow me." He walks up the beach, but I don't follow. He turns and sees that I haven't moved. "Oh, hey, sorry. There's a great spot to sit and listen to the waves."

"You know what? I'm freezing. I think I'm going to head back to the fire."

"I'm still making you nervous, aren't I?" He walks back to stand in front of me. "Look, I *like* the idea of us being friends. Come on," he pleads. "I promise, I'll keep my hands to myself." He makes a show of jamming his hand in his pockets.

I look toward the fire.

He wraps the blanket around my shoulders. "This should help. Come on. It's so pretty out, and you can see the stars better when you're away from the fire. *Hey*. It'll give us a chance to get to know each other better. We've never really had time to talk in depth."

We're not that far away and I'm probably making a big deal out of nothing. "Okay."

"*Awesome*."

He leads me to several large boulders set back in the tall grass. Again, I look back at the fire; more people are arriving.

I'm taken by surprise as he pins me against a massive rock and starts kissing me. *What the hell?*

"*Mmm*. I knew you'd taste good."

"Stop." I laugh nervously, thinking he's joking and nudge him to back off.

"I knew you were hot for me." He grips my chin firmly, crushing his lips painfully to mine.

I try to turn my head, but he has a vice grip on my jaw, squeezing hard. I shove at him, but he won't budge, the full weight of his body is pressing on me. He jams his tongue in my mouth, making me gag.

Asshole! I bite down hard and try to twist away. "Get off of me!" I scream. "Get the hell off!"

"You bitch!" He wipes his mouth with the back of his hand

then looks down at it. His face contorts into a vicious grin before focusing back on me.

I shove hard, trying to get my body free so I can run, but he grips me by the throat and slams my head against the jagged rock. Silver flecks drift in front of my eyes as the pain becomes unbearable. His hold on my throat tightens.

"Help!" I scream, but the words are barely audible. I feel lightheaded. I claw at his hand, attempting to loosen his hold. "Please, stop!" My heart is pounding as the fear of passing out overwhelms every nerve in my body.

"You know you want it," he says as he grinds against me.

"Why are you doing this?" I cry, tears falling down my cheeks as the reality of being trapped sets in.

"I'm sure you screw Cody every night. What's the big deal?" he snarls.

Suddenly, I feel his weight lifted, then see Josh sprawled out on the sand with Cody standing over him. He scrambles up just as Cody pulls back his arm and slams his fist into Josh's face.

My hands go to my mouth as Josh staggers back.

He regains his footing and circles Cody. "There you go again, interrupting our fun," he sneers, wiping the blood from his nose. "We were minding our own business and once again you go all crazy on me."

"Is that the way you see it, you sick bastard?" Cody shouts at him.

My body shakes violently as people begin to congregate around us. Cody looks over at me. Josh takes that moment to charge, tackling him to the ground. Sand flies everywhere as they wrestle, each trying to gain control.

"Fight, fight, fight!" the crowd chants. I look around

frantically as people laugh and point. I spot Shandler. She's staring at me with a look of sick satisfaction on her face.

I turn and run.

The tears are making it hard to see. My feet are bare and scraped raw from the road cutting into them, but I don't care.

How could I have been so stupid! My lungs burn, but I can't stop. *I have to get away from here!* I cry even harder. I trip and fall, skidding along the pavement, scraping my hands and knees. *I can't stop*. I wipe my eyes as I stand, then start running again. I see headlights coming from behind. The thought of Josh finding me lends new panic. I frantically look around for a place to hide, but there's nothing but grass on either side of the road. The lights get closer and slow down. *Oh my god! I can't*. I run faster.

The car pulls alongside of me, keeping pace. I'm trapped.

"Cassie?" Through the haze of terror, I recognize Cody's voice. "Get in the car."

"No. I have to go!" In shock, I continue to run.

"It's too far to make it on foot," he says softly. "Home is at least twenty miles away."

"He might be coming." I continue to run, but I'm suddenly aware of the pain in my feet, and I begin to stumble with each step.

"Cassie. Please. You're not thinking straight. It's okay. I'm not going to hurt you."

I look over at him. As the familiar face seeps past the terror, I stop.

"Come on," Cody says gently. "Let me take you home."

I look out into the darkness. My mind tries to process the

damage—mentally and physically—but it's all too much. I grip the roll bar and haul my battered body into the seat.

I briefly look at Cody, not wanting to make eye contact, but see the blood at the corner of his mouth, and that his eye is mostly swollen shut. Humiliation forgotten, I reach up and touch his cheek. "Cody, your face."

"Don't worry about it. I've been hit worse in basketball. Besides, you should see *him*." He laughs then turns serious when he sees my bloodied hand. He gently takes hold, inspecting it further. "Cassie," he says, picking up the other. "Did he do this?"

"No, I fell on the road." I pull them away, placing them in my lap, palms up. "I'm so sorry," I choke out.

"Why? You didn't do anything wrong."

"Yes, I did," I sob. "This is all my fault. You warned me."

"*Shhh*. No means *no*! He's the one at fault."

"Yeah, but if I hadn't gone with him, this would have never happened."

"Him *treating* you like that should never have happened. *Cassie*, you did nothing wrong."

Sickening images flash through my mind. "If you hadn't found me—"

"But I did and that's all that matters."

"He wouldn't stop!"

Reaching over, he gently wraps an arm around my shoulder, pulling me in to his side. "It's over. You're safe." I lay my head against his chest, hiding my face with my hand as tears roll down my cheeks. Cody's arms encircle me completely. "It's going to be okay," he soothes. "I know it's hard to believe at the moment, but it will be—you'll see."

"I should never have left the fire, but he made it sound like he was good with being friends." I straighten, looking at him in renewed panic. "Oh my god. I—"

"You trusted him. How would you know he would do something like that?" He cups my face in his hand and stares at me intently. I lean against it, taking in the warmth, feeling safe. "It's not your fault." He wipes a tear from my cheek with his thumb. "It makes me angry hearing you say that. No one has the right to force you to do something you don't want to do, regardless of the situation."

I break away and lean back against my seat. "Yeah . . . but—"

"No! There *are* no exceptions. What he did was sick and twisted, and I don't think you're the first girl he's done this too. The rumors are out there. It's even more disturbing to realize that they're true."

"He was so nice."

"He manipulated you."

"Yeah," I whisper quietly as I look out into the darkness. I want to shrivel up into something so small, it can never be found.

Cody's phone makes a sound. "We should get you home—get all your cuts cleaned up. Are you okay if I start driving?"

"Yes." A new realization hits me. "School," I groan. "Everyone is going to think I'm some kind of tease that changed my mind and overreacted."

"Let them think whatever they want. They're nothing to you."

My mind is whirling as he drives. The pain, what happened, the future, so much so, that I can't seem to focus on one thing, which is probably good, because if I did, I'd probably shatter into a million pieces.

. . .

We pull into the garage. I climb out of the jeep, wincing with each movement. There isn't a part of my body that doesn't hurt—especially my feet. I try to walk on the sides of them, but it doesn't help much.

"Here," Cody says, lifting me up, cradling me in his arms.

I don't argue, just lay my head against his chest as he carries me through the house. The lights are off, so either Roxanne and Jeff are in bed, or they went out.

Cody carefully sets me on my bathroom counter. I can see the worry on his face as he looks me over. "I'll be right back. Don't move."

"I don't think I can," I say, feeling weak, beaten . . . a victim. I look down at the holes torn in my jeans and the scraped flesh underneath.

Cody returns with a handful of medical supplies. "I checked on my parents. They're asleep."

"Good. I was worried they would hear us. I don't want them to see me like this."

"You should talk to them," he says. I start to object. "But we can talk about that later. Now, you'd better get those pants off, so we can fix up those knees."

I'm too mentally ruined to be modest. I wince as I begin to peel my them off—Cody steps in and helps.

His phone has been going off like crazy. I'm sure everyone wants to gossip about the night—get the inside dirt. "Maybe you should get that?"

"Get what?"

"Your phone. It's been making noises non-stop."

"Oh, sorry. I didn't notice." He takes it out of his pocket.

"I'll turn it off." Then slides it back in place. He reaches for a washcloth from a basket on the counter, gets it wet, then gently clean my cuts. When he's done, he sprays disinfectant, thoughtfully blowing on the stinging areas.

"Okay, your feet."

"Couldn't we just leave them until tomorrow?"

"Infection will hurt a lot worse."

"Fine." I plug the sink and turn on the water, letting it fill halfway. I swivel my body so I can set my feet in the water. I suck in air through my teeth. *Eff! that hurts.*

"Thanks for doing all this," I say when I finish.

"No problem. Here, let's get everything bandaged."

When we finish, I wiggle off the counter and stare in horror at my reflection in the mirror. My eyes are red-rimmed and swollen with black smudges of dried mascara everywhere. My hair is a knotted mess barely being held together by the hair tie. My shirt is stretched and hanging loosely on my body. I swallow back the hysteria that's threatening to spill out again.

Cody appears behind me in the mirror. He turns me around to face him. There's so much worry in his eyes. "I was so scared when I saw him attacking you. I've never been so angry in my life. I swear I could have killed him. I might have if somebody hadn't pulled me away."

I wish you would have.

I want so much to get in the shower and wash this evening off me, but then I'd have to get all bandaged again, and I don't think I have the strength to shower anyway. Tomorrow.

"Come on." Cody lifts me into his arms again. "Let's get you in bed." He sets me down carefully. "What do you want to sleep in?"

"Second drawer down, there are some big T-shirts." He finds

one, hands it to me, then turns his back. I pull off my shirt with my fingertips, staying away from the sorest parts of my hands. "I'm done."

"Here, let me have it." He reaches out for the torn shirt. "You don't want this anymore, do you?"

"No. Get my jeans as well. Burn them if you can."

He smiles. "How about if I just take them out to the garbage? We don't exactly have a fire pit in the backyard, not to mention it would probably wake the parents."

"True." He pulls the covers over me as I settle underneath. "Thank you . . . for being there."

He sits beside me and brushes a wisp of hair away from my face, then frowns as he slides his thumb across my lower lip. It feels like a salve on my abused mouth. "I'm so sorry," he says in a whisper. "Sleep."

I nod and watch him as he leaves, closing the door behind him.

As I close my eyes, the horror fills the darkness. Wracking sobs take over as the images play out behind my eyelids. I turn on my side, covering my mouth so Cody can't hear.

"Move over," he says gently nudging me over.

I'm surprised and overwhelmingly grateful as he turns me towards him. I put my head on his chest and curl into his side.

"Stop telling yourself that garbage you're filling your head with," he says after a while.

"Okay." My voice sounds so small.

He soothes me till I fall asleep.

15

THE NEXT MORNING, I wake up alone. My muscles ache, my mouth feels bruised, and my knees are on fire. Oh god! Nausea rips through me. I get to the toilet just in time.

After emptying my stomach, I lean back, slumping against the wall and cry. How can I face everyone, especially Cody? He saw it all happening. I feel so—so gross and dirty, invaded, and violated.

My skin crawls at the memory of Josh's hands on me. I have to wash the feeling away—get clean somehow. After getting the water to a decent temperature, I strip my off my clothes and step in, letting the water wash over me. It stings all the open wounds.

I start to wash, but I can't get rid of the sensation of his touch. I turn the heat up as hot as I can stand and scrub harder. It won't come off—it won't leave me. I lower myself to the shower floor, defeated. The hot water hits my back, the excess pouring over my bowed head. I watch as water droplets drip off my hair and lashes as I cry, releasing it all, until there is nothing left.

Spent, I stand up on wobbly legs. Feeling lightheaded, I lean against the shower wall and take several deep breaths. Eventually, I turn off the water and gently dry off.

My hands don't look as bad as yesterday, but my knees look raw. I cover them in the bandages Cody left on the counter. I'll leave the gauze wraps off my hands so no one will ask, but wrap my feet—they're way better than I expected, but still need to be covered. I can put socks over them. No one will know.

I look in the mirror, inspecting my face and neck for bruises. Surprisingly, they've disappeared since last night—mostly, anyway. I can easily cover what's left with makeup. The back of my head is painfully sensitive from where it hit the rock, but other than that . . . I can pass as if nothing happened—at least on the outside.

I dry my hair, but let it hang loose. I pull on some baggy shorts with an even baggier T-shirt. I feel almost human again. As much as I don't want to see anyone, it's Sunday breakfast, and if I don't attempt to eat, Roxanne and Jeff will know something's wrong and start asking questions.

"Morning," Roxanne and Jeff say simultaneously from the kitchen.

"Morning," I return. I sit next to Cody—not my usual seat—but I feel the need to stay close to him, regardless of my embarrassment.

He looks me up and down with distaste.

Oh my god! He blames me. The devastation is now total.

"You are *not* going to start wearing those crappy clothes again, are you?" He cracks a grin.

I furrow my brow at him, my mind slow to process. When I

clue in, my heart and mind breathe a collective sigh of relief. Now I want to smack the hell out of him for making me hurt like that.

Roxanne walks out from the kitchen with a platter full of pancakes, Jeff trails behind her with bacon and a bowl full of scrambled eggs. "What the *hell* happened to your eye?" Roxanne shrieks. She quickly sets the food on the table, then rushes Cody's side. Reaching down, she touches the side of his face. He turns toward me, rolls his eyes—well, eye, then turns back to his mom.

What if he tells her? I begin to panic.

"I ran into a brick wall." His casual reply allows me to relax.

"This is serious," Roxanne snaps back.

"What does the wall look like?" Jeff asks knowingly.

"Pretty busted up," he says.

Roxanne crosses her arms against her chest. Her eyes narrow at Cody as if waiting for a better response. When he ignores her and loads his plate with pancakes, she makes a sound of disgust and returns to the kitchen. Jeff busies himself by passing the eggs to me.

After I place a small amount on my plate, Cody squeezes my leg under the table. "Don't worry," he whispers.

"What was that?" Roxanne barks out, making me jump.

"Nothing," we say in unison. She pins us both with a look that says we better fess up. When neither of us respond, she lets it go—luckily.

I've done my best to eat, even though I'm not hungry. Now it's time to go.

"Okay . . . seriously. Cassie, *this* . . ." Cody yanks on my shirt, "has got to go. You are not hiding behind this ugly shit again."

Roxanne sucks in a breath. "Cody! How dare you say such a thing! I *thought* we talked about this!"

"Sorry, Mom." He drops his head as if being chastised. With head still bowed, he turns in my direction and grins. "I'm serious," he mouths.

I don't know why, but the scene is funny and makes me feel better. "Go to hell, prep-boy," I tease.

He shoves me. I shove him back, wincing slightly from the scrapes on my hand. The banter is a relief.

"I, uh, have a lot of homework to do," I say, needing some space. "Do you mind if I go get started?"

"You've barely eaten," Roxanne says.

"No, I have. It's just that watching Cody stuff his face made me lose my appetite." It's a good lie, putting the focus back on him.

"Whatever," Cody says. "I'll help clean up."

"Thanks." I pick up my plate and lay it in the sink, then do my best not to run to my room.

"Are you okay?" Cody asks from my doorway as I make my bed.

"Not really."

He walks in and sits at my desk. "You really should think about pressing charges."

"Cody. He didn't rape me. What are the police going to do? Arrest him for being rough and feeling me up? I'll just look stupid."

"Well, at least they would have something in their records."

I sit on the side of my bed, facing him. "No. I just want to forget about it."

"Okay. If you say so, but I think it's a mistake. What if he does it to someone else?"

I pause. "From what you said, he has. Did they file a report?"

"I guess you won't know until you talk to them."

"*Cody*, I'm sure you've heard how these things go. You report it, there's a big investigation, and basically the girl gets blamed. I don't want anyone else to go through what I did, but I also don't want to deal with the interrogations, and then be humiliated all over again."

"I think you're wrong. There were several people who witnessed what happened."

"Yeah. And a lot of people witnessed him holding me close by the fire. They'll twist it around."

"Who will?"

"*Everyone who saw it*, and then the police. Josh is super popular. *No* one at school will say anything against him—fear of retribution and all. *No* one wants to be on the wrong side of popular."

"That's stupid logic."

"Is it? You've always been there. You don't understand how all the underlings scrounge for the few lucky crumbs you people dish out in the hopes it will make them popular too." He starts to object, but I cut him off. "I know . . . it's pathetic, but it's a real thing. So no one is going to back me up."

"I will. I don't give a shit."

"I know, and I appreciate that, but it will just get turned around. Josh will make up some bullshit story and everyone will believe it. He had *me* fooled, and I wasn't even taken by the whole good-looking-guy popularity thing. I really thought he was a nice guy. Whatever. You don't need to be pulled into my nightmare."

"I was there, Cassie. I already am."

"I just need to keep busy and keep my mind off it as much as possible. Do you want to study or something?"

"Sure. We could do that." He gets up. "Let me go get my books."

"Cody." He turns at the door. "Thanks for staying with me last night."

"No problem. I'll take any excuse to snuggle up to a warm female body." He winks at me.

"You're such an ass!" I pick up a pillow and throw it at him, which he catches and throws back. It hits me in the face, messing up my hair. I smooth it back and smile at the empty doorway.

16

I DECIDE CODY IS RIGHT. I can't hide behind ugly, baggy clothes. It will look like I let him affect me, which it has, but I don't want Josh knowing it. I refuse to let him see the pain he caused.

I bandage my knees and wear jeggings with a loose-fitting shirt and tank-top underneath. You can't see the goose egg on the back of my head, and it's easy to hold my hands in a way so no one can see the palms. My feet are still a bit sore, but my flip-flops are squishy, so that helps. So far it's been bearable.

I pause at the school entrance, trying to construct a wall strong enough to shield me from the aftermath that's sure to follow. Cody offered to stay by my side, but I feel that would cause more talk.

The whispering starts as soon as I enter. Little by little, the wall crumbles throughout the day, and I'm humiliated all over again. By the time English rolls around, I'm ready to run away—back to New York, to Luigi and Maria, home.

The classroom door is in sight. At least in there, once class starts, everyone is focused on the teacher and not me. I keep my eyes to the floor, weaving in and around people as quick as I can.

If I don't see the stares then they don't exist, right?

I wish.

I make the mistake of looking up, it was only a second—a second too long. Josh and Shandler are right in my line of sight. He's leaning back against a locker, staring at me with a cocky grin on his face. Shandler's next to him with a similar expression. Seeing him makes my insides twist into knots as fear and revulsion take hold.

Wait . . . Is his arm around her? I stare at them, taking in the scene.

Are you effing kidding me!

Josh makes a show of pulling Shandler close, kissing her cheek, while staring at me.

I'm horrified and sick. Why? I don't understand.

There's a pause in my step as the answer slams me. It was all a setup! My body vibrates with disgust and rage. I want to throw myself at them, smashing my fists against any body part I can find, but I know I won't.

What do I do, ignore them?

Hell no! "Hey, Josh," I call out, as I slow my walk. "How's your face?" I add a pouty lower lip, taunting him. "It looks awfully painful."

No way I'm going to let either of them think they've got the best of me.

He sneers and takes a step in my direction. Shandler grabs his arm, pulling him back.

That one step has fear almost choking the air out of me. Somehow, I keep walking, doing my best to keep up the façade of indifference. But as soon as I reach my seat, my legs give out and I collapse into my chair, my whole body shaking.

How could I have ever thought he was a nice person? And Shandler? How can anyone be that evil? And why would they set me up like that? It's twisted.

I focus on my breathing—in for four, out for eight—trying to calm down.

"Hey," a girl says from behind me.

I ignore her. I can't deal with it right now, especially to my face. She taps me on the shoulder.

Eff! My rage-induced bravado is long gone. There's nothing left but a jellied mass of chicken shit.

I turn around ready to do battle anyway I can, but I'm instantly disarmed by the kindness I see in the warm brown eyes of a very small girl.

"Are you okay?" she asks gently. "I was at the party."

I move to turn away.

"Don't be embarrassed." Her words stop me. "The same thing happened to me about a year ago." She looks down and picks at the edge of her binder. "Unfortunately, no one came to my rescue."

I'm horrified. "I'm so sorry."

She shrugs her shoulders. "It's okay," she says, her eyes filling with mischief. "I kneed him in the balls—he barely laid a hand on me. Puto pendejo," she spits out the words like a vile taste. "I'm Mila."

"Cassie."

"Are you interested in some payback?"

"Excuse me?"

"Payback . . . as in making him suffer total humiliation and possibly some extreme physical pain. I've got lots of ideas."

"Thanks, but I'd really liket to forget the whole thing."

She leans forward. "That's how I felt. But after watching it happen to you—I can't stand by any more."

"Okay, everyone." I turn around as the teacher enters. "Settle down and let's get to it."

"Just think about it?" she whispers over my shoulder.

I wonder how many girls he *has* done this to. Making him pay does have its appeal. I can visualize all kinds of hell I'd like to unleash on his ass.

By the end of class, my confidence is slightly renewed and I'm revved up. I turn to Mila, "What do you have in mind?"

A slow, wicked smile spreads across her face.

We make plans to meet after work. I feel a little better knowing that I'm not alone in this. Yes, I have Cody, but having a female to talk to, especially one who's been through the same thing, will help.

Mila tells me how Josh pulled her into a room at a party. She'd just left the bathroom when he grabbed her.

"Luckily no one saw," she says. "It was easier to pretend it never happened. He harassed me for several weeks after, but eventually got bored, probably because I wasn't cowering—sick bastard probably gets off on it."

"Yeah, yesterday, Josh was standing with his arm around Shandler. Both with a smug expression on their face."

"He was with Shandler? Hmm. That's interesting."

"I think they set me up."

"It wouldn't surprise me. She's vicious."

"Why would she do that?"

"She's crazy jealous. It's probably because you live with Cody."

"As if I planned it," I mutter to myself. "How could Cody ever be with someone like that?"

"Guys are blinded by her beauty, then they dump her when she shows her true nature, unless they're just as messed up as she is."

"Like Josh?"

"You got it."

"I can't believe he played me like that. How could I not see it?"

"Don't feel bad. Not many can resist his charm and good looks—he has a way. *Hey*, why *are* you living with Cody? Did you get in trouble at your old school—get shipped away or something?" She bumps me with her shoulder, teasing.

I stare at her a second. It's weird talking to someone other than my mom about personal stuff.

"You don't have to tell me if you don't want to. I was just curious."

"No. It's okay. My mom died of cancer and arranged for me to stay with Cody and his family. I guess she was really close friends with his mom growing up."

Her hand slaps over her mouth in horror. "*Ohmygod!* I'm so sorry!" She touches my shoulder briefly. "I never imagined anything like that. I feel like a jerk for joking about it! Are you okay? I'm such an ass. Of course you're not okay. Oh, I feel so *bad* for you. How are you dealing with it?"

"I actually don't think I have yet."

"Yeah, I can't imagine. What was she like?"

"Honestly? I'm not sure."

"That's a strange thing to say."

I explain what I learned and how hard it's been to accept this new version of her. About how much it hurt, and how deceived I felt. Mila was really nice. She listened, which is surprising because she seems to have a lot to say about everything. It felt good to unload the thoughts.

"What about your dad? Isn't he around? Oh, no . . . did he die too? Or did he abandon you as a baby? Oh, I hate men like that. My dad sucks big time. He pretty much disappeared after he dumped my mom. Well?"

I chuckle. "I'll tell you if you let me get a word in."

"I'm sorry. I babble when I say stuff I shouldn't—which happens a lot." She takes a deep breath, exhaling loudly. "Okay. I'm good. So, what happened?"

Strangely, I tell her that part of my life as well.

"Wow," she says, after I finish. "That's some drama."

"Yeah."

"So, what are you going to do about him?"

"Nothing. The guy's a douche. I've got nothing to say."

"Aren't you the least bit curious?"

"*Not really*. Why should I be? He's an ass, and that's all there is to it."

"Yeah . . . I guess. Don't get me wrong, he's a total dick for what he did to your mom, but everyone has a story and people change. He was young and totally messed. Alcohol can really screw people up."

"I don't give a shit about his story. All the hard times Mom and I had were because we had to hide from him."

"True, but even though things were hard, you were tight with your mom—well, except for the mysterious past, but at least now you know why, right?" I hadn't really thought of it that way. "You're lucky. My mom and I barely talk. She's too busy with her boy-toy of the month to pay any attention to me."

"What do you mean?"

"My dad left her and married a younger woman—blond too, not even Hispanic. My mom calls her perra cachonda." I look at her like, *meaning*? She laughs. "It's something like slutty bitch."

"*Ahhh*. Got it."

"I think she feels the need to prove that she's still got it or something . . . I don't know. She says it's the hot Latino blood. I say she's acting like a Cougar. She got a shit-ton of money in the settlement, so she likes to take young, hot guys on trips—totally gross."

"And she leaves you alone?"

"Yup. Pretty much."

"I'm sorry. That would suck."

She waves it off. "I gave up caring a long time ago. Besides, going through the rough stuff makes you stronger."

"I've heard that, but I'm not sure I buy the logic."

"Oh, come on! Whoever learned anything from easy? It's the hard shit that makes you use your brain—problem-solve, cope, adapt. It builds character, life skills, and I'm sure in your case, being from a rough neighborhood—street smarts."

"What self-help book did you read that from?" I tease.

"Don't need a book." She taps the side of her head. "It's all in here. And don't you dare let Josh take away who you are. You fought back and beat him. He didn't take anything from you, right?"

"Well, actually it was Cody who beat him," I say meekly, making her scowl. "But you're totally right," I amend quickly. "He didn't beat me." Mila smiles triumphantly. "But he did make me feel incredibly violated and dirty."

She softens and sighs. "I know. I went through it all as well. But dirt can be washed away, and violation is a state of mind, as is feeling like a victim. Like I said, it all makes us who we are. Who you choose to be is up to you—weak, beaten, or *kick ass strong*!"

"Thanks. You're right." I was strong, until this happened—it really beat me down. But her logic makes sense.

"It will take time, don't get me wrong, but you'll get through it, and I'm here if you need me."

"Thanks. I appreciate it. Where are you from?"

"Oakland." She looks offended. "Why?"

"I didn't mean like, *as in what planet*? I was just wondering, because of your accent?"

"Oh, mi madre and her family are from Puerto Vallarta."

"Nice."

"*So*, when are you going to talk to your dad—you know, make it okay? It's not good to hold all that negative energy in—like, it's totally toxic."

I could *not* survive in her mind for a second. I think my brain would explode. "Let's save that for another time. I've got enough to deal with right now."

"Fair enough," she says. "Let's get down to business . . . Josh."

"I've given that a lot of thought. As much as I would like to make him hurt for what he did, I think we should wait a bit. If anything happens, I'm pretty sure I'll be the first person he'll come after, and I don't want to do anything to provoke him. Maybe I'm chickening out or maybe it's an intelligent decision—I'm not sure—but I want to wait."

"I'm sure we could come up with something without him knowing it was us, but I get what you're saying."

We end up discussing possibilities for therapeutic purposes. She's had a year to think about it, so there were lots of ideas—some inventive, some bordering on crazy.

When Cody got home, I told him about seeing Josh and Shandler together, and how I thought she set me up. He was furious, saying it was a new low even for her. I wanted to tell him what happened to Mila, but I knew he would hassle me again about going to the police. Besides, it's her secret to tell, not mine.

As I drift off to sleep, Mila's words of wisdom replay in my mind. We are the perils we face, and I have faced my fair share lately. But I haven't fallen apart—well . . . not completely. Regardless, I won't let what he did define me.

17

Cody has been super nice since the whole Josh episode. We spend a lot of time together at home—doing homework, watching TV, or just talking. Life seems better when he's around, less overwhelming and complicated.

Pretty much everyone at school has stopped giving me the stink-eye. Ignoring Josh was the best advice. I think he got bored of trying to torture me, so now he mostly leaves me alone. Seeing him around school still makes my knees feel wobbly, my heart race, and my skin crawl, but I'm doing my best to not internalize it.

Mila and I sit together at lunch now. She's got a lot of energy, which is great, because it takes my mind off of pretty much everything. It takes a lot of focus to keep up with her mentally.

And Shandler. I never see her around any other girls. She is definitely the main bitch at school, but there isn't a mean-girl posse behind her. She's a singular walking nightmare.

How can anyone be that vicious—to set a person up like

that? I wonder if she knew how far he would take it? Or did she just think he was going to humiliate me somehow? She's been hard to deal with. She continually bombards me with insults. I'm either a slut, a whore, or I stink, and where did I get my clothes . . . Wal-Mart? And on, and on.

Most days I want to punch her in the head, but settle for returning her insults with comebacks I learned from my old school. Sometimes, it shuts her up, others, we really get into it. I hate days like that, because it draws a lot of attention, and gossip usually follows. Mila is in the loop, so I hear it all from her.

"Hey, gorgeous," Mila's voice booms as she enters the restaurant. In a way, she reminds me of Anna—small, loud, and fearless.

She sits down at one of the tables and motions for me to sit with her.

"What are you doing here?" I ask, pulling out a chair and parking my butt on it.

"Can't a friend come by and say hi?"

I give her a look like, *you're full of crap, what do you really want?*

"You're astute as always." She leans closer and motions me to do the same. "I've got it."

"You've got what?" I eye her suspiciously.

"The revenge plan."

"I thought we were tabling that."

"Come on." She squirms in her chair excitedly. "We'll sneak out and plastic wrap Josh and Shandler's cars, then spray paint graffiti all over them."

"I am not vandalizing their cars!" I hiss.

"It's not really vandalizing . . . well, it is, but we're spray painting the plastic wrap—it won't hurt the car. I saw it on

YouTube." I start to say no, but she continues. "I figure it's been a couple of weeks since the whole thing went down. They would never suspect you, and definitely not me."

"Josh has been fine, though. It's mostly Shandler."

"So! After what he did to you, I would think you would want to get back at him most of all."

"I think I'd rather let it be. Like I said, he hasn't been bothering me, and I'd like to keep it that way. Besides, don't you think they'd be a little suspicious with us hanging out together?"

"No way. How could they possibly know?"

"Mila, Josh isn't stupid. He must know that we've talked."

She waves me off like it's a minute detail.

"Let me think about it," I say.

"What's there to think about?" I don't respond. "Okay, let's just do Shandler's car—the evil bitch has it coming."

I take a moment to think about it, a grin spreading across my face. "*That* I could do."

Mila cocks her head to the side. "You hear from your father?"

"Oh my god! Squirrel moment? No."

"Gonna call him?"

"No."

"Not gonna talk about it?"

"No."

"Want me to set you up with Chris Hemsworth?"

"No. Wait. What?"

"Ha!" she says pointing at me.

I laugh. "Dork."

Tony comes over and sets a slice of pizza in front of each of us. I smile up at him. "Thanks, Tony, but I didn't ask for this."

"You have a friend, and you feed friends when they come to visit."

I laugh, dismissing the lecture. "This is Mila."

"Hello." He smiles.

"Hola. Nice to meet you." She smiles in return.

"Can I get you two a soda?"

"Yes, please," we say in unison.

She turns back to me with a look of determination. "So, let's go buy a crap ton of plastic wrap and get some spray paint." She rubs her hands together mischievously.

"When do you want this whole thing to go down?"

"I'm thinking late Sunday night. That way she'll be totally screwed for Monday when she tries to go to school."

Tony puts down the glasses of pop, eyeing us both. "What are you two up to?"

"Nothing." I smile innocently at him.

"*Humph.*"

She giggles as he walks away. I shake my head and smile. I'm so glad I met this crazy, little spitfire.

"Hey," Cody says from my doorway. "Can I come in?"

I close the lid to my computer. My brain's not working anyway. "Sure. What's up?"

"Nothing. Just wanted to see how you were doing?"

"With what?"

"You know . . . school, the whole Josh thing." He sits on my bed facing me. "I've been leaving the subject alone, but now I'm not sure that was the right thing to do."

"No. I'm doing good."

He looks surprised.

I shrug a shoulder. "What? If I let him affect me, he wins, right?"

"I'm impressed."

His statement ends, but his focus on me continues. My body starts to buzz under his stare. What's he thinking?

I should say something, but I can't think of anything.

Cody clears his throat. "Okay, well . . ." He stands up like he's going to leave, but looks around as if he's trying to find a reason to stay. I'm about to ask him if there's something else, when he takes a step toward my nightstand and casually picks up my sketchbook. "Is this the one I got you?" He turns to the first page.

"Hey!" I jump up from my desk, trying to grab it from him, but he lifts it out of my reach and continues invading my personal property.

I try again, but he turns his body and flips over a few more pages. "Cody! Give it back!" I reach around him, but he twists his body even farther. "I'm serious!" I swipe at it again. "I know you have problems with personal space . . . property . . . and anything else along those lines—but seriously. Give." I smack his arm. "It." *Smack*. "Back." *Smack*, *smack*.

"All right, okay," he says, laughing. I watch as his eyes take in our close proximity. A cocky grin spreads across his face.

Realizing I'm pressed up against him, I step back. "What?" I snap.

He shows me the page he's on in the journal. It's a drawing of him that time I came across him working out in the garage.

Crap!

"Oh, *pshh*." I wave it off like it's no big deal. "I'm always drawing random stuff, I rarely look back through it." Which is a bullshit lie.

I jump up and yank the book out of his hands, then slam it closed.

"Not a big deal, huh?"

"What are you . . . like twelve?"

He puts his hands up in defense. "Hey. Sorry."

Ahhh! Of all the drawings he had to come across, why did it have to be that one? I give myself a mental smack on the forehead. I know my face is neon red, but I hold my chin up just the same. "It's equivalent to a diary, okay?"

"What do you mean?"

"What I mean is . . . you looking at it is embarrassing."

He looks puzzled. "Why?"

I roll my eyes at him like he's a moron. "Instead of writing about instances, I draw them, like a snapshot in time."

"So your drawing of me . . ."

"Is no big deal!" He gives me a look of disbelief. "I—I just liked the way your muscles looked. I mean . . . I liked the lines of definition." Crap. "As in, your perfect anatomy." *Ahh, frick!* "What I'm trying to say is—"

"I love it when you get all flustered," Cody teases. "Your cheeks get all red and blotchy, and you get this little line . . . just there." He touches the spot between my eyebrows.

I smack his hand away, but the sentiment makes me want to melt. Damn him! I hit him with my sketchbook. "Don't be a dick!"

"Ow! I'm not. It's totally cute."

God, he's such a flirt. I give him a hard stare. "Okay, you can go now."

"Fine, I'll leave. But your pictures are amazing. I had no idea."

"Thanks."

He continues to stare at me. If he doesn't leave soon, I'm going to tackle him to the bed and tell him exactly how I feel about him. Then we'll both be embarrassed when he sputters out a rejection.

With an irritated sigh, I point to the door. "*Leave*. I have homework to finish."

"Fine," he says, but stops at the entrance. "Hear any more from your dad?"

"Oh my god! Really? Go!"

He crosses his arms defiantly.

"I don't want to talk about it!"

He throws his hands up. "I'm gone."

"Finally," I grumble to myself.

"But, you should contact him!" he hollers from inside his bedroom. "It's a big deal, don't you think?"

I'd rather just go back to thinking he doesn't exist. "It's none of your business!" I yell back.

I try to settle back into writing my paper, but all I can think about is shit for brains—the look he gave me, his words, our bodies together.

Oh, hell.

Luckily, this assignment isn't due till next week. I close the laptop and take the sketchbook over to my bed. Leaning back against the pillows, I look through the drawings. Luckily, I got the book away before he saw the millions of other sketches I drew of him. He'd tease the hell out of me.

Can I help it if he's good subject matter?

18

"This is going to be so much fun." Mila vibrates with excitement as she clasps onto the side of my arms.

"How is vandalizing someone's car supposed to be fun?"

"Just imagine the look on Shandler's face—looking stunned, maybe a bit confused at first, then her raging temper-tantrum when it finally hits her—it's priceless."

I visualize the moment and a wicked grin creeps across my face.

"See? Told ya."

"You're a bad influence. What if we get caught? Do you even know where she lives?"

"We won't get caught, and, duh . . . Internet. Addresses are easy to find."

We head to the checkout line with all our contraband. The checkout lady looks at us like she knows we're up to no good. I start to fidget nervously under her scrutiny.

"So, what's it like living with Cody Stanton?" Mila says his name like he's royalty.

I look through the magazines on display, trying to project indifference. "It's fine. No big deal."

From my peripheral vision, I see her arms-crossed stance as she looks at me speculatively. When I turn to face her, she raises an eyebrow, adding to the look of knowing satisfaction. "No big deal, huh?"

"Yeah! *No big deal*."

"Bullshit! You've totally got a thing for him."

Once again, trying to look disinterested, "No. I don't."

She punches me in the arm. "You're *such a liar*! *Oh my god*. And you live with him—*Awk*ward."

"Tell me about it," I slap my hand over my mouth and stare at her with wide eyes.

"Ha! I knew it!" She points an accusing finger at me.

I groan as I drop my head back, momentarily staring at the ceiling. "And his bedroom is right across from mine."

"I know. You poor girl. Does he know?"

"No."

"He could be into you."

"Not in *that* way. It's more of a sister slash friend sort of thing."

"That sucks."

I roll my eyes. "Yup."

Mila parks down the block from Shandler's house, shuts off the lights, and turns to me. "You ready?"

"Do we really have to wear all this black stuff? No way am I wearing this ski mask."

"Do you want someone to identify us if we're spotted?"

"No."

"Exactly!"

"Fine!" I say, pulling it over my face. "But I feel ridiculous."

"You look it too." She giggles as she fixes hers in place.

We look at each other and burst out laughing.

"This is crazy!" I laugh even harder.

"Payback is a righteous bitch!" Mila points at me. "You . . . should . . . see . . . yourself," she says, gasping for air between each word.

Seeing just eyes, lips, and nose all scrunched up in humor, I nod my head in agreement, but can't get the words out.

As the laughter plays out, we each take a deep breath.

Mila says, "Let's do this!"

"Yeah." I try hard to stifle the laughter that won't settle. We need to get this done.

It's close to midnight as I follow her into an alley that runs behind all the houses on this block. I look up at the monstrosity Shandler calls home. "Damn that's big!"

"Yeah, whatever, mine's bigger."

"Say, *what*?"

"No biggie," she adds somberly. "There's her car."

I'm surprised it's not in one of the five garages. It's pitch black except for a streetlight way down the street.

When we near the garages, a light with a motion sensor clicks on. "Shit!" we both say and quickly hide behind Shandler's car.

"Let's get out of here," I say.

"No. Just wait."

When the light clicks off. Mila stands up and walks around the vehicle, the light doesn't go on again—her car must be out of range.

"Perfect." Mila takes the plastic wrap out of the gym bag

that's slung across her body. She finds the beginning of the first roll and gets me to hold it between my fingers as she starts the wrapping process, giggling and leaping around the car like a maniacal fairy.

Mission completed, we stand back, admiring our work.

"She's gonna have a hell of a time getting in her car," Mila whispers as she hands me a can of red spray paint. "You should have first honors."

I ponder a moment, then shake the can and write, *I pick my nose when no one's looking* on the side of the car and *Wicked Witch of the West* across the front.

"Nice," Mila says, taking the can from me, then walks to the back of the car.

"Perfect!" I say with admiration when she finishes.

It reads, *Child of Satan,* across the trunk.

"I know." Her expression is a mixture of amused spite and satisfaction.

"I am so glad I'm on your good side. You're scary."

"You bet your *sweet ass*."

Someone from across the alley starts dragging a trashcan out.

We both crouch down. "We're totally screwed," I whisper.

"Chill." she says, placing a hand on my shoulder.

We watch as a man in his bathrobe and slippers deposits the can in the alley and goes back into the house.

We look at each other and breathe a collective sigh of relief. A nervous giggle escapes me. I cover my mouth, but it doesn't help. I feel the laughter bubbling up again.

"Come on!" Mila grasps my hand and yanks me in the

direction of her car. "Let's go before your uncontrolled behavior gets us caught."

She sounds like such a mom. Now, I really can't stop laughing.

"*Shhh.*" she hisses, pulling me into a run.

"Who's there?" a voice says from behind us.

We round the corner going full speed. I stumble but regain my footing as Mila uses her key fob to unlock the doors. As soon as we're in the car, we hunker down out of sight. Mila's so small she almost fits under her steering wheel.

Still laughing hysterically, I pull my mask off.

Mila yanks hers off at the same time she strikes out with her foot, kicking at me. "*Shhh!* You could have gotten us caught."

"What do you care, Queen of the Rebels?"

"My mom would kill me."

I stare at her like, *as if you care.*

That gets her going and laughter fills the car.

"We should look and see if he's gone," Mila says.

"I will." I stretch up to take a peek. "Oh my god!" I drop back down.

"Mierda! What?"

I start giggling again.

"You bitch! There's no one there!"

"Nope."

Her eyes become angry slits. "What did you say about getting on my bad side?"

19

EVEN THOUGH IT'S a Monday and I'm exhausted from the late night, it's been an amazing day, mostly because of the speculation surrounding Shandler's car. Apparently, she's been storming the halls, intimidating anyone she thinks might be involved and grilling them into a confession—which is pretty much everyone, since no one likes her. Luckily, she hasn't found me. I'm not sure I could stand up to the pressure, not to mention that I suck at lying. But all in all, I feel vindicated and *very* proud of myself. I wonder what my mom would think? The old her—the one Roxanne describes—would have led the way, probably come up with the idea herself. The Mom I knew . . . I don't know.

"Cassie." Cody pulls me aside in the hallway.

"Yeah?" I say, still revelling in the glow of my handiwork.

"Did you have something to do with what happened to Shandler's car?"

"Do what?"

He glares at me. "Cassie?"

"*Me?*" I say, placing a hand to my chest with a dramatic flair of innocence.

"Are you *nuts*!"

"Oh, don't get your Underroos in a wad! No one found out, and it felt good to finally do something."

"I'm glad to see you so . . . liberated, but still. You shouldn't mess with her. If you're not going to the police, then let it go."

"Okay, *Mom*."

"*I'm serious*."

"Don't worry. I'm good now."

I'm writing my name and date on my English midterm—a total downer from my vengeful buzz—when the realization of how close the holidays are hits me. It's going to be the first Thanksgiving and Christmas without Mom. And just like that, my vindicated glow turns into a somber reality. Damn! Hopefully, once I get through this year and all the major firsts are over, things will get easier.

At home, Luigi and Maria would close the restaurant and we'd have a massive Thanksgiving feast with all their family—which is *huge*. The day after, Mom and I would take the subway to where the Christmas trees were being sold, then half-carry, half-drag one back. We tried taking it home on the subway once, thinking it was late enough and wouldn't be crowded, but it was and the people stared at us like we were crazy. We had a good laugh.

After hefting the tree up six flights of stairs, we'd string up the lights and strategically place all the homemade ornaments on it. We made new ones every year, feeling they were nicer than the store-bought ones. I garbaged them all when I was packing—something I totally regret. Stupid choices made in pain.

"That exam was *hard*," Mila says on our way out of class.

"Yeah," I say distantly.

She takes my arm, stopping me. "Hey, you okay?"

"I don't know. Not really. I was just thinking about the holidays coming up. It's going to be hard with my mom gone."

"Oh." Mila winces. "Yeah. Well, on a positive note, *you* don't have to endure endless holiday parties with all of my mother's crappy friends and admirers."

"That bad, huh?"

"It's worse than bad. It's a nightmare. They get all dressed up and dole out their yearly quota of phony affection—giving each other air hugs and kisses, all while wishing each other a jolly, effing Merry Christmas."

"Bah-humbug?"

She laughs. "Pretty much."

I follow her as she starts to walk. "What about Thanksgiving?" I ask.

"What about it?"

"Does your mom do the big feast?"

"No, she usually heads off to Cabo with her friends or friend, depending on who she's doing that week."

"Wow. So, you stay at home alone? That's so sad."

She dismisses the comment with a wave of her hand. "It's not a big deal. Thanksgiving is just as commercial as Christmas

—a way for businesses to make extra money. Besides, I'm used to my mother's total lack of maternal instincts and inappropriate behavior. She's a selfish, self-centered person—not much I can do about it."

I stop walking. "That is so depressing. Well, on the upside, at least you know what your mother's about. She may be a sucky person, but at least she's honest about it."

She pulls me forward so we're walking again. "Your mother had legitimate reasons for hiding her past. It wasn't like she was deliberately trying to deceive you. I mean, she was, but not in the way you're taking it—she was trying to keep you safe. It sounds like you had a special relationship, and she loved you a lot. Isn't that all you need to know? I mean, isn't that what really matters?"

"I guess. It just—"

Mila releases a frustrated breath, "Oh my god. *Enough* already. She was protecting you. She didn't do anything wrong! Be happy with what you had."

"Tell me how you really feel." I joke. Her bluntness doesn't bother me, because I know it's just Mila being herself. "No. You're probably right."

She smiles triumphantly. "You know I am. I need to get to class. See you at lunch?"

"Yup." I pause. "Hey, you know what? You're coming to my house for Thanksgiving. Roxanne is doing the whole feast thing. Have I told you about Sunday brunches?"

"Yes, several times. But I don't really know them—it would be kind of awkward. I'd feel like I was intruding."

"Welcome to my world. It's better than sitting at home feeling sorry for yourself."

She looks indignant. “I *do not* feel sorry for myself. I just don’t give a f—”

“Good then. You’ll come with me. We can feel awkward together.”

She huffs as she walks away, throwing a dismissive wave.

20

WELL, I wouldn't say Thanksgiving was awkward, but it was definitely an experience—*hole-ee*! With Roxanne and Jeff's extended families invited, it was like an in-house tornado of people, loud noise, and food that left a disaster in its wake. But it was worth it. Even Mila had a blast.

I turn the corner and slam into someone. "I'm sorry," I say as a natural response, then realize who it is.

Josh's hands grip my arms, steadying me. I'm taken back to the day on the beach. I look around wildly, looking for someone to save me, but no one's in the hall. I'm all alone—again.

He smiles down at me as if nothing had ever happened. "No, it's my fault. I should have watched where I was going."

I'm confused by his attitude. Realizing his hands are still on me, I shake him off and step back.

The corner of his mouth lifts. "I'm glad I ran into you. I've been thinking about everything. I feel extremely bad about the way I treated you at the party, *and* at school. It was all Shandler's idea. She got me so worked up with all the shit she was saying about you, and . . . well, there's just no excuse. Can you forgive me?" he asks, looking remorseful.

I gawk at him. Is he insane?

Catching myself, I step around him and continue on my way.

"Aw, come on! Cassie!" he shouts. "I'm sorry."

I don't turn around. My legs feel like Jello. I need to get to class and sit down. I thought I was past letting him affect me, but having him touch me, and being that close . . . I shudder. *I am not a victim.* I say over and over to myself as I walk to class.

Cody and I are watching TV, Roxanne is in her office, and Jeff is at a friend's house talking to him about a renovation. In conversation, I casually relay the events with Josh. "What game is he playing now?" Cody fumes. "He *obviously* didn't get the message the first time I kicked his ass. He must need a reminder."

"*No*, don't. Just leave it alone. It'll only make things worse. I shouldn't have even told you," I snap.

"What does that mean?" he fires back.

"Exactly what I said. I didn't tell you so you could jump on your white horse and save the day. I can take care of myself."

"*Cassie*," he says harshly, before stopping himself. "I didn't mean to make it sound like you're some kind of weakling. It's just that I care about you . . ." He picks up my hand absentmindedly and flips it over. "And I don't trust him."

"I don't either. He's . . ." I'm distracted by Cody's gentle touch as his fingers trail over the scar that remains on the palm of my hand. When he stops, I look up. Our eyes lock—neither one of us are diverting our gaze.

My body is buzzing with the thrill of possible meaning, but then his expression quickly changes from, I'm not exactly sure what, to empathetic concern, confusion, then finally embarrassment. He pulls his hand away and directs his attention back to the TV.

Internally, I wilt from the rejection. "Can you believe that story about Shandler making him do it?" I say, recovering quickly.

"Yeah. Um . . ." His focus remains on the TV. "Hard to say. She's a total nut job, and more than likely fuels Josh's sociopathic ego. Don't *ever* underestimate her . . . or Josh." He looks at me briefly.

"No, I won't."

Should I leave? It's so awkward now.

If I did, what would that say?

"Um . . . why doesn't Shandler have any friends?" It's a stupid question, but I had to say something.

He looks at me curiously. "I don't know . . . I guess she's burned every possible friendship. I could never figure her out. Her mother seemed pretty nice, but, in all the time we were together, I never met her father."

"What did you ever see in her?"

"I don't know. Just thinking with the wrong head, I guess."

I punch him in the chest. "Gross!" Now this feels normal.

He recoils from the impact. "Hey. Gentle. I'm sore from working out."

"You're such a pig!"

"No, I'm not. I just made a mistake."

"Yeah, a quantum one."

"Ooh, big word!"

"Dick."

"Bitch."

I laugh, thankful that we're back on track.

"Sorry for overreacting earlier," he says. "For some reason, I'm ridiculously protective of you. I never had a sister before—maybe that's it."

Bam! Kill me now, why don't you!

21

"WHAT DO YOU MEAN, he *talked* to you!" Mila explodes when I tell her the following day.

"*Shhh!*" I look around to see if anyone's paying attention. "Calm down. Cody already did the whole over-protective thing. I don't need it all over again." I shut my locker and start walking to the lunch area. Mila follows alongside, mumbling her trademark Hispanic expletives.

"So, what did the dickhead say?" she says. I open my mouth to speak. "What could he possibly have to say? He has no right to talk to you. What a slimeball!" She turns her focus to me. "Are you going to tell me what he said, or what? God! I can't believe it—kid's got cojones!"

"Oh my god, Mila! Shut up and I'll tell you! Sit!" I point to a chair at a table I picked out.

She plops herself in it and crosses her arms defiantly across her chest. "Are you going to let me talk now, or what?" I ask.

"*Maybe*." She's acting like an indignant child.

I raise an eyebrow. "Seriously?"

"*Fine*. Sorry."

I laugh. "*Holy-man*, you get wound up."

"Well, he's an asshole! Remember . . . he attacked me too."

"You're right," I say, feeling bad. Sometimes I forget. She acts so tough all the time. "You have every right to react. But do you have to make such a scene?"

She gives me a lopsided grin. "I wouldn't be me if I didn't. So, Cody was pissed?"

"Yeah."

"*Really?*" Mila says, pumping her eyebrows.

"I wish. When I commented on how crazy he got, he said it must be because he never had a sister before."

"*Ouch*. That sucks."

"Yep."

"Maybe he just meant that he's never had anyone he felt the need to protect before."

"I'd like to think that, but hoping and wishing are destructive to my already battered self-esteem."

"Order up!" Tony yells.

I finish wiping down a table, then pick up the order. I turn back and Josh is standing there. A jolt of adrenalin shoots through me. "Josh. Um." *I'm in a safe place*. I remind myself.

"I just came to say hi. You won't talk to me at school, so I figured I could corner you here." He smiles politely, but the play on words isn't lost on me.

"I was just heading to the back. Um, have a seat. Someone will be with you in a minute."

Marco's cutting up tomatoes when I come up beside him.

"Josh Trainer is out there, and I don't want to deal with him. Can you get his order?"

He turns around, his blade pointing at me. "Cassie, I don't wait on tables."

I push the knife to the side. "Just do it! Please," I beg.

He looks at me like I'm mental. "Fine, but Nona and Nono are going to ask why I'm waiting on him."

"Tell them I'm not feeling well. I'll go wait in the bathroom."

He shakes his head while wiping his hands on a cloth, gives me one last look of confusion, and heads out to take Josh's order.

I high-tail it to the bathroom but leave the door open a crack so I can watch. Marco is talking to Josh, but I can't hear what they're saying. I quickly shut the door when they both look in my direction.

"Cassie," Marco says, knocking on the door softly.

I open it looking around.

"He's asking for you."

"Why can't he just leave me alone?"

"What's happened?"

"As if you don't know."

"Know what?"

I open the bathroom door further. "Seriously? He attacked me? At the beach?"

"What!" The look in his eyes turns deadly.

I quickly reach out, grabbing his arm, and pull him inside. "Don't!"

"Why not?" he seethes.

It's odd to see a normally subdued person rage. "No. The

last thing I want is Tony finding out. He'll chase him out with a butcher knife. I don't think that'll be very good for business."

"Why is he here?"

"'Cause he won't let it go. He wants me to forgive him. But I think he's up to something. I don't trust him."

"Smart girl. Don't worry. I've got this. I'll give him my asshole special—extra toppings of saliva and pepper flakes on his pizza."

"*Ew*, but appropriate."

He starts to go, then turns back. "Oh . . . uh, I told Nona that you weren't feeling well. Sorry about that."

"Why are you sorry?"

"You haven't had one of her remedies."

"I'm confused."

"All I can say is, you'll wish you'd come up with a different excuse."

I shake my head in confusion as he leaves. As soon as I close myself in the stall, I hear the bathroom door open. "Cassie, it's Anna. Marco said you don't feel so good. I've got something to make you better."

"'Kay. Just a second." I flush the toilet for no reason and open the door.

"You look pale. Drink this!" She shoves a glass into my hand.

I sniff it.

"It doesn't taste so good, but it will make you better, so drink!"

I put the cup to my lips. She tips it, forcing me to drink it all or have it spill down my shirt.

She lets go of the glass when it's empty. "*Ahhh!* Anna. That's horrible!"

"It is," she says smiling. "But it makes you better. Mamma's recipe."

"*Ack!*" I shudder. "What the heck's in this stuff? It tastes like dirty socks?"

"A little of this, little of that. Don't you insult Mamma's cure!" she scolds.

"Sorry. It's just nasty."

She smiles. "You feel better, no?"

"No! Now I feel like throwing up."

"Yes. You throw up, and then you feel better. It's the cure!"

"Oh, god!" I run into the stall and puke it back up.

"There! You see? Better. Come out after you rinse your mouth and wash your hands," she says, then leaves.

I groan and do as she says.

There's a knock again.

"*What?*" I yell, angry as hell.

The door opens. "It's Marco." He peeks his head in. "It's all clear." He looks me over. "So . . . you had the remedy."

"Don't even mention it, or I'll puke again. Why didn't you warn me?"

"I did."

"You could have told me what happens when you *drink* it!"

"Where's the fun in that?"

"You're a dick!"

"Hey. I got rid of him for you, didn't I?"

"What did you say?"

"I said you were in the back puking your guts up and couldn't talk right now."

"Oh, perfect." Of all the things he could have said, he picks that. *Nice.*

"That's not what got him to leave. As soon as he took a bite of my fiery hot pizza, he started gagging, then drank an entire glass of saliva-filled pop. Pretty sure that's what did it. He threw some money on the table and left."

"Tony is going to be *so* pissed."

"*Naw* . . . he didn't even notice. If he had, I would have told him that I saw Josh bullying some kids and he would have been all-up-in-it." He grins.

"Marco!" Tony yells. "Delivery is ready!"

"Thanks," I say, punching his arm.

He smiles. "No problem."

22

CHRISTMAS. Wow! The lights and decorations, and the *tree*—Roxanne went all out. I've never seen anything like it, except maybe in the department stores in Manhattan—Macy's and Saks—that kind of thing. I guess if you have money to burn, why not? And she *is* a designer, so she probably can't resist all the sparkle.

"Get up!" Cody yells, banging on my door.

"*Aah!*" I groan and roll over. "Go away!"

He whips it open. "Get up!"

My pillow is suddenly yanked out from under my head, and the covers are ripped from my body.

"Are you nuts!" I sit up. "You about tore my head off!"

He rolls his eyes, then stares at my body with a stupid grin on his face.

I look down at my tight tank and very short boy boxers, then grab the covers back and yell at him to get out.

"It's Christmas morning, come on!"

"I'm coming!" I smile. With his childish excitement, it's hard not too. "Get out, so I can change."

"Do I have to?" he says, wiggling his eyebrows impishly.

I give him a look like, *get going before I claw your eyes out*, mixed with an undertone of, *I wish you were actually serious.* That's when I notice he's only wearing pajama bottoms. I groan as my insides heat up. "You know . . . it's kind of chilly, maybe you should put a shirt on."

"What? I thought you liked looking at my near-perfect anatomy."

I growl and hurl myself at him, pushing and shoving, trying to get him out of my room, but his big, meaty body won't budge. He laughs as he takes hold of my wrists and pins my hands against his bare chest. I'm pretty sure if a person could spontaneously combust, I'd be a pile of cinders right now.

As he stares into my eyes, his mood turns serious, like he's trying to figure out life's deepest mysteries. Meanwhile, my heart's pounding so hard that I feel dizzy. Then he plants a quick kiss on my lips, making a loud smacking sound, shoves me on the bed, then runs out of my room laughing like a loon.

"Jerk!" I yell after him.

I touch my fingers to my lips. *What the hell?*

Did that *really* just happen?

Was that a sisterly kiss?

Do brothers kiss their sisters on the lips?

I don't think so.

Should I be hopeful?

Get a grip! It's just another one of his flirtatious, means absolutely nothing, moments. He's driving me nuts!

. . .

We open gifts like a family, and I mostly keep my emotions in check. It's hard with Mom not being here, but Cody's actions in my room have kept my mind occupied, distracting me from sinking too low.

Cody and I basically got each other gag-gifts, mostly inside joke stuff. It's been fun.

Over the Christmas debris, I notice Roxanne look at Jeff, who nods in return. "Cassie, there was a gift delivered to you this morning by messenger," Jeff says from the couch.

I look back and forth between them, confused.

"It's from your father," Roxanne adds.

I'm stunned as he holds out a small, expertly wrapped gift box to me.

"You don't have to open it if you don't want to—it's up to you," Jeff says. "But we realized after you went nuts on us, that keeping things from you is a mistake," he teases. "You're old enough to make your own decisions. You're a strong person, Cassie. I know you would never let him push you around, and if need be, you have a family behind you to kick some ass."

I reach over the massive pile of wrapping paper to take the gift from him. "I appreciate that. I think I'll wait till later to open it, though. I don't want it to ruin the day." Even hearing mention of him has scarred the moment. *Asshole!*

"Sure. We understand," Jeff says.

"I don't know about you guys," Cody says, "but I'm starving."

"When are you not?" I retort.

He answers with a playful shove before standing up.

Beaming up at him, I kick my leg out, nailing him in the back of his calf muscle, making his knee buckle.

"*Oooh!*" he says before tackling me to the ground. "You are in so much trouble." He sits on me, pinning each arm under his knees, and starts tickling me.

"*Ahhh!*" I yell and thrash about. "Let me up! You weigh a freaking ton!"

"Okay, kids," Jeff says. "No horsing around. I don't want to be waiting in the emergency room on Christmas day."

Cody gives my head a swirly before standing up.

I flip the tangled mess out of my eyes. "*Dick.*" Then hook my foot around his ankle as he tries to walk away, making him trip.

He turns, giving me a lopsided smile. I swear he couldn't look any sexier if he tried. "Mom! Cassie has a potty mouth!"

I stick my tongue out at him.

"Oh, real mature," he returns.

What a nug.

Breakfast was amazing, as usual. After helping clean up, I go to my room, determined to face whatever's in the mystery box. I shake it. There's muffled movement.

I sit down on the floor, leaning against the foot of my bed, and tear into the expensive wrapping. I open the lid and move the tissue aside. There's another box which reads iPhone. I shake my head. *What the heck?* I open the lid. There's a note folded up inside.

Cassie,

I know I haven't been there for you, and I take full responsibility for that, but I want to try and salvage some kind of a relationship. So much time has been lost, and I will do everything I can to make it up to you. But that's near impossible when you won't talk to me, and I realize confronting you the way I did might have been too aggressive. I don't like feeling like a stalker in my own daughter's life, so I hope you will accept this gift as a way to open a line of communication. You can call me anytime, or if that's too forward, you can just text or email me. My information is already programmed into your contacts. Just turn it on and it's ready to go.

Brent

I pull off the lid and take out the phone—it feels foreign in my hand. I stare at it, not even sure how to turn it on.

"Hey. What did you get?" Cody asks as he enters. "Sweet . . . an iPhone. Now we can message each other."

"Why would we need to do that? We live together, you moron!"

"That's just what people do."

"Well, it's stupid." I stare at it again. "Uh . . . how do you turn it on?"

"Seriously?" He laughs.

I give him an evil glare. "You know I don't have a phone."

"Yeah, but it's just so weird."

"Do you want to help me or not?" I snap.

"Jeez, chill." He sits on the floor next to me and takes it.

"Okay, so you press this circle button," he says, demonstrating. "And it will turn on." The phone comes to life. "Voila."

He hands it to me. There is a picture of me and my father building a sandcastle. I immediately throw the phone away from me, like it's a bomb about to go off.

"Whoa!" Cody says, placing his hands on top of his head. "That's super expensive, ya know?" He retrieves the phone. "What's the matter?"

"The picture." I point at the phone.

"What do you mean?" he touches the screen and it lights up again.

"Awesome. That's exactly the way I remember you."

I jump up and start pacing. "He has *no right* . . . to . . . to . . ."

"Cassie, calm down. It's just a phone."

"It's not just the phone! How dare he throw some bullshit moment in my face?"

"He's your dad."

I whirl on him. "No!" I'm super close to tears and fighting for control. "He lost that right the moment he abused my mother."

His voice softens. "People can change. He went on to get his life together and became very successful."

"*Oh!* So because he's famous . . . that gives him a free pass back into my life?"

"I doubt that's what he's thinking. I'm sure he feels awful and wants to try and fix things."

"Well, he can't!"

"Cassie, you're being kind of stubborn, aren't you?"

My eyes widen in shock.

"Well . . . come on. He's spent the last fourteen years trying to find you. Shouldn't that count for something?"

"Oh my god! Seriously? What . . . you feel, what . . . sorry for him?" I shriek, making him cringe. "Are you fucking kidding me!"

Cody shrugs his shoulders looking helpless. "Sorry, I guess I'm not helping."

I place my hands on my stomach. I feel sick. The tears begin to flow despite my intended control.

He jumps up. "Shit! Cassie. I didn't mean to upset you." Reaching for my hand, he pulls me close, wrapping his arms around me. My arms hang limp as the dam breaks and all the hurt I've been trying to hold in—my mom, the move, Cody, my father, Josh—comes pouring out. *Shit*. Why does he have to see me lose it again?

I vaguely hear Roxanne as she says, "Cody, I heard yelling . . . is everything—oh my goodness, what happened?"

"It's okay, Mom. I've got it."

"Cassie," Roxanne says. "Are you okay?"

"*Mom*. I've got it. *Shhh*," Cody soothes as he strokes my hair. "It's okay."

Racking sobs take control and my knees feel like they're about to give out. He scoops me up and cradles me in his lap on the bed.

I cry and cry. I want to stop, but I can't seem to get past the dark, emotional pit that wants to swallow me whole. It's too much. I feel like I'm drowning.

Eventually, the heart-wrenching sobs turn into short fits of despair, followed by a deep, shuddering breath. Tears are wiped from my cheek.

Through blurry, swollen eyes, I see Cody's thoughtful expression and I'm instantly pulled into the light.

"Hey, beautiful."

I give a snot-filled snort. "Funny." I realize where I am and start to get up. "I'm so sorry. I swore I was done crying."

He holds on tight as he reaches for tissues from the box on my nightstand—my body moving with his. "No . . . it's okay. I'm totally getting used to the angry-moody girl who likes to leave snot and mascara smudges all over my shirts."

"Thanks," I say, blowing my nose.

"*Holee*, that's gross."

I try getting up again, but he wrestles my head back to his chest then plants a kiss on top. "Stay. I kinda like this."

I laugh at him, then sigh, snuggling in closer—his chest is solid and warm against my cheek. I don't care if this is another one of his insincere flirtatious moments. I wouldn't move if you paid me. "Sorry. I guess I kinda lost it."

"Kinda?"

I lean back and glare at him. "You don't need to rub it in."

"Oh, stop." He playfully shoves my head back against him. I wrap my arms around his waist and squeeze tight. "You probably needed it. It was bound to happen sometime. I'm surprised it took this long."

He's right. And I do feel a lot better—hollowed out—but better. "Yeah . . . well I'm sorry you had to be the one to see it . . . again." I reluctantly crawl off his lap and grab another tissue. "Did I hear your mom come in?"

"Yes, but I told her I had it covered, so she left. Probably hung outside the door for a while though, to make sure it was *really* okay."

I gape at him. "*Really?* Oh my god! How embarrassing."

"No, it's cool. I'm sure she understands."

"I doubt she would understand why I was on your lap."

"She either didn't see, or figured it was innocent, which it was," he quickly clarifies. "If it wasn't, she'd have ripped my head off for seducing you, then kick the crap out of me."

How do the girls at school deal with this? The thoughtful flirtiness. I guess that's why they're always following him around like little hens, picking up the crumbs of affection he throws out.

I've become one of the hens.

Ugh!

He grabs me by the hand and pulls hard. I tumble onto the bed next to him.

"What was that for?" I say, laughing.

He leans over me, his eyes alight with humor. "I don't know—just seemed to fit with the rest of the day, minus the volcano of emotion that just exploded."

I guess *that's* true.

His nearness is befuddling my brain. I watch as his gaze travels to my mouth. The humor disappears as his expression turns serious. My insides flutter and my heart pounds as his eyes drift up to mine searing me with an intensity I have no experience with. Suddenly, his lips are caressing mine. No more flutters, just fire everywhere as the kiss intensifies.

Before I can process what's going on, he pulls back, breathing heavily. I can feel him shaking, or maybe it's me.

What the hell just happened?

"I'm sorry," he says. "I shouldn't have done that."

Disappointment rakes across me. "Oh . . . yeah. Right. I don't—" I stand up, needing to make a quick exit.

"Wait," he says, grabbing hold of my hand.

I stare into his eyes as he pulls me between his legs. The look . . . is it regret? Indecision? *What?* I can't tell. .

"Why did you do that?" I finally ask. The silence is killing me.

"I don't know. I'm as surprised as you are."

Not the response I was hoping for. I start to pull away, but he holds me in place, his eyes searching mine.

What? Don't leave me guessing.

He grabs my other hand and pulls me closer, guiding my body down until I am straddling him. I watch him, mesmerized as he touches his lips to mine once more. I'm scared. I want him too bad for this to be some game he's playing. That's what it's been all day today—fun and games, right?

But he feels *so* good.

His lips travel down my neck, then back up again, leaving a trail of raised flesh. Everything inside me is screaming to let him explore all he wants. So I'm disappointed when he pulls back, only to have my heart tug at his gaze silently questioning if his actions are okay.

Oh, god. I don't care if it is or isn't. I wrap my arms around his neck and get lost in him. Time slips away. So do all my fears, frustrations, and sadness as I drift in and out of heaven.

Far, far away, I hear a noise. I don't think much of it until it gets louder. I have a hazy realization that I'm on my back with Cody half on top of me. Smooth. Didn't even feel the maneuver.

"Cody!"

He jumps up. I'm a little slower to respond.

Roxanne's staring at us with her arms crossed, looking angry. "How can you be so insensitive? Taking advantage of this during this emotional time."

He grins at me. "I told you she'd blame me. Sorry, Mom, just got lost in the moment, probably the damsel-in-distress syndrome. It won't happen again."

"It better not, young man or I'm shipping you off to military school!"

My mind is still foggy. What just happened?

"Cody, could you give us a moment?"

"Sure." He moves toward the door.

"And you and I will talk about this later." She glares at him a moment longer before turning her attention to me. "Are you okay, honey?" I look over her shoulder and watch Cody leave.

Why can't life be cut and dry—just straightforward: this is how it is, no guessing or thought processing involved?

"I'm sorry about Cody. His behavior is *completely* unacceptable."

"Um . . . Yeah." I'm still dazed by what just went down.

"What set you off? Was it the gift?"

I snap back to reality. "Oh, yeah." I retrieve the phone, touch the screen, and hand it to her.

She puts her hand to her mouth. "Oh, Cassie." She looks at me. "I can see why this would be upsetting. Was there a note?"

I pick it up and hand it to her.

She hands me the phone and takes the letter. After she reads it, she looks up. "It's a nice letter," she says cautiously.

"I guess."

Ding!

The phone vibrates in my hand. I look at Roxanne in fear. "What do I do? It has to be him. No one else has this number." I hand her the phone. "I don't want it."

She touches the screen. "Are you sure?"

I look at the phone like it's some kind of demonic device, then nod my head rapidly.

"I understand. Give it some time."

"I don't know if time will do much. I don't want any part of him."

"It's your choice, Cassie. No one is going to make you do something you don't want to do."

"Thanks for understanding and sorry about the whole Cody thing. It's nothing, really. I plead temporary insanity due to mental trauma."

She laughs, setting the phone on my bed. "I've got my eye on you two. I'm thinking it might be a good idea to move you to the guest room near us. I'm not comfortable with what I just witnessed."

"No, don't. I really like my room. Don't worry. I'm sure it didn't mean anything to him."

"And to you?"

I shrug my shoulder and look at my feet. I quickly realize my mistake and look up at her.

She puts her arm around me. "As much as I'd love the two of you falling madly in love, now isn't the time. You live together, and friends would be the healthiest way for your relationship to move forward, at least until you are about thirty," she jokes. "There will be *no* hanky-panky in this house, young lady."

I choke mid-swallow, followed by a coughing fit. "You don't have to worry." I clear my throat before continuing. "I'm sure it was a momentary lapse in judgment."

"I wouldn't be so sure," she says as she leaves. "I'm serious. I will be keeping my eyes on you two."

I'm exhausted when I finally climb into bed for the night. I snuggle under the billowy duvet with my emotions running somewhere between love sick mushiness and tortured angst.

I've barely seen Cody since the whole . . . kissing episode, and when I did, I got an awkward smile. What the hell does that mean? Roxanne did her best not to give us a minute alone, but still . . . he could have at least said *something*.

I stare at the ceiling.

Maybe I could sneak over to his room and, you know . . . ask him. And if I'm lucky, get a repeat.

No. I don't want to chance rejection.

But still . . . I kind of want to get *some* kind of clarification. I mean, if he thought it was a mistake, I'd rather him tell me now so I can deal with it and move on. Not knowing is making my stomach hurt.

I should just pull on my big girl panties and go ask him. I flip over on my stomach instead, pulling my pillow over my head.

No . . . I kind of feel like the ball's in his court. I know what *I* want; he's the one that has to come to grips.

Although . . . he may not *know* what I want. And maybe he's feeling uncomfortable about making such a bold move.

I sit upright. I need to go talk to him! I yank the covers off and scoot to the edge of the bed.

But it's not like I held anything back—that should speak loud and clear.

I slump forward, then flop backward.

Screw it. There is no way I'm going over there and humiliating myself.

23

IT'S BEEN six days and Cody still hasn't said anything about the kiss. It's not like he's been rude or avoiding me, but he hasn't brought it up either. And since I'm too much of a chicken-shit to confront him, I've pretty much made myself unavailable. The disconnection is *killing me*.

"Do you want to drive down to the beach with me?" Cody asks me at breakfast. "It'll be a little chilly by the water, but we could dress warm."

I stare at my plate a moment before answering. "Um—"

"Come on. The sun is out. Christmas vacation is almost over. It'll be good to get some fresh air. What could be better than going to the beach on New Year's Eve?"

Where is he going with this? He's barely said anything and now he wants to take me to the beach?

Well . . . I guess it's big-girl panty time? Decision made. "Sure. When?"

"Now?"

"Oh . . . *okay*. Sure. Just give me a minute to get ready."

"Is that, like, girl-time get ready? Or normal time? We don't have all day."

"*Aaah* . . . normal time? You should know by now . . . I don't do 'girl time'."

He slams me with his dimpled smile—so unfair.

I throw my bathing suit on. I have no idea why—the water's too damn cold. I shake my head and take it off, exchanging it for ankle length spandex and a long-waisted sweatshirt. I quickly throw my mess of hair into a fan bun.

Cody comes out of his room at the same time I do. He looks me up and down, then extends his hand forward. "After you."

I feel the back of my sweatshirt lift up, making me turn.

"Nice view."

I turn, smacking his hand away and grin. "Do you mind?"

"Not at all. In fact, a shorter top would be more stylish."

"*Pfff*. Man-whore."

"Sceeze."

Back to normal? Maybe he just wants to forget the whole thing—pretend it never happened. I guess that would be a lot less stressful. Anything's better than the way things have been lately.

"Mom!" he calls out.

Roxanne pops up from behind the kitchen counter. "What?"

"Hey, Cassie and I are going to the beach."

"Why are you going there?" She nails us with a suspicious look. "It's kind of cold, isn't it?"

"Not really. Besides, we want to hold hands, kiss, and make mad passionate love on the sand. Let's not forget the blanket, honey," he teases.

Roxanne's eyes bug out. "Cody Stanton!"

I smack his arm. "That's not helping," I hiss.

"Mom! I'm just joking, chill. We want to get some fresh air and go for a walk. It's so nice out."

With her hand over her heart, she takes a deep, cleansing breath. "Cody, that was not funny."

"Sorry, Mom. Just trying to keep it light."

"Don't be late," she says irritably. "Dinner's at six."

"We won't," I say, looking at her apologetically. There was absolutely no need for Cody to get her worked up.

On the drive, Cody is back to being unusually quiet, making me nervous. I'm sure he's finally come to the realization that it was all a big mistake, and he's taking me there to give me The Talk.

Frick! Now my stomach's all in knots.

I step out of the jeep after he parks. He's put the soft top on. "*Burrr*. The sun isn't out."

"Have a little faith. You brought a jacket, right?" I nod my head, yes. "You'll be fine."

I kick off my flats and throw them on the floor mat under my seat. I hate walking on the beach with shoes. I don't care how cold it is—it just feels icky.

I pull my jean jacket tightly around me as I follow him down to the water's edge. He seems distracted, but so am I.

We walk along in silence. I'm careful not to get too close to the water. Last thing I need is a rogue wave coming up and soaking me.

When the sun finally decides to make an appearance, I stop. Closing my eyes, I lift my head to take it in. The sand heats up immediately, feeling amazing under my feet. Another great advantage of living in California. No way I would be doing this on the east coast this time of year.

Cody takes my hand. I open my eyes abruptly, looking at him as he faces me, he picks up the other one. Oh crap! Here we go. "Cody—"

"Just hear me out," he says.

Yep, here comes the rejection.

"I really like you," he says.

And *bam*, there it is . . . the I Like You But speech.

"I know it's totally wrong . . . because we live together . . ."

Okay, now my heart's jammed itself in my throat. *Shit!* Just get it over with. He could have just done this at home. It's not like the beauty of the location is going to make it any easier.

My attention focuses back on him when I realize he's staring at me, not saying anything. Did I miss something?

"I think you feel the same way. Am I right?" he asks, looking hopeful.

What's he talking about? I nod my head, yes. Better to agree than not—whatever he said. I mean, it all sucks anyway.

His smile says he's relieved as he lets go of my hands. I feel my heart breaking a second before he takes me in his arms, his lips suddenly on mine.

Wait, what? Is this the goodbye kiss?

Who cares! I drape my arms around his neck, kissing him back with everything I've got. All the pent-up tension and need comes pouring out. He pulls our bodies closer together—not even air can flow between us.

Hold on. This doesn't feel like a break-up kiss. I pull away from him, confused.

He looks concerned. "What's wrong?"

"Can you explain to me what just happened?"

"Cassie." He shakes his head slightly side to side. "What do you mean? Are you having second thoughts about us being together?"

I feel lightheaded and take a step back to steady myself. "You want us to be together?"

"Well, yeah."

"I have to sit down."

"Don't worry, we'll figure it out," he says sitting beside me, sounding concerned. "I know it's going to be difficult—us living together and my parents."

"I just . . ." Could this really be happening? "Wait. I am so confused. You want us to be"—I motion between the two of us —"together, as in a couple?"

"Well, yeah. That's what we were just talking about."

Is that hurt in his eyes? "Why?"

"What do you mean, *why*?"

"I don't know. Where did this all come from? You never . . . I mean, you've *never* acted like you were into me."

"No? You think I would caress and hold just any crying female?"

"Well . . .yes, and I just figured you felt sorry for me."

"*Pfff*. Hardly." He grins, then turns serious. "You know that first morning you were here—when you crashed into me? You placed your hand on my chest to steady yourself?"

"Yeah?"

"It was the weirdest feeling. It was like I suddenly found a part of me that was missing—one that I didn't know was gone, and life somehow seemed right again. It's hard to explain. I didn't quite get it at first. It took some time, but little by little, I realized that the part of me that was missing . . . was you. I was only four when you left, but I can still remember being devastated.

"Then there were the logistics—we live together, you thought I was a spoiled, self-centered, womanizing brat. But we became friends anyway. Oh my god . . . and I wanted to be around you all the time, but like I said, we live together, and my parents—just so many things to think about. Like what if I made a move and you were totally against it? Or we started and things went bad? Then when I kissed you . . . I just didn't care anymore. So, here we are."

I punch him as hard as I can in the shoulder.

"Ow! What the hell was that for?" He rubs his arm, looking dumbfounded.

"I've been miserable all this time, having to contain my feelings, when you were feeling the same damn thing?"

"I guess so."

My mind starts whirling. I stand up suddenly and start to pace. "This is crazy. I can't do this."

"Do what?"

"This whole relationship thing—especially with you."

"What's wrong with me?" He sounds offended.

"There's nothing *wrong* with you—it's just, you're *the* Cody Stanton."

"Cassie, seriously? That is *so* stupid." He stands up and grips my arm holding me still. He glares down, looking angry. "You should know by now that that's not me—that's everyone else's perception of me. It doesn't mean anything."

I look into his eyes, trying to find a hint of untruth, but all I see is sincerity. Feeling like my heart is going to burst, I throw my arms around his neck. "So . . . you really like me?"

"*Yes,* you moron." With the tips of his fingers, he caresses a feathery trail down my cheek, then touches his lips to mine.

I close my eyes and thank the powers that be for this moment.

I pull back suddenly. "This could get really complicated."

He kisses my nose. "Shut up."

"I'm just saying."

We spend the day talking and fooling around. This was the *last* thing I expected when he asked me to go to the beach. I'm *still* in shock.

We agreed to keep our relationship a secret—for sure at home, because of his parents, but also at school. Kids talk, parents talk, and news of our relationship could get back to Roxanne or Jeff and that would complicate things. I'm not news, but our relationship would be.

I notice the sun going down and remind him that Roxanne wants us home by six. We walk back to the jeep holding hands. The feel of him physically connected to me . . . it's soft, yet electric. He makes my legs weak, but I feel powerful enough to lift a car—so many contradictions. I don't want any of this amazingness to disappear.

"You should text your dad back," Cody says after we get strapped in, "maybe set up a meeting. I could come, you know . . . for moral support."

"Where did that come from?"

"A quick combination of thoughts."

"Well, un-combine them. Let's stick to the happy moment of you and me."

He pulls out of the parking lot and toward home. "Look,

you've got to deal with him sometime. You can't hide from him forever. Let me be there for you."

I groan. "I love that you want to be there and all, but I totally *don't* need to deal with him."

"Okay, but he's your dad."

I don't respond.

"Wimp!" he teases.

"Oh, whatever!" I pause, trying to gather my words. "Look, if I contact him, it will give him false hope, and he'll think it's going to lead to more."

"Okay, okay. But let's just say . . ." I glare at him, but he continues anyway. "Let's just say that no one's perfect, and sometimes people have a hard time, or totally screw up—like I'm sure most people do at least once in their life. Don't they deserve a second chance?"

"Maybe in someone else's world, but not mine. And this isn't just a little screw up . . . what *he did* was life altering."

"I know. I get that. But still. No one's perfect and people can change a lot over time. I'm sure he has a story. Don't you want to at least hear him out?"

"Not really." I stare out the window. "Can we just drop this please? Let me enjoy the inner glow I'm feeling from having you declare yourself to me."

He laughs. "Sure."

I can't seem to keep my hands off him on the way home.

"That feels so good," he says as I caress the back of his neck, just below the hairline.

"Yeah?" I lean over, kissing the smooth, silky area I just touched.

"Cassie, you better stop that. I need to focus on the road."

I sit back. "You're right."

I put my hand on his leg, then start drawing imaginary swirls with my finger.

"Cassie."

I giggle. I can't help myself. Who is this person? I've never met her before. My swirls travel toward his lap.

"Cassie! Oh my god! Stop! Are you trying to get us killed?"

"Sorry," I say with mock innocence.

"You are *so* going to get it when we get home."

"*Oooo*. I'm scared." Wow, we're *already* home.

"You should be." He pulls into the garage, quickly opens his door and hops out.

Realizing he wasn't kidding, I squeal and jump out, making a bolt for the door. I barely get it open when he catches me and lifts me up, throwing me over his shoulder like a sack of flour. I pound on his back. "Put me down!"

"What's going on here?" Roxanne yells as we pass her in the kitchen.

Cody smacks me hard on the butt.

"Ow! I was only kidding," I holler.

"Cody, put her down, right now!" Roxanne says, sounding shocked and horrified.

"No can do, Mom."

He carries me out the back porch, opens the screen door, and steps toward the pool.

"You wouldn't . . ." And over I go. "*Daaare!*"

I come up sputtering. "It's so cold," I say, teeth chattering.

I wipe the wet hair and water out of my eyes and see Roxanne yelling at Cody. I swim quickly for the edge.

"Have you lost your mind?" she yells at him. "Why would

you do such a thing? Cody Stanton, you are *so* grounded! Help her out of the pool this minute! It's the middle of winter."

Cody doesn't even look at her—just stares at me, grinning proudly.

"It's okay, Roxanne. We were just joking around," I say, shivering uncontrollably as I reach out my hand to Cody. "It just got a bit"—he takes hold and I yank hard. Cody flies over the top of me—"out of hand."

Cody makes a massive splash, soaking Roxanne. She, in turn, throws her hands up and storms into the house muttering to herself.

Cody dunks my head under the water. I come up splashing water in his face, both of us laughing. I'm in heaven. It takes everything I have not to lean in and kiss him senseless, but Roxanne might be watching.

He looks toward the window at the same time I do. "This really sucks," he says. "I want to be with you and not have to hide it. I didn't have to with any of my other girlfriends. The parents didn't care as long as I as I left my bedroom door open."

I splash him in the face. "I can't believe you just said that!"

He splashes me back. "Jealous?"

"*Probably!*"

He pulls me to the side of the pool, both of us gripping the edge. "Nobody has ever made me feel the way you do," he says.

My heart squishes from the honesty. "No one has ever said that to me before."

"I *hope* not!" He looks mortified, but it fades into a slow, easy grin. "How about you? How do you feel?"

"Honestly? Alive, thrilled, wonderfully happy, and dreamy. I feel like I could float to the clouds. All those ridiculous clichés rolled up into one."

"Wow, that's one big, happy bubble."

"Yup! Now let's get out of here, before we catch pneumonia."

"Well, you two . . . that was *some* show," Roxanne scolds, as we walk in with towels wrapped around us.

Jeff comes walking in. "What's that, honey?" He opens the fridge and rummages around for something.

"These two." She points at us.

He shuts the door and looks at us with our towels and wet clothes, taking a bite of a carrot he says, "Looks like *someone's* been having fun." He taps Roxanne on the nose with his carrot and leaves the room.

"He," she says, throwing her hands in the air, "is *so* oblivious."

"*Mom*. Don't get all goofy. There's nothing to get worked up over. We were just being idiots."

"Yeah," I say. "It was an awesome day."

"Oh, *really*?" She crosses her arms over her chest, looking at us speculatively.

"Oh, give it up, Mom. It was a beautiful day. We walked along the beach looking for seashells, we talked, goofed off—she got me riled up on the way home, so I threw her in the pool."

"Hey," I say, looking at Cody. "I'm really tired. I think I'll go dry off, and just lay down for a bit."

"Yeah, sure." He looks concerned. "Are you okay?"

"Absolutely." I smile ear to ear. "Just wiped out."

Warm once again, I snuggle into bed and relive the day in slow motion, enjoying every moment all over again. I am totally and utterly in love—a huge contrast to how I've felt since Mom passed away. I wish she was here so I could share it with her. I miss her so much.

"Cassie?" Cody rubs my back softly.

"*Whaaa?*" My room is dark. "What time is it?" I open and close my eyes a couple of times, trying to get them to work. "I must have fallen asleep." I turn over and sit up.

"It's around six. Mom was wondering if you want to help with the lobsters. It's a New Year's Eve tradition."

"*Uhhh*, yeah, sure. I just need to wake up a bit."

He leans in and places a warm, seductive kiss on my lips.

"Okay. That'll do it," I laugh.

"Come on," he says pulling on my hand, half dragging me out of bed.

"Okay, okay. I'm coming."

"I've got her!" he yells down the hall.

"Oh, good," Jeff says, clapping his hands together as we near the kitchen. "You're in for a treat."

"Cody said something about helping with lobsters?"

Roxanne holds up a live lobster. "That's right!" She wiggles it side to side, making it dance.

I chuckle nervously. "*Okaaay?*"

"Come around here." Jeff motions for us to join him. He hands Cody a lobster, then extends one out to me.

I look at him like, *are you serious?*

"Oh, don't be such a girl," Cody teases.

I take the writhing creature, its leg flexing like a giant spider. "This is so disgusting," I squeal. "Take it, take it." I try to hand it off to Jeff, then Cody. They both extend their lobster toward me, indicating their hands are full.

"It's okay," Jeff says. "You'll get rid of it soon enough. Okay, everybody ready?"

"For what?" I dare to ask.

"For hypnotizing them," Jeff says, like this is the most normal thing ever.

"*Ex-cuuuze* me?"

"You can't just throw them into a boiling pot of boiling water—they'll scream," Roxanne explains.

"Oh my god! Who are you people?"

They all laugh at me.

"Just put the lobster on its head like this." Roxanne flips hers upside down on the newspaper, standing it up on its head, then proceeds to rub its tail from body to tip.

"You have *got* to be kidding me."

"Stop being such a wuss," Cody says. "Just do it!"

I glare at him as I flip my lobster on its head, its rubber band clasped claws lay splayed out on the newspaper, like, *help me*—its little legs flailing in midair. "This is disgusting." My face scrunches up as I shudder, completely repulsed. With one finger, I rub its tail as shown, while keeping my distance. The lobster calms down.

"Time to put them in," Jeff says, walking over to the stove. He lifts the lid off of a large pot of boiling water and gently sets his in.

"What? No! This is horrible! It's totally inhumane! I can't kill the thing after I've bonded with it!"

Cody gives me a sideways glance and smirks as he dumps his in, followed by Roxanne.

"It's going to die anyway," Jeff says sympathetically. "It's been out of water, and it's not like you can go throw it back in the ocean."

"You've eaten lobster before," Cody says. "How do you think it ends up hot on your table?"

"This is rich people food. I've never had it before."

Jeff and Roxanne exchange a look like, *we're a bunch of insensitive shmucks.*

"Sorry," I say. "I didn't mean to be a jerk. I'm sure it will be good."

"Do you want me to put it in the pot for you?" Jeff asks.

"Yeah, I don't think I can do it."

I hand Ed over to him. Yes . . . I've already named him.

He places him in, putting the lid on the big pot, sealing Ed's fate.

I look at the pot sadly. Cody puts an arm around my shoulder, squeezing me to him. "Come on, killer. Let's go set the table."

I look at him, horrified. He laughs his head off, then dodges the punch I throw before running out of the kitchen.

"Not funny," I yell.

Dinner was amazing, although I didn't eat much lobster. I couldn't help thinking I might be eating Ed. After everything was cleaned up, we played Monopoly. Man, I never figured Jeff for the competitive type—*total* personality change. After that, we turned on the TV to watch the big crystal ball drop in Times Square with Ryan Seacrest.

It made me homesick. Every year, when I was old enough to stay awake, Mom and I went over to Luigi's and Maria's apartment and watched it on their television. It was so much fun.

"Oh my god! It's almost midnight," Roxanne announces.

"Really? Already?" I say. The night went so fast.

Seacrest starts the countdown: Ten, nine—Roxanne hands out New Year's Eve hats and noise-makers—five, four, three, two, one.

"Happy New Year!" we all cheer together and start blowing our horns. Cody hugs me and whispers in my ear. "Happy New Year, Cassie." Then kisses my cheek. We separate with me beaming up at him. I look over at Jeff and Roxanne to see if they noticed the exchange, but they're lip-locked in a steamy kiss.

"Gross, you guys!" Cody teases.

They separate, looking at me, embarrassed, then hug Cody and me.

"Well, Kids." Jeff says. "We're off to bed. Don't stay up too late, okay?"

"Dad, that's what kids our age are supposed to do on New Year's Eve."

"I suppose you're right," Jeff says.

Roxanne sends Cody a warning look, before they head off to bed.

"So? What do you want to do now?" Cody asks.

"Dunno. Any ideas?"

"We could go swimming?"

I laugh. "Uh, been there, done that. No thanks."

"Figured."

Cody takes my hand. "Come on." I let him lead me down the hall to the entrance of his room.

I stop in the doorway. "I should get to bed," I say, feeling nervous at what he might be expecting.

"I'm not going to bite." I look at him warily. "Seriously, it's not like that."

"Good, because I'm not ready for *that*." He raises an inquisitive brow. "Yep, seventeen and still a virgin."

"Get your mind out of the gutter." He feigns insult. "I don't *do* that on the first date anyway. What do you take me for?"

I laugh. "This is our first date?"

"I'd say so."

"Best date ever." *Only date ever.*

We lay on his bed—him leaning against the headboard, me on my stomach next to him, keeping our distance in case his parents come and check on us. Roxanne has been watching us like a hawk.

"How come you're not at a party?" I ask.

"I wanted to be with you."

"I'm glad, but won't your friends miss you?"

"I see them every day at school and at practice."

"Yeah, but it's a special occasion. Don't you have a wingman that's going to be lost without you?"

He laughs. "No. I don't really have a 'best friend', just lots of people I hang out with."

"So, even though you have all these people around you, you don't have a close connection with any of them?"

"What? Are you my therapist?"

"No. I just find it interesting."

"Why? What's wrong with me liking my downtime?"

"Nothing. It just surprises me is all."

"You like having *your* space."

"Yeah, but I'm a self-professed loner, you're . . . What did your mom call you?" I pause for effect. "Mr. Social?"

"You think you have me pegged, don't you?"

"Actually, no." I sigh. "You continually surprise me."

"It's not all black and white, Cassie. A person isn't one way or the other, there can be several shades of gray in-between."

"Well, at least you're not the fifty shades fucked up kind."

He laughs. "Nope, I've only got the good hues."

I climb up on my hands and knees and kiss him on the cheek before plopping back on my stomach. "You know what? I believe you."

"Finally! And I'm just going to throw this out there, but your father might have some decent shades as well."

"Don't go there." I growl.

"Okay, fine. Another time maybe." I give him a dirty look. "Or not."

This day has been amazing and I'm not going to let the anger toward my father wreck it. I change positions, snuggling into his side and putting my head on his chest. I've decided I'm all for risking it. His parents *must* be asleep by now, right?

I still can't believe how the day played out. Never in my wildest dreams would I have thought we would be a thing. It still doesn't make sense, but . . . "You know . . . there is no reason you should like me," I say, thinking out loud.

"Cassie, don't start."

"No, I was just going to say . . . but I'm glad you do. And I like that you continually surprise me—you're not the person I pegged you for. I'm not sure why I always think the worst."

"Probably easier. You'll never be disappointed if your expectations are low."

"I guess. Maybe a bit of insecurity too—the feeling that

shiny things are out of my reach—that I don't deserve them—or I'm not good enough for them."

"I'm shiny?" He grins down at me, looking amused.

"Very." I stretch up and kiss his on the neck. He is irresistibly kissable—it's going to be hard to get enough.

"Well, you deserve more than shiny, you deserve sparkling brilliance. You're a good person, Cassie. Anyone with half a brain can see that. Good, exceptional people outweigh shiny any day."

We stay up till almost sunrise—talking, kissing, snuggling. I couldn't ask for a better way to bring in the New Year.

24

Yep, Christmas vacation is definitely over. Back to the grind, torture, and overall boredom of school. And Cody is totally pissing me off!

He's basically been ignoring me the whole day. Then I see him leaning against a locker next to some girl, whose face is way too close to be anything but intimate. *Like, what the hell?*

"So how was Christmas?" I ask Mila on our way to English.

"Shitty. I'm sick of all my mom's fake friends, with their fake smiles, fake body parts, telling their same old fake stories, in our fake house."

"That good, huh?"

"I swear she had a party every night. It was a real *effing* Merry Christmas."

I place my hand on her shoulder. "Sorry." Then I see Cody and stop suddenly.

"Yeah. Well. It's par for the course. What are you staring at?"

"Are you freaking kidding me!" I almost shout. Cody is

standing talking to Shandler, and there's not much space between them.

"What's wrong with *you*?" Mila follows my line of my sight. "*Ahh*," she says spotting them. "That sucks."

"I can't believe he would do that after—" I stop myself.

"After what?" She steps in front of me, eyeing me curiously.

"Nothing," I grumble. "Let's go."

"I don't know. I'm pretty sure I saw you shooting daggers at the back of his head."

"I don't want to talk about it."

"Usually when someone says that, it's because there's something really juicy to talk about. *Sooo?*"

I huff out a loud, frustrated breath. "Now's not the time. I'll give you my cell number and you can call me tonight."

"Wait! You got a cell? Did the skies open up and rain frogs?"

"Ha, ha . . . *funneee*. My father gave it to me for Christmas."

"You talked to your dad? Holy shit! Your holiday had more drama than mine."

"Yeah, a lot has happened."

"Why don't I pick you up after work, and you can fill me in? Here, let me have your phone." I pull it out of my bag and hand it to her. With lightning speed, she puts her number in my contacts. "Just text me when you're ready."

"Okay, sounds good."

"Cute picture."

"What?"

She hands me back the phone. "Your screen saver."

"Don't go there," I growl.

She puts her hand up in defense. "Hold on there, sister. I'm on your side, remember?"

"Sorry. I'll explain later."

"I can't wait," she grins. "This should be *very* interesting."

"Yeah, a whole bowl full of dysfunctional."

Eff this hurts. I'm glad I only have one class left. I want out of here.

"Cassie. Hey."

Josh joins me as I walk to my next class. *Great!* "What do you want?" I snap, trying not to lose my shit.

"I just want to see if we're good. I'd feel better knowing that you've forgiven me. I should never have listened to Shandler. Man, she really has it in for you. What did you do to her?"

"Breathe."

"Yeah. It doesn't take much to piss her off."

"I have to go." I walk quickly away.

"So, we're good?"

I don't answer. I just need to get this day done.

"Okay," he says, yelling. "I'll see you later."

"There's my girl," Tony says as I walk in. "Anna! Cassie's here," he yells.

Anna comes out of the back and hurries toward me. "Ah, my Bella." She cups my face in her hands and pulls me down, kissing both cheeks. Her hands move to mine, grasping them as she holds my arms out. "Tony! She's too skinny!"

"Anna! Leave the poor girl alone! She just got back. You wanna make her run back out the door?"

"*Bah!* You didn't eat over vacation. I let you off for a week and you don't eat! *Santo Cello!* Sit down while Tony brings you a nice big piece of lasagna."

"But, Anna, I'm not hungry."

"You will sit and eat! And I will hear no more!" She declares before turning on her heel and returning to the back ktichen. I smile after her.

"I guess there's no point arguing, is there?" I say.

"None," Tony says, sitting across from me. "Did you have a nice holiday?"

"Yes. Thank you for giving me the time off."

He brushes the compliment away with a wave of his hand. "With school out, it's slow. Marco, with me and Anna, can do just fine."

"Marco didn't take any time off?"

"He didn't want it. He wants to make his money so he can go to that fancy cooking school of his!" He sounds bitter. I make a face like, *what's your deal?* Tony smiles back at me. "I know. We've got our old way, but that's what we know."

I place my hand over his. "I like the way you are."

He blushes.

Marco comes out and sits down with us.

"Did Anna tell you to come out and make sure I'm eating?"

He looks sheepish. "Maybe. You know how she is. She means well."

"Hey, girl." Mila voice booms as she walks through the door.

Perfect timing. "Want some lasagna?"

Tony eyeballs me.

"What? I'm not hungry."

"No, thanks." She sits at our table.

"Too bad," I sigh.

Tony gets up. "I'll go put your food in the oven."

"Thanks, Tony, but you really don't have to."

"Yes, I do. I don't want Anna yelling at me."

"She's *always* yelling at you."

"No. That is just talking loud. You don't want to see her mad."

"Fine," I say.

"You two want drinks?"

"Sure," we both say.

"I've got to get back to work," Marco says, getting up.

Mila leans to the side so she can see around me. "What are you looking at?" I ask.

"Marco."

"Say what?"

"He is so hot!"

"Marco?" I follow her gaze. "Yeah, I guess he could be considered good looking."

She eyes me like, *I must be blind or something.*

"So, come on. The suspense is killing me."

"I'm not done working. I just got here."

"You're not busy. Spill."

"I don't want anyone to overhear. Pick me up at seven."

"*Fine*," she says as a boatload of kids come in. She gets up. "See you soon. Tony, thanks, but I don't need that drink. I'm not staying."

He looks at her and waves.

I make my rounds and hand the written orders on the counter in front of Tony, then tell him not to worry about my food, since I was busy now. He gives me a hairy eyeball and tells me it's my funeral if she finds out.

"Spill," Mila says as soon as we get in her car.

I explain the whole father drama on the way to my house.

"Coming in?" I ask when we pull up outside.

"Oh, *hell* yeah! You still have to give me the Cody update."

I groan.

Jeff is just finishing the dishes as we enter. "Did you have a nice holiday?" he asks Mila.

"It was okay. You?"

"Fantastic."

"We're just going to my room to hang out," I tell him.

"Okay. Sounds good."

We pass Cody's room—it's dark. He must have a late practice—basketball's started.

We make ourselves comfortable on my bed.

"That's pretty cool that your dad gave you a cell phone."

"I guess."

"Have you texted him back?"

"No."

"*Why not?*"

"I don't know. I'm not ready, I guess."

"Well, get ready. It's time for you two to meet up. Why don't you text him now?"

"No way. I wouldn't know what to say."

"Just tell him thanks for the phone. That's probably a good start. Here, give it to me." Quick as lightning, she jumps off the bed and grabs the phone from my bag.

"Hey," I protest.

"There. Done."

"Done? *Done what?*" I sputter, panicking. She hands me the phone.

"I told him you want to meet up?"

"*I what*?" I shriek.

"You would have taken forever to get to the point, so I saved you a lot of time and stress. It's best to just get to it."

Ping!

I look at my phone. "Oh my god! He texted me back. *Shit*, Mila!"

"What does it say?"

I open up the message.

Brent: Thank you so much for texting back. I would love to meet up with you. I could take you for lunch or dinner. Whatever you want, just name the time and place.

I show her.

"This is good," she says. "Right?"

I stand up and start pacing. "This was *your* doing, not mine. *You* go meet him!"

"Oh, sit back down. *Jeez*. Grow some cojones!"

I look at her, annoyed. "*Excuse* me?"

"Yeah, grow a pair! Come on . . . don't be such a chickenshit."

I glare at her silently. Mila mimics my expression. "Fine!" I say finally. "What should I say back?"

"Give it here." She motions for me to hand her the phone.

"Oh, no!"

She laughs. "Fine. Do you want to do dinner or lunch?"

"I don't know . . . someplace I can take off and not make a scene if I have to. Maybe a park or something?"

"Zoro's. It's an awesome restaurant on the beach—it's outside and totally chill. You could meet him around two. There shouldn't be many people there that time of day."

"Fine, but it will have to be a Saturday, because I don't think Cody has practice that day." Mila gives me a big toothy grin. "What? He said he'd go with me if I decided to meet with him.

Brent probably won't be able to make it on such short notice—being that he's a big-shot director."

"Just text it."

"*Fine.*"

"Oh my god! You take *forever*."

"Hey, I don't ever text."

He replies instantly that he will be there.

My stomach does a flip-flop. I hold on to it. "I think I'm going to be sick."

"Oh, come on. You can totally do this."

"Frick!"

"Now. Enough stalling." She stares at me expectantly.

"What now?" I sound annoyed.

"Cody?"

"*Ugh.*" I pull my knees up and drop my face into my hands. "It's nothing. He just irritates me sometimes." I lift my head, looking at her, hoping she'll let me leave it at that.

"I call bullshit. What happened?"

"*Nothing*," I say, but wishing I could share.

"Does he feel the same way?"

"He says he does." I slap my hand over my mouth. "Crap! How do you *do* that?"

Her eyes get huge. "No way!"

"Don't make a big deal out of it—*please*."

"It's Cody Stanton. It's a big deal."

"You can't tell anyone. That's why I wasn't going to say anything."

"Why not?"

"Because if it gets back to his parents, it could be bad."

"It's okay," she says reassuringly. "I won't tell anyone. I promise. So? What's the deal?"

"You're not going to let this go, are you?"

"Definitely not," she bubbles.

"Things got . . . affectionate between us over the holidays."

"You guys hooked up!"

"*No!* We kissed." Her expression says she wants more. "And hung out and stuff."

She punches me in the arm. "Good for you. And?"

"And?" I pause for effect. "He may have said he wants us to be a thing."

Mila squeals.

"*Shhh!*"

There's a knock at the door. Cody walks in before I can reply. "Hey, beautiful, why are you squeal—" He stops short when he sees Mila.

"Hey, yourself, handsome."

Cody looks uncomfortable.

"Cody, you remember Mila, right?" I ask nervously.

"Since kindergarten," he says it cautiously, like he's trying to assess the damage his words might have caused.

"Oh, sorry. Right." I stammer. "And she was just here for Thanksgiving."

"Didn't you used to pull my braids?" she asks, teasing him.

He looks at me suspiciously before he answers. "Only because you wouldn't stop chasing me around the playground. How else was I supposed to defend myself? I wasn't allowed to hit a girl."

Mila snorts. "So you and Cassie, huh?"

"Mila!" I shout.

"You *told* her?" He looks furious.

"Oh, don't get your skivvies in a bunch," Mila says. "I won't say anything."

Cody looks at me like he wants to get his hands around my neck.

"Cody, chill," she says. "I think it's great, and I wouldn't want to do anything to wreck it. But keep in mind . . . if you do anything to hurt her, I'll make you regret it."

"*Pfff*," he responds.

"Look," Mila says, looking back and forth between us. "I've got homework to do. I need to get home."

"I'll walk you out," I say, wanting to give Cody a minute to cool down.

"Hey, don't worry about me. You two stay and have it out. I can find my *own* way."

Great.

"Why don't you shoot those daggers in another direction," I say to Cody after she's gone.

"How could you tell her?" he says through clenched teeth. "I'm trying to protect you . . . us."

"You mean protect your sweet reputation."

"Why would you say that?" he says, looking astonished.

I look at the floor. "Nothing."

"Seriously . . . why would you say something like that?"

"You totally ignored me at school today."

"I did not."

"Yes . . . you did! Not only that, but you were totally flirting with some girl, then the ultimate slap in the face—I saw you talking to Shandler. Like, what the hell! After what she did to me?"

"What are you talking about?"

"I saw you!" I poke an accusing finger in his chest. "Don't even try to deny it. Cody, I don't need this hurt. I've had more than I can handle."

"You're overreacting. I have lots of friends." I roll my eyes at that. "As for Shandler . . . she came up and started talking to *me*. And I didn't see you."

"Whatever. Fine. I get it. This whole secrecy thing—it works for you. You still get to be Cody Stanton, the school stud, and your friends won't make fun of you for hanging with me."

"Are you serious right now!" he yells.

"*Shhh!* Your parents."

"They went to the grocery store," he says, glaring at me.

I stare back, holding my ground.

"I don't need this shit," Cody bites back suddenly. "Maybe this *was* a mistake."

I feel like the air was just knocked out of me. "Maybe it was!" I try to save face.

He whips open the door. "Fine!" he bites back.

"Fine!" I yell as he throws my door closed and then slams his.

I flop backward on the bed, arms crossed over my chest, wanting to scream. I slam my fists down repeatedly at my sides, then stare up at the ceiling.

Slowly, the anger gives way to confusion, then to gut-wrenching fear. What just happened? Everything was amazing and then, *poof*. . . it's all gone. I don't want to feel like this—I don't—I can't.

My door opens and Cody peeks his head in. "Cassie?"

I sit up. The look of remorse on his face washes away the pain instantly. I catapult off the bed and into his arms, wrapping myself around him, squeezing hard.

"I'm so sorry," he says. "I just don't want anything to mess this up."

"I'm sorry too," I say against his neck. "I'm scared shitless."

"About what?" He carries me over to the bed and climbs on with me still attached. When he lays out, I release him and snuggle into his side.

"Pretty much everything, but right now . . . losing you. Waking up one day and finding out that this thing between us was a dream—reality's biggest joke."

"Hey, I'm scared too. I've never felt like this before. And I can't say I won't screw up. We both will. But if we keep talking —not just jumping to conclusions—I think we'll do pretty good."

"You're right. And for the record . . . Mila tricked me into telling her."

"How?"

"Trust me . . . she has her ways. You don't have to worry, though. She's one of the few people I trust, and it felt good to have someone to confide in."

He kisses the top of my head. "I understand, and if it was any other situation, I'd be good with you standing in the middle of the basketball court, announcing it to the whole school. Hell, I'd be by your side. But—"

"It's okay. I know. We don't know how your parents will react. Speaking of which . . . you better get out of my bed. We're in a pretty compromising position. Your parents could come home any minute."

"This is hardly compromising." He rolls on top of me, pressing me into the mattress. "Now *this* might be considered compromising."

"Yeah." I cough. "And I can't breathe."

He rolls off and stands up. I take in an exaggerated breath.

"Ha, ha. I've got to study for a test tomorrow. Do you want

to study with me? We could go out to the kitchen table and make Mom happy."

I climb out of the bed. "Sure."

It's pretty scary trusting your heart to someone. Knowing that at any minute they could wound you deeply with a careless word or rip your heart to shreds with a thoughtless action. Trust isn't an easy thing for me, and opening myself up the way I am takes a lot of it.

I roll on my side and pull the covers up to my chin. It's a risk worth taking.

25

OH, crap, crap, crap! I can't believe I'm doing this. I blame Mila.

This drive is hell. Why did I ever agree to this? *Seriously*. I'm in total panic mode—my stomach's all twisted up, my mouth's dry, and my hands are sweaty.

"Cassie, calm down." Cody reaches over and places a hand on my leg. "It's going to be okay."

I'm going to text him and tell him I can't do it.

"We're here."

"Shit! Cody—"

"Don't you *dare* chicken out! Come on. You can *do* this."

I glare at him. "I hate Mila!"

"No, you don't."

"Right now, I do."

He shakes his head and with a resigned sigh, gets out of the vehicle. "Come on." He shuts his door, then walks around the front of the jeep, finally opening my door.

I grip my seat. "I can't get myself to move," I tell him.

"Yes, you can." He extends his hand. "Hold on to me. We'll get through this together."

If I just focus on Cody—on his eyes, his lips. Man, he has beautiful lips. As I take his hand, some of the tension leaves me. Gently, he pulls me out.

"You know, if you keep looking at me like that, I'm gonna pin you to the side of the jeep and have my way."

I laugh nervously. "You would not."

He presses his body to mine, pushing us backward. "Try me."

I put my hand on his chest, stopping the advance. "Okay, okay. You made your point. Now my heart is *really* racing. Do you want me to start hyperventilating?"

His smile would melt an Ice Queen's heart.

I stretch up on my toes and kiss him. "Thanks."

"For what? Befuddling your brain further?" He gives me a sly grin.

"You wish." No way am I adding to his already inflated ego. "No. For helping me get this far."

"Come on, we still have several steps to go." He pulls me toward the restaurant, which looks like a dilapidated shack with a deck overlooking the ocean.

I falter the moment I see my father. He is sitting at a table along a railing overlooking the ocean. Cody grabs my arms, steadying me. "it's going to be okay," he whispers in my ear.

He hasn't seen me yet. Maybe it's not too late to bail. Just as I think it, he looks over at me and smiles.

Damn!

He gets up and walks toward us.

My legs feel like soggy noodles. Cody wraps his arm around my waist for support. I lean against him.

The distance between us closes in a blink of an eye. My father takes me from Cody and pulls me into a suffocating hug. I stiffen and my arms hang by my side.

"Oh, Cassie," he says, setting me away from him, looking me over. "I'm so glad you came. I know this must be really hard for you."

"Well—"

"Come on," he says, cutting me off. "Let's sit down." He motions us to his table.

The waitress comes over immediately. "What do you want to drink?" she asks me.

"Water's fine." My throat is so dry. I can barely swallow.

"For your friend?" my father asks, eyeing Cody.

"Oh, sorry. This is Cody."

He pauses. "Cody! As in Roxanne's Cody?"

"Yep. That's me."

"I thought you looked familiar. Wow! You've grown." He reaches his hand across. Cody does the same, and they shake.

The waitress starts to look impatient. "I'll just have water too," Cody says. "Thanks."

"Great," she says, irritably. "I'll get *right* on that."

Brent stares at her back, then turns to us and smiles. "I have to say, I'm a bit nervous." He smiles awkwardly.

Cody takes my hand under the table.

There are so many ways I could respond to that statement —none of them nice—so I stay silent.

"So . . . how are you liking California?"

"Fine."

"And school?"

"It's okay."

The waitress comes and sets our waters down. "Do you

know what you want, or do you need a couple of minutes?" she says, sounding snarky.

"I'll let you know when we're ready to order." Brent says with cold authority.

It doesn't sound like he's too impressed with her people skills either.

"Fine," she says in a huff, and walks away.

What a bitch. Tony and Anna would rip my head off if I ever treated a customer like that. I didn't tell them I was having this meeting. They'd have freaked out and gotten all worried. I figured it best to keep it quiet until I see what's what.

"So, school is good?" he repeats the question.

I look at him like, *are you senile or what?*

Cody kicks the side of my foot.

"You're in your senior year, right? Both of you?" he asks, looking anxious.

"Yes," we say in unison.

"Wow. I can't believe how grown up you both are. You two used to be inseparable."

"How would you know?" I snap. "From what I hear, you were never around."

Cody kicks my foot again. I turn and glare at him through narrowed eyes. *Kick me again, I dare you.*

He gives me a slow, easy smile, making my insides mush. *Jerk.*

I thought I could do this—keep it light—but the longer I sit here, the angrier I get.

"Are you okay living with Roxanne and Jeff? They're really—"

"Brent." I say in a flat tone meant to deflate whatever momentum he's been trying to build. He looks at me, surprised. I can tell he thought things were going smoothly. "I know you want to do this whole happy reunion thing, but that's not why I'm here. I came for answers, nothing more."

His eyes turn sad. He looks out at the ocean a moment, then turns back, looking resigned. "All right, Cassie. You're right. I guess I was just hoping." He pauses. "Go ahead. Ask whatever you want."

"Why?" Direct, as hell, but it encompasses everything. Can't skirt around *that* question.

"Right. Let me start by saying I'm sorry." When he pauses, I stare at him like, *yeah, so*? "I let the industry get the best of me. I drank, did drugs, and was half out of my mind most of the time. That part you probably already know, but after your mom left, it got worse. It took another year before I completely hit the bottom. Shortly after, I checked myself into rehab. It was the hardest thing I've ever done, not only dealing with quitting, but the reality of what I did—what I'd lost.

"As soon as I was healthy enough to leave, I hired a private investigator." He looks at Cody. "I hounded your parents relentlessly." Then back to me. "I think the full force of my actions came when I realized that Roxanne genuinely didn't know where your mom was, that I was that much of a monster, she couldn't even tell her best friend where she was—that she had to completely disappear in order to feel safe. Dealing with those emotions on my own without chemical help was an extreme struggle."

Struggle . . . screw you. You don't know the meaning of the word.

Cody squeezes my hand. I'm not sure if it was for support, or to tell me not to respond.

"My AA mentor suggested I start to focus on things I *could* control, so I put everything I had into my career." He laughs to himself. "I even thought if Allora saw I had became successful —saw through the media I was sober . . . maybe she would contact me, even come back. But it never happened. I never stopped looking for you, though. I didn't." He looks earnest. "I made my investigator a very rich man." He jokes. His smile fades when he realizes that no one else is laughing.

"Allora must have missed something in her attempt to hide from me, because I was listed as next of kin on one of her legal documents. I never would have known anything had happened to her otherwise. What you must have gone through."

"You have *no* idea."

He looks pained. "Look, I wish I could say more than sorry, but that's all I can give at this point. I screwed up and hurt an amazing woman. I missed out on my daughter's life. Believe me, I've suffered."

I stand up ubruptly. "Suffered? You have no idea what suffering is. We barely had enough to pay rent, let alone enough food to eat. I started working at fourteen to help us get by. Then, when Mom got sick, seeing her in so much pain . . . We had no insurance!"

"She could have called me, that was her choice to cut me out of your lives," his façade breaks and bitterness seeps through. "I could have been there, taking care of both of you, or brought you here. She never gave me the chance!" He stops himself, finds calm, and continues. "Cassie, I'm sorry. I never—"

All my restraint snaps. "Are you kidding me!" I glare down at him. "Never gave you a chance? I'm pretty sure she gave you more than you deserved."

Cody stands up next to me. "Cassie."

"You know . . . I could never figure out why we had to live in New York. There were plenty of states . . . cities that would have been cheaper to live in. But she was so terrified of you, a total monster, that she buried us in the farthest, most densely populated area in the US. Where you're a face among millions and nobody gives a shit.

"But the worst part of all this . . . you know the worst part? After seventeen years, I find out the woman who I trusted and loved above all others, was a complete stranger—she never told me about her past—she lied to me about who I was, where we came from, and that you were alive. I was angry, *so* angry at her—angry at the person I was closest to. She was my best friend, my only constant. And she had to keep everything hidden from me because of *you*!

I look at Cody. "I need to go."

He puts his hand on the small of my back to lead me away.

Brent stands up. "Please. Don't leave it like this." He looks beaten. "Maybe we could try again another time?"

"I seriously doubt it." I turn to Cody with an expression of, *get me out of here*. "I got my answers. There is nothing more I need from you."

We head toward the exit. I feel my hand being taken and held firm, stopping my escape. I turn, looking up into my father's pained eyes. "Cassie, please don't shut me out. I will do whatever you want, but please, let's keep talking. We can go to family counselling. I'll do anything."

I bark out a contemptuous laugh as I shake my hand loose of his grip. "Family? That's a laugh." For some stupid reason, guilt hits me, needling me. I've never unleashed like this on anyone. And as much as I hate him—hate everything he's done—I know that treating him like this is wounding him deeply.

I'm just not that vicious . . . not really. "I don't know. Maybe. Maybe we can talk again sometime. I don't know."

"Okay. Fair enough."

His hopeful expression starts me seething again. I want to exhale loudly and roll my eyes like a bitter child, but I stop myself. Instead, I turn and focus on the door—my escape route.

As soon as I'm in the jeep, I bury my face in my hands. I try to catch my breath. I'm shaking and I feel sick.

Cody gently rubs my back. "Come on. You don't want him to see you like this."

I take a deep breath and sit up as he starts the engine.

"Well, that went well," I say as he pulls out of the parking lot.

Why did I do this? What was the point?

I guess I thought, *maybe* I would have a better perspective after meeting with him—be okay with some things, move forward—have a little peace, instead of resentment. I don't know. It was stupid. I shouldn't have come. All I did was make a scene. The answers I got did nothing.

"Cassie, hey . . ." Cody takes a hold of my hand. "Don't be so hard on yourself. You did great."

"Then why do I feel like such a bitch?"

"Because you were." I gape at him. "But you had every right to be," he clarifies quickly. "Look, you knew this would be hard. Just give it time. Let it all settle in."

I stare out the window for a while, then rest my head against the seat and close my eyes against the sun.

. . .

"We're here," Cody says, shaking me gently.

I open my eyes and straighten up. "Sorry, I guess I fell asleep."

"Yeah. You were sawing logs."

"I was snoring?" I look at him, mortified. I don't snore.

"Just a little," he smiles. "It was cute."

"Snoring is *never* cute." I sound surly.

He leans over, cupping the side of my face before kissing me. "I am *so* proud of you," he says against my lips.

A sigh of contentment escapes me.

"Come on," he says. "The longer we sit out here, the more suspicious Mom's going to get."

Roxanne rushes toward us as soon as we enter the house. "Are you okay?" She hugs me so hard, I can barely breathe.

"I'm good."

She steps back, appraising me. "Are you sure?"

"It was hard, but Cody helped me get through it. But, I'm done . . . drained and brain dead, so if it's okay, I'll let Cody fill you in." I point down the hall toward my room. "I need to shut down for a while."

"I completely understand," Roxanne says.

I drop my purse on the floor and plop face first on my bed, grab my pillow, bunch it up and lay my head into the soft folds. How do I process this? I don't even know where to start.

26

"I'M SITTING RIGHT HERE, you know," Mila says.

"Sorry." I put my phone away, then pack up my lunch. "I never thought I'd be one of those people who would text all the time, yet here I am." When Cody and I talk at school, it's platonic. The texts? Not so much.

"No problem. I get it," she says, winking at me. "Have you contacted your dad since you went full-on-psycho-bitch-from-hell on him?"

"Have I told you how much I hate you for setting me up?"

She looks perturbed. "Daily."

"No. But I'm sort of considering it."

I appreciate that he hasn't tried to reconnect. At first, every time I thought about the meeting, I wanted to explode, but now it's down to a low-grade fury. It's better than fantasizing about how I could annihilate the man. I consider that a major improvement. And I get how alcohol can turn people into monsters—you hear about it all the time, but there are so many "buts" every time I have this conversation in my head. I've gone around and around making myself dizzy.

My final consensus is that he figured it out, got his shit together, and has been sober for . . . I guess, twelve years. So, I have to assume the monster's gone and will never be back.

It's just that so much damage was done, two lives were altered—three if you include his. But like Mila said, I wouldn't be who I am if I didn't have the life I've had. I wonder what I would've been like if I'd been raised with all that wealth. It's weird to think about. Lots of "buts."

"Hey, Cassie," Josh says, sitting down next to me.

I briefly look over at Mila, whose expression screams, *are you friggin' kidding me?*

"I just—" he starts, but the bell signals the end of lunch, cutting him off.

"Well, I uh . . . got to go," I say. Getting up quickly, I walk to where Mila is staring at him with murderous intent. I take hold of her arm, pulling her away before that fiery-hot temper of hers decides to unleash.

"Pendejo!" she spits out. "Sitting down with us, acting like nothing happened."

"I know. He won't let it go. He keeps trying to talk to me like everything's normal and we're, like, best buds. I'm not rude, but I'm not nice either. I thought if I stay neutral, he'd lose interest and leave me alone—apparently not."

"He's up to something. This whole trying to get your forgiveness thing doesn't fit. He's only lived here for two years, and from what I've experienced, he couldn't give a shit about anyone but himself."

"He's only been here a couple of years?"

"Uh-huh. Girls were all over him."

"Where did he move from?"

"I'm not sure, but I think it's just him and his dad."

"You'd think that girls would stay away from him, given his reputation."

"You'd think, but no. Who wants to believe rumors when a guy's *that* hot? Besides, he doesn't seem to go for easy targets—sick bastard likes a challenge. And then, of course, new girls. They wouldn't have a clue."

"Aren't *I* lucky. I've got to get to class. Call or text me later, okay?"

"Watch out for him, Cassie."

I nod my head in agreement just as my phone pings. I smile and wave goodbye as I start to read Cody's text.

Before I know what's happening, I'm knocked to the floor. I look up as Shandler walks past me. "Wow, Cassie, you should be more careful. It takes a lot of coordination to walk and text at the same time."

I look around me as I get up. I see lots of sympathetic expressions, but no one dares to get involved. "Bitch!" I bite out.

She cocks her head and flashes a malicious grin, then walks away. I'm tempted to go after her . . . *so* tempted, but what am I going to do, jump her in the hallway? As much as the image tempts me, fighting's never been my style.

Now I'm wishing we didn't bother with the plastic wrap on her car and just used the spray paint.

On my way to Antonio's, I realize I forgot all about Cody's text. I pull out my phone and see I also have a message from my father. Shit! So much for him leaving me alone.

I respond to Cody's text, then debate whether to read my father's.

Curiosity wins out.

Brent: I'm not trying to pressure you, but do you want to go to a movie or something?

I snort. A famous movie director asking to go to the movies.

Am I ready for this? I could get Cody to go with me again, or not see him at all—that would be easier. I don't know. Mom didn't want me having anything to do with him. She died with this secret, and I feel that if I move forward with this relationship, I'm going against her. But at the same time, she's gone and this is my new reality.

I hear Mila in my head saying, "Grow a pair."

I guess, at this point, it's about having the guts to see this through one way or the other.

Me: Sure, but I don't have a car.

Brent: Really? Okay. I'll send one to pick you up. Does Friday work, around six?

Me: Okay.

What does he mean by, "I'll send one to pick you up?"

He must mean a cab. A movie will be good—can't really talk, so no deep conversations. I can probably handle that.

Ping!

I need to get Cody to show me how to change the sound on this thing—it's annoying.

I walk into work reading Cody's text.

Cody: You're coming to my game tomorrow night, right?

Tomorrow night? What day is it? "Tony, what day is it?" I call out when I enter the restaurant.

He looks at me like I'm nuts. "Thursday!"

"Thanks." Wow, this week went fast. Shit! I don't want to

miss Cody's game. I text my father to see if we can change it to Saturday—he says no problem. I text Cody back and get lost in the conversation.

"I dunno why kids always have to be on those things," Anna gripes. "You gonna work or play with your phone!"

"Work," I laugh. "Let me just say goodbye."

"*Bah!*" she says, and walks over to Tony. "Kids! They waste *too* much time!"

Ping!

"Again with the phone!" Anna throws up her hands in exasperation.

It's Mila wanting to know if I'm going to the game and if I want a ride.

"That man bother you anymore?" Tony asks randomly, as I place an order slip on the counter.

"Who? Josh?"

"No! The older one. The one says he's your father!"

"I actually met with him."

"What you say!" he yells.

"It's okay," I soothe. "Cody went with me."

"Good boy. What he want? He's no right to bother you!"

"I know. Cody and Mila talked me into it." He starts to object. "It's okay. I think it was a good thing—really hard, though."

"I don't like it!" he declares, waving a knife over his head.

I look over my shoulder, concerned about the customers. Luckily, no one seems to be paying attention. I turn back to him. "It's okay. Really. I got to hear his side of it."

"What side he got? He don't have a side!"

"Seriously. *Shhh*. You're going to start freaking people out."

"What's does freaking people out mean?"

"Scaring people."

"Who's scaring people? You don't make any sense. I don't like hearing you with this man. Luigi's not going to like it either. You forgive too easily!" He slams his hand down on the counter.

People's heads snap up. I smile reassuringly at them. "Tony, calm down." I whisper at him. "People are staring."

He looks around me. "*Bah!*"

"And I didn't say I forgave him, but he is my father. I guess I should at least give him a chance. I don't know. He's the only family I've got left."

"You've got lots of family! Me and Anna, Luigi and Maria, and the family you live with. You don't need that man! He's no good for you!"

I laugh. There's no use arguing with him. "Okay, okay, Tony. But you know what I mean."

"*Bah!*" he says again. "What's this Tony business? You call me, Zio!"

I smile at him. "Got it." I think Zio means uncle.

"Here!" He shoves a pizza over the counter at me. "You can't stand here talking to me all day. People are waiting!"

The man is priceless.

27

"HEY," Mila says when we get settled at Cody's game. "You know that guy you work with at the restaurant?"

"Tony?"

She laughs. "No, the other one."

"Marco?"

"Yeah. Is he seeing anybody?"

"I don't know, why?"

"I told you . . . he's hot!"

"I know, but Marco?"

She smacks my arm. "You must be blind."

"Apparently," I say, rubbing the sting away.

"You totally have to set us up?"

"How?"

"*I* don't know. Figure it out."

"Why's it my job to figure it out?"

"Because you know him. And that's what best friends do for each other."

"Oh. Okay. Can't you just bulldog him like you do with everything else?"

"You calling me a bulldog?" She looks insulted.

"No, I mean, how you're bold and loud, and not afraid of anything."

She laughs. "I know what you meant. I don't want to come on too strong, just put a good word in for me . . . maybe introduce us."

"I could do that."

She smiles. "Good, because he's here. Let's find him during intermission. You can introduce me and ask him to come sit with us."

"You already had this planned out."

"Pretty much."

Cody's on fire. He's hit four three pointers, and it's only the first quarter. The gym is packed. The sound is almost overpowering with all the squeaking shoes, whistles from the refs, and cheers from the crowd. I'm actually kind of glad when the buzzer sounds for half-time. My ears need a break.

Mila is yanking on my arm to get up. "Let's go find Marco."

"Hold on." I tap Roxanne on the shoulder. "Would you or Jeff like something from the concession?" Roxanne leans over and asks Jeff, who is talking to a guy next to him. He shakes his head, no. "We're good, Cassie. Thank you for asking."

"No problem."

Jeff looks up as we start to move away. "Thanks, Cassie."

"Yup."

"Chill your dill!" I say as she drags me down the bleachers. "You're gonna make me trip."

She turns to me, rolling her eyes. "It's not my fault if you're a klutz."

We weave through a crowd of people with Mila leading the way—obviously.

Wham! I get shoulder checked. "Sorry," I say, apologizing to the unseen force, then look behind me. Shandler is smirking at me. She flips her hair over her shoulder and struts away.

"*Bitch!*" That's the second time she's done that. At least I didn't land on my ass this time.

Mila turns. "Did you say something?"

"Shandler just shoulder checked me," I say, rubbing at the sore spot.

She storms past me. "Where is the skank? I'll kick her ass. Puta!" she hollers in Shandler's direction.

I chase after her, grabbing her arm. "Hold up, Holly Holms."

She stops and stares at me like, *who the eff is that*?

"One of the top female MMA fighters? Or used to be."

"How would you know something like that?"

"ESPN is on a lot at our house." I shake my head. "Just leave it. We should go find Marco."

She pauses for a minute. I can see her mind working—kick Shandler's ass or go find Marco. "Fine! We'll deal with her later."

We find him waiting in line at the concession.

"Hey," I say.

"Hey."

"Who are you here with?" I ask.

"Just friends."

Mila clears her throat behind me. I step aside, introducing her in a way that, I hope, doesn't sound like a total set up.

"How's it going?" he says.

"Really good," she returns, smiling like she wants to devour him—typical Mila.

Mila pinches my side, making me jump. Taking the hint, I say, "You and your friends should come and sit with us." The words sound mechanical and scripted. *Ugh!*

He gives me a funny expression. "Sure . . . yeah. I'll ask them."

I'm surprised. I expected her directness would have intimidated the crap out of him. Apparently not.

"I think that poor boy is crushing on you," Mila teases as Marco walks away.

"No, he's not. I'm not interested anyway."

"Obviously! You've got Cody." She elbows me in the side. "I'm not worried. Once I set my sights on someone, I don't give up easily."

"Mila, you're scary."

"Yes, I am."

We work our way back to our seats. I passively scan the crowd, and somehow zero in on Shandler. She's sitting next to a really pretty girl with short, pink, spiky hair—she must be new. Poor thing doesn't know what she's in for.

I can't imagine the kind of parents that spawned that piece of horror. Maybe she was just born evil, like the child of Satan or something. Cody did say she's always been mean. She's definitely the scariest person *I've* ever met—next to Mila. I snicker to myself.

I see Marco heading over. The only spot open is next to Mila. I'm sure she planned it that way.

"Where are your friends?" I ask after he sits down.

"They didn't want to move."

The game starts and Roxanne turns to me. "Cody's having a good game."

"Yeah, he is."

I glance over at Mila and Marco, their heads close together, talking. There's a commotion, something must have happened. I turn my attention back to the court just as Josh pushes Cody and Cody shoves him back twice as hard.

What the hell?

Josh points his finger in Cody's face and yells at him viciously. I can't hear what they're saying with everyone freaking out. Cody steps back and drills Josh in the face, sending him stumbling.

"Oh my god!" Roxanne exclaims as Jeff jumps up. Mila grabs a hold of my arm.

Josh recovers and comes at Cody, screaming. He looks insane as he tackles Cody over the player's bench, knocking water bottles everywhere. Coaches rush in and break them apart. Everyone is silent now—watching, waiting.

Cody strains against the person holding him. "You piece of shit!" he yells at Josh. "I told you to stay away from her!"

"Fuck off, Cody!" Josh manages to yank his arms free from his restraints. "What's wrong with me trying to get a nice piece of ass now and then?" he sneers as he's retained again.

I feel an icy chill run up my spine. *No, no, no. This can't be happening.* Cody tries to charge him again, but arms continue to hold him back.

There's shocked silence with a few murmuring whispers as they're both escorted to the dressing room.

I feel sick as the panic wells up inside me. I clench and

unclench my hands as I take deep breaths, trying to hold it together.

"Cassie." Mila's places a hand on my shoulder.

There's a shrill whistle, and the game continues.

Roxanne and Jeff turn, looking at me expectantly. "Judging by the expression on your face, I'd say this has something to do with you," Roxanne says, looking worried. "Cassie, what's going on?"

"Can I explain at home?" I ask cautiously. "This isn't the place to go into it."

"Fine," she concedes. "But we are discussing this tonight, not tomorrow, not next week—tonight."

"No. I know."

I look over at Mila and Marco. Both are wearing sympathetic expressions. Unfortunately, this does nothing for the massive knot that's formed in my stomach.

Jeff turns around and looks up at me. "We are going to leave at the next whistle. Are you coming with us?"

I look over at Mila, pleading. "I can take her home," she says to Jeff.

I need some time to process what and how much I want to say.

"I wonder what Josh said to Cody to set him off," Mila says on the ride home.

"Who knows? Something vile, I'm sure."

"Probably."

I tap my hands on my legs, then push up straight in the seat as I take a deep breath. I'm terrified of what's to come.

"This could be good . . ." She looks at me briefly.

"What could be?"

"Talking about this. Getting it out in the open. Maybe they can talk some sense into you—get you to report what happened."

"*You* didn't."

There's silence. "I didn't have anyone to tell. My mom was in Aruba at the time—not that she would have been supportive. She'd probably have blamed me—said that it was my fault."

"I'm sorry, Mila. I shouldn't have said that."

"It's okay. I know you're freaking out."

What am I going to say? Maybe there's a way to explain without having to get into the horrid details. *I* could do that—leave out what happened at the beach and just say he's been aggressively pursuing me. That *might* work.

We pull up to the house. "Can we just stay in the car a bit longer? I need another minute."

"Sure. So . . . you're seeing your dad tomorrow?"

I breathe deeply. Great. Change one stress for another.

"Sorry," she says, picking up on my apprehension. "Marco and I are going out tomorrow night," she says quickly, changing topics.

"Wow!" I say, trying to sound enthusiastic through the nervousness. "You work fast."

"Life's too short. I just say it like it is, and either they're in or out. And he is definitely in."

"*You* are amazing."

"I don't know about that. I've just seen my mom work, you know? All her bullshit games with men. I figure if you don't like me . . . fine. There's no need to waste anyone's time."

I look toward the house. "Well, I might as well get this over with."

She gives my hand a squeeze. "You'll be okay."

"Thanks. For everything."

"No problem. Good luck with Daddy Big Bucks."

I give her a wry smile. "Not funny."

"Yes it is."

I watch her as she drives away. I look at the house, knowing I have to go in, but can't get my feet to move. Why did this have to happen to me?

They're all at the dining room table when I walk in. I look questioningly at Cody.

"Have a seat, Cassie," Jeff encourages.

I watch Cody's expression as I sit next to him, trying to read his thoughts. His face is already starting to bruise. I hate that I'm the cause. He takes my hand under the table and caresses the top with his thumb. The reassurance helps me relax a little.

"Now, will you two *please* tell me what's going on?" Roxanne demands.

I take a deep breath as the revolting images of my ordeal invade my mind. I decide in that moment that Cody and Mila are right; I need to tell them the truth.

"We need to go to the police," Roxanne says hysterically when I've finished.

"Cody! Why didn't you tell us?" Jeff says. He is livid—a side of him I would have never thought possible.

"It wasn't up to me," Cody says. Jeff starts to lose it, but Cody cuts him off. "I tried to get her to go, but she wouldn't. It was and *is* her choice."

"Well, we have to go right now!" Roxanne says, getting out of her chair.

"No!" I yell, alarmed at the implications.

"They need to know." Roxanne is adamant. "What if this happens to someone else?"

I shake my head no. "What if the police agree to investigate and it gets out? I've already been through enough."

"Look, Cody's right," Jeff says, with a resigned sigh. "We can't make you go."

"*But*," Roxanne sputters, looking at him helplessly. "We can't just let him get away with this! He attacked Cassie, and Cody has been in a fight over it."

"Roxanne," Jeff says, taking her hand and guiding her back into her chair. "It's not up to us to decide. Only Cassie can do that."

"But—"

Jeff's expression stops her from saying more. Roxanne looks at me, then back at Jeff. "Cody," she pleads, "you have to talk some sense into her."

"I've tried."

"Cassie," Roxanne says with tears welling in her eyes. "Baby, we're supposed to protect you." She stifles a sob.

I get up and walk around the table, sitting in the chair next to her. "It's not your fault."

"Oh, honey." She pulls me in and holds tight. "I'm so sorry this happened to you."

"I know." I gently pull from the embrace. "But I just want to let this go, okay? It happened months ago. I'm okay. If I start into this again, I won't be."

She wipes her eyes and nods her head in agreement. "But if you change your mind, we'll be here for you. Whatever it takes," Roxanne declares emphatically. "I need you to know that."

"I do. And thanks for understanding." I look over at Jeff. "Both of you!"

Sometime in the night, I wake up to a warm body spooning me and an arm draped over my waist. "You awake?" Cody asks as he nuzzles the back of my neck.

I smile to myself then slowly turn to face him, wiping the sleep out of my eyes as I do. "I am now. What are you doing here?"

"I couldn't sleep. I was worried about you."

"What time is it?"

"Around two."

I snuggle in closer. "You shouldn't be in here."

"They're long asleep."

"I'm sorry you had to defend me again."

"*I'm* not. He is a scumbag. I'm glad coach kicked him off the team."

I sit up abruptly, alarmed. "Because of me? No! Everything was manageable—now . . ."

"There was nothing I could do to prevent it, even if I wanted to—*which* I didn't. He was a cancer on the team anyway."

"Yeah, but—"

"*Shhh*. Coach pulled me into his office. He threatened to kick *me* off the team if I didn't explain my actions."

"You told him?" I ask incredulously.

"I told him the details, not your name. I said I couldn't. He was very concerned, and just like *everyone else*, advised me to encourage 'The Girl' to report this to the police. I told him I tried."

"Cody, Josh is going to blame me. He's going to make my life a living hell."

"I'm sorry, Cassie. I just snapped. If you heard what he was saying . . . Well, I just couldn't help but knock his teeth up into his demonic brain."

I groan loudly.

"It'll be okay. You'll see."

"Explain how this could ever be okay."

"We'll talk about it in the morning," he says, maneuvering me back into a spooning position. He kisses the back of my head. "Get some sleep."

"I'm sorry about your bruises."

"Don't be. It gave me another excuse to beat the crap out of him for what he did to you."

"Cody?"

"*Hmm?*"

"What am I going do? I'm scared."

"It'll be okay. Between me and Mila, we won't let you be anywhere alone."

"That's impossible."

He doesn't respond. I hear the even tone of his breathing.

Great. Glad *one* of us can sleep. My nerves are on hyper-drive as I envision every horrid scenario I can think of.

Eff!

28

THIS IS such a crappy day to be meeting my father. I barely slept, and I'm on edge about going to school on Monday. I could have cancelled, but I don't know . . . I just didn't.

Cody is hanging out with a friend, so I'm alone waiting by the front door. He offered to come with me, but I should do this alone.

There's a knock at exactly 5:30. "I got it!" I yell before swinging the door open.

A hard looking, giant of a man stands in front of me, hands clasped looking at me expectantly. "Miss Cassie?" Confused, I nod my head, yes. "I'm Harold, your driver."

My driver?

"Mr. Carson sent me to pick you up."

I stare at him a moment. "I thought he was sending a cab?"

"No, Ma'am." He waits patiently as I stand there like a dumb-ass. "Shall we go?" he politely asks.

"Oh. Sorry." I step out and close the door behind me, then follow him to a long black car. It's not a limousine, but close.

Harold gets there first and holds the door open for me. I feel like a long-lost princess or something. This is so weird. "So," I say, climbing awkwardly into the back seat, "it's not just in movies."

The side of his mouth lifts into a grin. "No, Ma'am. I suppose not."

Harold's gentle demeanour and proper etiquette seem at odds with his appearance. He looks more black-ops military than a gentleman chauffeur.

His smile is warm and kind as he climbs into the driver's seat—a gentle giant, I decide.

I wasn't sure what to wear. He said we'd have a quick bite before the movie. I figured quick meant casual, so that's how I dressed. At least I'm comfortable in my clothes—wish I was in my head.

Frick!

I can't stand how awkwardly quiet it is. "So, Harold?"

He looks at me in the rearview mirror. "Yes, Ma'am."

The "Ma'am" thing is so cute coming from him. From anyone else it would probably piss me off. "Are you a full-time limo driver? Do people hire you out?"

"No, Ma'am. I just drive for your father?"

I raise my eyebrows in surprise. "Really?"

"Yes, Ma'am. Going on seven years now."

"I guess that's normal for a big shot like my father, I mean, Brent."

He smiles. I can see the mistake isn't lost on him. "He's a very busy man."

"I guess he would be," I mumble. Staring out the window, my mind races from one issue to another—my father, Mom,

Josh—mostly Josh. I don't want to have to be looking over my shoulder every minute, but what choice do I have?

I don't get it. It seemed like he was fine. He was apologetic after the attack, even tried to be friends with me. I guess it was all an act, but why? For what purpose?

The car pulls up alongside an outdoor café. I reach for the door handle, but Harold is already there, opening the door with his hand out to me. I give him an awkward smile as he helps me out of the car. "Thank you."

"My pleasure," he smiles. "Enjoy your dinner."

I take a deep breath and blow it out loudly when I see my father waving at me from a patio table. Harold gently elbows me, leans over, and says, "You've got this."

"Do I?" I reply nervously. He nods his head and winks at me.

He's right. I can do this. I straighten my shoulders and then force my feet to move toward the café.

I pass the hostess, gesturing that I know where I'm going. My father stands up slightly when I reach the table. "You look very pretty," he says, before sitting back down.

"Thank you."

A waitress comes over. "What can I get for you, Mr. Carson?"

"Cassie? What would you like to drink?"

"A Coke? A Coke is fine."

My father smiles at the server. "Make that two."

She smiles politely. "Very well, Sir."

"How does she know your name?" I ask as she walks away. Maybe he's got a thing for pretty, young waitresses. Or she knows that he's famous and tips well, so she's a suck up. He is still really good-looking for an older man.

And *why* do I care?

Arg! Because I don't want him to be a creep, and I also don't want some gold-digger after him.

I think I'm confused about my role here.

"I come here a lot. They have great food, and it's close to my office. You should come by the set sometime, we're just starting a film with Gerard Butler and Channing Tatum."

"Oh my god! No way." Shit! I sound like a star-crazed fan. "Sorry about that." I smile sheepishly. Mom and I didn't have a TV, but we watched movies at the theatre when we could.

"Don't be," he laughs. "It's a standard reaction."

There's an awkward silence. I wring my hands in my lap. My brain is blank. This was easier when I was raging with anger. I had an agenda. Now I have to figure out what the hell to talk about.

"What do you like to do in your spare time?"

Whew! Okay. Good question. "Not much. Between work and school, I don't have a lot of extra time. I'm trying to save up money for school," I quickly clarify. I don't want to sound like a total bore—not that I care—oh, hell, I think I care.

"Good for you. Where do you want to go?"

The waitress places our drinks down.

"Are you ready to order?" she asks, looking between us.

I haven't even looked at the menu.

"Cassie?"

"Um." I open the menu and order the first thing I see. "I'll have a chicken Caesar salad."

"And for you, Mr. Carson? The usual?"

"Yes, Michelle. That would be fine. Thank you."

They know each other's name. Maybe they have a thing going.

"Coming right up," she says happily.

She's way nicer than that horrible waitress at Zoro's, but still . . . none of my business. Well, it kind of is. I don't know. At this point he's just a sperm donor, but he could be more if he's not a lame-ass skirt chaser.

"So?"

I stare at him. *Sooo?* "Oh, yeah. What school do I want to go too? Um . . . I'm not sure."

"There are a lot of excellent schools in California."

"True, but I think I want to go back East."

He looks disappointed.

"Only because it's my dream to go to Pratt." I say it without thinking. Old habit I guess. "But I don't want to go there anymore."

"So, you're an artist?" he says, looking pleasantly surprised.

Shit. Wasn't ready to share that. "I guess. It was something Mom encouraged me to do. When she died, the enjoyment kinda died too."

Sadness flickers in his eyes, then disappears. "Well, you must be good to even consider going to such a prestigious school."

"Yeah, I'm okay."

He smiles. "Can I see some of your work sometime?"

"I destroyed it all."

"Why would you do that?" He looks stunned.

"It was a bond I had with Mom. She's gone, so . . ."

"That's kind of extreme, isn't it?"

I look at him like, *who are you to judge?* Mixed with, *what the hell do you care?* Then I remind myself that I was going to keep the bitterness out of the evening.

"I'm sorry. I didn't mean to . . . I just mean to say that I'm sure she would be very disappointed that you've stopped."

I take a drink of soda to give myself a moment to calm down before I answer. "Probably. Cody basically said the same thing. He bought me a sketchbook and pencils for my birthday. I've done a bit of drawing, but that's it. No big deal. Next subject. Did you ever get remarried, have any other kids?"

"I would have liked to have been there for your birthday. Maybe the next one." I shrug my shoulders indifferently. He continues anyway. "No, to the wife and kids. I was too busy with my career, and it just didn't seem right. Your mom and I were never officially divorced, and I was always hoping I would find the two of you."

"Fair enough." I give him points for the answer.

He kept the conversation light for the rest of dinner, which I appreciated. We mostly talked about his work—films he's done, neutral stuff like that. He didn't flirt with the waitress—they continued to be professionally polite, so I guess he's okay there.

We decide on the new *Star Wars* movie. I remember watching the old ones with Mom at a vintage theatre that showed classics. It's ironic that I'm watching the new one with my father.

"So, do you get recognized wherever you go?" I ask as we wait for the movie to start. That could be another reason the waitress knew his name.

I *seriously* need to let that go.

"No, I'm behind the cameras, never in front."

"That's probably a good thing. It would suck to have paparazzi following you everywhere."

He leans the bag of popcorn my way. "True. Us behind the scene people have it easy that way."

I take a handful, and pop a few in my mouth.

"Did you leave many friends behind with the move?"

"None. No time. I had to work."

He looks pained. I'm not sure why this bothers me, but it does. Maybe I don't want him to see me as pitiful. "Mom and I had a lot of fun together, though. And whatever time was left after school and work, I spent on my art, so no time for friends."

"It doesn't sound like you had much of a childhood." He sounds sad.

I didn't really want to get into this. "It wasn't easy, but I have a lot of special memories, and we had Luigi and Maria. They were as close to grandparents as I'll ever have. I spent a lot of time with them—they helped raise me." And I really miss them. "Are your parents still alive?"

"Yes, but I haven't spoken to them since your mother left."

"Maybe they might want to meet me?"

"I'm sure they would."

The previews start as the lights dim.

I guess I'm moving forward with this thing after all.

The movie was fun with lots of action.

"*Ah*," my father says, "here's Harold." The car magically pulls up right as we exit.

"Thanks, um . . ." I stumble over what to call him, "for the night."

"You're welcome. Thanks for seeing me again. After the last meeting, I didn't dare keep my hopes up."

"Well . . ."

"No, it's fine. I deserved it. Thanks for at least trusting me this much."

Not knowing how to respond, I give a shoulder shrug and a non-committal smile, then walk to where Harold is waiting with the door open. "Hi, Harold," I say as I climb in. He's the best part of the evening.

"Miss Cassie," he says with a nod before shutting the door. He seats himself behind the wheel. "Did you have a good time?"

"Yes, thank you."

My father waves goodbye as we pull away from the curb. My emotions are really screwed up. I have no idea how to feel about him. Do I let go of the past and try to salvage some sort of relationship with my only remaining blood relative? Or do I say, *screw you*, and get on with my life?

I notice Harold studying me in the rearview mirror. "What's on your mind?" I ask.

"If you don't mind me saying so, Mr. Carson is happier than I've ever seen him. I just thought you should know."

"How did you meet him?"

He briefly makes eye contact in the mirror. "That's a story for Mr. Carson to tell."

"Okay." I wonder what that's all about. "Have you always lived in California?"

"No, Ma'am. I grew up in Texas."

"Why did you leave?"

"I enlisted."

That explains the hard look and massive build. Harold pulls up in front of the house. He's out of the car with lightning speed.

Once again, he takes my hand and helps me out. "Harold,

I'm capable of opening the door and getting out of the car myself."

He grins at me. "It's part of the job, so I guess you'll just have to suffer the hardship."

"Funny guy," I tease.

"Glad you think so." He grins. "I hope to see you again soon?"

"For my fathers sake?" I return.

"Yes, and my own. You grew on me pretty quick." The corners of his eyes crinkle in humor.

"Yeah, I kinda like you too."

"Hey," Cody says, coming out of his room. "I thought I heard you." He slides his hands on either side of my face and tangles his fingers in my hair, then kisses me.

"So? How did it go?" he asks, detaching his lips from mine, leaving me wobbly kneed.

"Give me a minute for the blood to go back to my brain and I'll tell you."

He smiles, looking arrogantly pleased with himself.

I lean up and kiss him on the cheek. "It went good."

"Just good?"

I step into my room with Cody following behind. "I think so. Me not wanting to smash his face in seems like a pretty big improvement to me."

"*Yeesh! I* guess."

I sit on my bed, my back resting against the headboard. Cody takes a diving leap, landing on his stomach next to me. "So, what's the next step?"

"I'm not really sure. I guess spending more time together. He asked if I wanted to come to the set next Sunday."

"That sounds interesting."

"Do you want to come with me?"

"I think you should spend some time alone with him."

"Yeah, maybe."

He reaches for my sketchpad on the nightstand. "Any new sketches of me?" He maneuvers his body so he's sitting next to me and starts thumbing through the pages.

"*Excuse me* . . . none of your business." I make a grab for it, but he holds it up high, out of my reach.

"Really? We have to do this again?"

"Hey, art is supposed to be shared by all."

"Only when the artist feels it's finished." I reach for it again. "These are just sketches."

He grips my chin and plants a loud smacking kiss on my lips.

I shove him. "Hey."

He winks at me as he settles the book on his lap. "All's fair in love and war, baby."

"*Fine*," I huff. More for show than anything. Resting my head on his shoulder, I relive the moments as he views them for the first time.

"That's Dad working in the garden. You've got to show him this. How do you draw a person's personality?"

"I don't know. It's just how I see it."

"Now this," he says, pointing to a picture of Anna in suspended agitation, "is Anna in true form." He kisses me on the head. "You are amazing."

"Thanks," I snag the book away from him then shove it under my pillow. It's hard to share my work—too personal. It's not just art, they're my feelings, something I don't want anyone to judge.

Cody grabs me and flips me underneath him. Liking the precarious situation, I grin up at him, and the toe-curling make out session begins.

Please don't ever let this end.

29

Ping!

"*Ahhh!*" I wake up, startled. Placing my hand over my heart as it pounds, I look around wildly, trying to figure out what just happened.

Ping!

Frick! My body drops backward on the bed, my pillow making a *puff* sound as I land.

That alert is *so* annoying. I've gotta get Cody to do something about it—change it or something. Why are people so obsessed with these things? They're ridiculously intrusive.

Ping!

"All right, already," I holler at the phone. I rub my eyes, trying to get them to focus so I can see the screen.

Mila: I had so much fun with Marco. How was hanging with your dad?

Mila: Hello!!!!!!!

Oh my god! Hold on a minute. I rub my eyes again and text back.

Me: You woke me up! It was good. Glad you had fun.

Mila: Let's go to the beach. It's supposed to be warm today. See if you can get Cody to come. Marco said he's in.

Me: Okay.

Whoo-hoo! It's brunch time in-the-hoouuse!

I quickly throw on some clothes and run out to the kitchen, the smell of bacon leading the way. Best day of the week."

Cody's already at the table—barely dressed as usual. I definitely don't mind the view now, especially since it's mine to enjoy.

"How did it go with your father?" Roxanne asks, squelching my less than innocent thoughts.

I scoop up some scrambled eggs. "It was fine."

"Are you sure?" Jeff asks. "We were worried about you."

"No, it was good." I snag two pieces of bacon. "We didn't talk about anything heavy, so that helped."

"Cassie's going to apply to some art schools," Cody blurts out.

"Cody!" I snap, my mouth full of food. "I never said that."

"Mom, you should *see* her sketchbook—it's amazing."

I stomp on his foot.

He looks at me, surprised. "Ow!" He jabs me in the ribs with his elbow. I giggle and smack him on the shoulder.

"Do I have to separate you two?" Jeff teases.

"I would love to see it sometime," Roxanne interjects, giving us both a hard look.

"Go get it, Cassie," Cody says, shoving me out of the chair.

I stumble to my feet. "Not right now. We're eating." I sit back down.

"I'll get it." He takes off.

"Cody!" I holler after him, then turn back and look at

Roxanne and Jeff. I shrug my shoulders. "He's my biggest fan," I laugh nervously.

Jeff smiles warmly. "I can see that."

Cody is back in a flash and hands the book to Roxanne who opens it immediately. "Cassie." She turns over several pages, taking time to absorb each one. "These are amazing. Jeff, look." She angles a page toward him. "It's you with your flowers."

A smile spreads across Jeff's face. "You really have a gift."

Uncomfortable with the praise, I fiddle with the food on my plate. "I was just messing around. It's not that big a deal."

"Oh, Cassie, you're wrong," Roxanne says, her expression sincere. "These are spectacular. I can feel the images. They sort of remind me of Norman Rockwell and how he captured moments."

"That's what *I* said," Cody joins in. "Who's Norman Rockwell?"

"Google it." Roxanne shakes her head. "Man . . . kids today."

I smile at her gibe.

Cody is already searching his phone. "Yeah, that's it! You're a modern-day Norman Rockwell."

What a nug. This is embarrassing. I feel like they all discovered I have breasts and need to make a big deal about it.

Roxanne leans forward. "Do you want help getting your application together?"

I turn and give Cody a death glare. He returns it with a ridiculous smile.

"Roxanne. I—"

"*Please*, let me do this for you. It would mean a lot to me. I know that's what your mother would have wanted."

I concede. "Okay, sure. I guess." I don't want to burst her bubble.

Roxanne claps her hand together in excitement. "We'll do it today!"

I groan inwardly. "Well, I think we"—I motion between Cody and me—"might have plans. Mila invited us to go to the beach with her and Marco. Cody?" I stare at him like, *you better say yes or you're dead.* Then to further my point, I pinch his side low enough that Roxanne can't see. I do not want to spend the afternoon cooped up filling out university applications.

He squeezes my leg slightly above my knee, making me jump. "I don't have any plans."

"*Okay!*" I yelp. "We should go, right?" I turn and smile sweetly at Roxanne and Jeff.

"That sounds a lot like a double-date." She looks at Cody accusingly.

"*Pfff!*" Cody retorts. "We're all just friends. I'm sure there will be other kids from school hanging out with us."

"Yeah. Totally," I say, trying to sound innocent.

I notice Jeff looking at Roxanne, like he's questioning her point. He looks at Cody, then at me. "Sounds like fun," he says, comfortably oblivious.

Roxanne's suspicious gaze travels between the two of us.

"I'll just go . . . ah . . . text her."

I'm giddy as I shut the door behind me. I've never been so happy. I wonder what Mom would say—maybe lecture me, give me the birds and the bees speech for the third time, or just take me in her arms and say something like, "My baby's first love . . . tell me everything."

I text Mila back to tell her that we're in and make arrangements to meet at 12:30.

I hear Roxanne and Jeff talking to Cody as I walk back toward the family room. Something in their tone makes me stop. I stay in the hallway, unseen, and listen.

"Cody," Jeff says. "Your mother is right."

"Dad, I don't see her like that—we're just friends. What's the big deal?"

"The deal is—you obviously like her," Roxanne says sternly.

"Well, yeah. She's awesome. I'm just having fun, just like I do with a lot of other girls." His words are like a punch in the gut. "We live together—the friendship's convenient," he says flippantly. "Plus, I kinda feel sorry for her, with everything that's happened."

Sorry for me? I shake my head, confused. Is this a joke or a ploy of some kind?

"It looked like more than a friendship when I walked in on you kissing her senseless on Christmas."

"What!" Jeff says, shocked. "How come I didn't know about that?"

"Jeff, some things are on a need-to-know basis, and this was one of them."

"I don't like the sound of that," Jeff sputters.

"Come on, Mom. I just got caught up in the moment. She was hurting—I had to do *something* to get her mind off it."

Am I seriously hearing this right now! What? I'm some sad, sorry mental case that needs the Cody Stanton lip-lock cure-all?

"Cody," Roxanne says, "it's more than a convenient friendship to *her*—you've *got* to know that. I've seen the way she looks at you. You're leading her on, and it isn't right. She's going to get hurt."

"Mom, you're making a big deal out of nothing. We both

know what's what and where we stand with each other. Nothing is happening that we're both not aware of."

I hear him head my way. I make a quick break for the bathroom, get undressed, and stand under the shower, letting the water fall over my head. All the amazingness I woke up with is gone. I don't want to believe he was serious, he can't be, but hearing him say the words makes them real somehow. I'm trying not to internalize it, but insecurity is taking over.

Cody is standing in the hall when I open the bathroom door. My breath catches—I still need a minute. He takes me by the shoulders and looks directly into my eyes as I try to look clueless. "You heard what I said, didn't you?"

I reluctantly nod my head yes. I could lie, but what's the point? It'll have to be dealt with eventually.

"You know I didn't mean any of it, right?"

I turn my head away.

"Come on. Seriously? You've seen how she's been acting lately—she totally knows something's going on. I had to say *something* to throw her off."

"It didn't seem like that's all it was," I say quietly as I half-heartedly push away from him. "Cody, I don't need this."

"Oh, come on, not again." He takes my arm and pulls me into his room, shutting the door behind us. "Stop acting like an insecure twit."

"I can't help it. You wanting me was ludicrous from the start."

He throws his hands in the air. "Why is me loving you so difficult to believe!" He looks at my blank stare, then turns away, growling in frustration before turning back. "Why are you being *so* stubborn?"

"Isn't it obvious?" I know I'm screwing things up, but I can't seem to stop it.

"No! It's not. Maybe you don't want to get hurt. Maybe you have trust issues—I don't know," he says, grabbing my shoulders and giving me a shake. "Did you hear me? Cassie . . . I love you."

I continue to stare at him, my mind slow to process. He turns away, sits on the end of his bed and drops his head into his hands. Finally, everything he said filters past all the crap I was telling myself. "Really?"

"Really!" he snaps back.

"Oh."

He stands, scoops me up, chucks me on the bed, then jumps on top of me, his lower body resting between my legs.

"God, you piss me off!" His lips come down hard on mine.

"Cody! Your parents!" The words come out garbled against the onslaught of the kiss.

"I don't give a shit!" He kisses my cheek, my throat.

"*Yes* . . . you do!" I push against his shoulders.

He buries his face in my hair and groans. "Okay, so I do. You know? You're a real pain in the ass."

I wrap my arms around him, holding him tight.

He lifts himself up on one elbow and caresses the side of my face. I look into his eyes. "I love you too," I say.

He leans down and kisses me once more, gently this time. His lips are soft and his tongue tantalizing. My hands are all over him, as his are all over me. I pull his shirt up at the back so I can feel his skin. He leans up and whips it over his head. I can feel every muscle in his back, his arms. He lifts my shirt up from my waist. Kissing my stomach, he moves upward.

I feel out of breath and my body is shaking. "Cody," I say firmly, needing him to hear me.

He drops his forehead between my breasts and groans. "I want to be with you so bad, it hurts."

I don't know how to respond.

"Come on," he says, getting up, pulling me with him. My legs feel like rubber. "We better get ready and go, we need to pick your friends up in"—he looks at his phone—"like in fifteen minutes."

"Oh my god! I totally forgot about them."

He stands, grinning at me. I notice the bulge in his pants and turn bright red.

He sees my expression and laughs.

"Don't laugh at me. I just. I don't . . . you know. It's all new to me."

"Don't worry. It's totally cool. If we ever . . ." His expression turns serious. "I would never pressure you or anything. But when you're ready . . ." He smiles as his eyebrows pump up and down.

"I really do love you. I'm sorry I didn't trust you. There's just been so much—I'm not myself. Losing my mom was so painful, losing you would be a close second, and that scares the hell out of me."

"I understand. You know, you could crush me just as easily."

"I never really thought of it that way. So, I guess we're both in a vulnerable spot."

"Yep. Pretty much."

We pull up to Mila's house. Cody honks the horn. "So, does this kid Marco know about us?"

"I'm not sure. I don't think so. Mila wouldn't tell anyone without asking me first. If he knows, it's something he figured out on his own."

"I'm not sure if I can keep my hands off you."

"We *could* tell him. He's a very private person. We could just explain and tell him to keep it quiet."

"I'm not ready to take that risk, are you?"

"No, I guess not. Well, then you better keep your dang paws off me."

"I'll do my best."

Ping!

I reach for my phone.

"Mila?" Cody asks.

"No. It's my father saying he enjoyed last night and hopes we can get together soon."

"Nice. I'm glad for you, Cassie."

"I'm not letting him off the hook that easy."

"I know. But you met with him, alone. It's a start."

"We'll see."

It was a perfect day. The sun was warm but not too hot. Cody and Marco hit it off—not that it was a major surprise, but you never know if a group will gel or not.

I thought Cody and I pulled off the whole platonic thing really well—at least I thought we did until Marco confronted me on the way back to the vehicle. I tactfully tried to steer the conversation in another direction, but he countered by saying it was nice to see me happy. My response was a bashful smile and accusations about him looking like a lovesick puppy the way he trails behind Mila. He told me I was full of crap.

We all had dinner at a seafood place on the beach. I totally stayed away from the lobster, *eesh*! Cody felt obliged to dance his crab in front of my face and call him Bob.

Jackass!

30

I'M DREADING DEALING with the weekend fallout. It's not knowing what Josh will do that has me stressing. I'll avoid him as best I can, but at school, it won't be an easy task.

"Hey. You okay?" Mila asks as soon as I enter school.

"Were you waiting for me?"

"Well, duh! I wasn't going to let you handle it all by yourself."

"Thanks."

"No problem."

She insists on walking me to class even though Mila's is in the opposite direction. I tell her I don't need a babysitter, but you can't budge the pint-sized terminator when she sets her mind to something.

"*Great.*" I turn to Mila. "Here comes Shandler."

"Oh, chill. It's fine."

Instead of her usual onslaught of verbal abuse, she turns her head away the moment she sees me.

"What, no shit-talking from the Wicked Bitch of the West?" Mila's words lash out when Shandler is next to us.

Her head snaps in our direction, eyes narrowed into angry slits.

"Oh my god! Shandler!" I take a step toward her. The side of her face is swollen and severely bruised. You can tell she's tried to cover it with makeup, but it's still visible.

"Don't." Her tone is hard and flat and quickly walks away, disappearing in the crowd of students.

"What the hell?" Mila looks at me, eyes wide.

"Do you think Josh did that?"

"If he did, he's completely lost his mind."

Half of me feels like she got what she deserves, after setting me up like she did. The other half feels awful. I guess she thought she could control him.

Somehow, I managed to dodge Josh the entire day. I kept expecting him to corner me and spew his verbal filth. Maybe he's waiting for the right time to spring. I hate that I have to watch my back all the time. But after seeing Shandler, he's capable of anything.

Psycho.

Cody and I have a history test in a few days, so our textbooks and notes are spread out all over his bed.

"You really should try to talk to Shandler," Cody says. "See if you can get her to talk to someone. Too many people are getting hurt, and no one is standing up to him."

I drop my eyes to our study questions. The truth of his words sting. "No way she'll talk to me. She can't stand me."

He touches my hand. "Sorry, Cassie. That wasn't directed at you. I understand the choice you made, but at the same time . . . he has to be stopped."

If anyone should have gone to the police, it's Shandler. She has physical evidence. Although, if no one was around to see it, how can she prove anything. It's her word against his, and just like me, she probably doesn't want to bring it out into the open. Maybe she feels ashamed—if that's even possible.

It's morbid, but I can't get the images of what he might have done to her out of my head. Was it rape, or did he just hit her, or both? "Oh my god! Was this my fault?"

Cody looks up from his notebook. "*No way*. Why would you say that?"

"Maybe he was angry at me, and she got in the way?"

He moves all our stuff aside and reaches for me, pulling me into his arms as he leans back onto the pillows. I snuggle against him, needing his comfort desperately.

"How can you be responsible for something he created—something you had no control over?"

"I don't know. I just feel sick about it."

"You didn't do anything wrong. You were a victim of a vengeful set-up from two twisted individuals."

"Logically . . . I get everything you're saying, emotionally . . . not so much."

I try to relax by focusing on the rise and fall of Cody's chest. I'm so tired.

"Cody, Cody!"

What the hell? My brain is foggy with sleep. Why is the earth shaking?

"*Cody!*" The harsh sound snaps me awake. Roxanne is standing over us, shaking Cody and looking pissed. Jeff flips on the light switch, blinding me.

I quickly separate myself from our entangled bodies and shove him hard. "Cody, wake up!"

He squints his eyes and looks up at me lovingly. "Hey, beautiful."

"Both of you out here, *now*!" Roxanne yells, throwing a pointed finger toward the door.

Cody looks around, disoriented, then it hits him. "Shit!"

My stomach twists into knots as Roxanne storms out of the room with Jeff following behind her.

"What happened?" he asks.

"We fell asleep with me basically on top of you."

"Nice. Just where I like you."

I punch him. "Be serious! *Now* what are we going to do? We're screwed." A horrified thought crosses my mind. "What if they make me go live with my father?"

"You're overreacting."

"Am I?"

"Come on," he says, pulling me off the bed. "We'll figure it out. It will be fine."

"I wish I shared your confidence," I grumble as we walk down the hall of shame.

Roxanne and Jeff are sitting at the kitchen table looking impatient. Well, Roxanne does, Jeff just looks bewildered.

"Have a seat," Jeff says, motioning for us to sit in front of them.

"How serious is this?" Roxanne asks as we take our places.

I start to deny any wrongdoing, but Cody interrupts me. "Look, the thing is . . . we love each other and you're just going to have to deal with it."

I look at him in horror. Of all the sensitive, diplomatic, mature things he could have said, *that's* what he comes up with?

Jeff and Roxanne stare at us with their mouths hanging open.

"What he means is . . . well . . . that is . . . um. We, uh—"

"Oh, yeah . . ." Cody looks over at me. "That's a *whole* lot better."

"Cody," Jeff says. "So all that bull you fed us on Sunday? I don't like being lied to, son."

"I'm sorry, but I'm sure you can understand why I didn't want to tell you. You reacted exactly the way we figured you would."

"Maybe if you would have talked to us ahead of time."

"Really?" Cody says. "You think that would have made a difference?"

"But you're just kids," Jeff says. "Love is a big deal."

I can't even believe I'm part of this conversation.

"Dad, Cassie is everything to me."

Roxanne's eyes suddenly get large. "Have you, you know . . . been together?"

"Mom! *That's* the first question you're going to ask?"

"Well . . . I had to." She looks over at Jeff, who looks a bit sick, then back at us. "It's a legitimate concern. You are both living under our roof. So? Yes or no?"

"Shit, Mom! Give me *some* credit."

"Look," Jeff says, placing a hand on Roxanne's arm. "This is unexpected. Your Mom and I need to talk this through."

I reach for Cody's hand and squeeze hard.

As if reading my mind says, "They're not going to make you live with your Dad."

"Cassie," Roxanne says in a gentle tone, "baby . . . we would never even *think* of doing something like that." I drop my head and sigh in relief. "We'd kick *Cody's* sorry ass out."

My head snaps up, and I burst out laughing.

"Funny, Mom," Cody retorts.

"Well." Jeff stands up. "This has been an eventful and . . . enlightening evening, but it's getting late."

"Yes, and I have an early meeting with the pickiest woman I have ever had the displeasure of dealing with. She's changed her mind four times—*on a living room*. Thank god it's not the whole house." She sounds more like herself, the anger gone.

Cody drapes an arm around my shoulders as we walk back to our rooms. "I told you it would be okay."

"I guess."

He pulls me into an embrace, holding tight. I could stay locked like this forever, but I'm exhausted. "I think I'm going to go to bed."

He gives me puppy dog eyes.

"Alone!" I laugh.

"*Fine*." He kisses my forehead, then my nose, before settling on my lips for a quick kiss. "Goodnight."

"Night."

Climbing into bed, I stare up at the ceiling, playing the evening over in my head. I'm relieved that we don't have to hide our relationship anymore, but nervous about how it's all going to play out, especially at school.

He told his parents he loves me! It's one thing to say it to me, but to hear him say it to them makes it more real. I can't believe this is really happening.

31

THE NEXT MORNING, there is a typed-out list of rules taped to our doors.

House Rules:

1. The bedroom doors will remain open, unless you are getting dressed.

2. No sex.

3. No making out in front of the parents.

4. No sex.

5. No fooling around in front of the parents.

6. And definitely, no sex.

Cody comes out of his room as I'm reading it and plasters me against the wall with his body. "Nothing on the list about this," he says, before his mouth begins to devour mine.

There isn't a place on my body that isn't tingling with heat. He slowly separates himself from me, wearing a provocative smile on his lips. I want to yank him back, but he spins me around and smacks my butt, sending me toward the bathroom.

"*Ow*," I rub the sting.

He laughs. "Hit the showers."

"I'm goin'." I give him a mischievous grin. "Want to join me?"

He makes a move like he's going to chase me. I squeal and run into the bathroom, slamming the door and locking it behind me. I lean against it and smile.

"That's what I thought." I hear him say.

"Good morning," Roxanne says as I enter the kitchen. Her words sound clipped.

Damn! I thought we were good.

"Aren't you going to be late for school?" she asks.

I'm totally paranoid now. "I think Cody is almost ready."

"What about breakfast?"

"I'll just grab a granola bar. I'm not sure about Cody."

Jeff comes in and pours his coffee into a travel mug. "All right, my love. Time to go make the big bucks." He kisses Roxanne on the cheek. "See ya, Cass."

"Okay. Yeah. See ya."

Roxanne doesn't say anything as she cleans the dishes—she probably wouldn't anyway—but now I'm self-conscious.

"So . . ." I say cautiously. She looks up. "Um . . . is everything okay? You seem kind of mad this morning."

"Honey, it's not so much that I'm mad. I'm more concerned than anything. I know you're not kids anymore—you both graduate this year—but I'll be honest . . . I'm kind of struggling with this. Call me old-fashioned." She pauses a moment, lifting a bowl to dry it, and suddenly smiles. "Your mom certainly would."

"Yeah?"

"Yeah. She was always saying I was worse than an old fuddy-duddy, and to loosen up. I was from a very religious family, so I was a prude—what can I say?"

"It's hard to imagine her saying that. What were my mom's parents like? I wish I could have known them. Were they strict or religious?"

"Neither. They always seemed really supportive to me. Allora really took it hard when they died. How could she not? I think you were about a year old when they had that car crash. They sure loved you."

"I guess I have grandparents from my father's side. He said he hasn't talked to them since my mother left?"

"Doesn't surprise me. Allora told me they knew he had a drinking problem and tried to intervene on several occasions."

"What are you talking about?" Cody comes in smelling all heavenly clean.

"My father's parents."

"Oh, yeah. Come on, we better get going."

"Is there a reason you're so quiet?" Cody asks on the way to school.

"I was just thinking about us."

"What about?"

"Since your parents know . . . our relationship doesn't have to be a secret anymore. I was just wondering what the plan is, you know . . . at school?"

"Oh, well. I was thinking we'd hang all over each other and

make out constantly so everyone can see us, like every other couple at school."

I snort. "Never."

For some reason, my mind wanders to Shandler and how Cody probably made out with her all over the school as well.

"Why are you frowning?"

"You dated Shandler. Did you love her too?"

He takes a hand from my lap, bringing my fingers to his lips. "I've never said those words to anyone, *ever*—well . . . other than my parents."

"But you were in a relationship together."

"It was never really a relationship. It was me being an idiot and thinking with the wrong head."

"I regret asking."

"Sorry, but it's true. She basically threw her body at me, and I couldn't think logically, and before I knew it, I was sort of stuck with her. It was a nightmare."

"I can only imagine. Was she your first?"

"Actually no. Summer camp when I was fourteen. It was co-ed."

"You went to summer camp?"

"Doesn't everyone?"

I give him a dirty look.

He catches my expression. "Oh . . . sorry."

I shrug a shoulder. "Wow, that's pretty young for the whole sex thing."

"I guess so, she was a lot older."

"You slept with a camp counselor?"

"No! Get your mind out of the gutter," he teases.

"Oh, what*ever*."

"No, she was seventeen. I was almost as tall as I am now, and I looked older than I was."

"So, you wuza *player*."

He gives me a sideways glance. "Hardly. It was hot, I was young and horny, and she was willing."

"Again, sorry I asked."

He takes my hand as we walk through the parking lot. I'm generally not an insecure person, but I feel like I'm upsetting the social balance right now. When we get into school, he pulls me into his arms and kisses me so intensely that I forget where I am.

My head feels light when he releases me. I find myself looking around and adjusting my clothes—feeling exposed in front of all the people staring at us, slack jawed.

Shit!

"See you in history," he says, smiling at my obvious discomfort.

"*Dick*," I mutter under my breath.

"What was that?" he says loud enough for everyone to hear. "You love me?" I quickly walk away from him, heading to my first class. "I love you too, babykins," he shouts after me.

I turn around and give him the finger before heading off to class, smiling like an idiot.

"So . . . the news is out?" Mila asks as we sit down for lunch.

"Yeah, I guess so."

She looks at me with a twisted smile. "You guess so? It's all over school."

"Don't people have anything *better* to talk about?"

"It *is* pretty big news. Not only is it Cody Stanton, but the fact that you guys live together makes for even juicier gossip."

"People need to find more important things to concern themselves with. I mean, seriously, with the stuff going on in the world—this is big news?"

"Oh, get off your soapbox." She waves me off with a flick of her wrist. "Gossip makes the world go 'round. What about his parents? I thought that was the whole reason you were keeping things quiet."

"Got busted sleeping together."

"They walked in on you having sex!" she shrieks.

"*Holy hell*, Mila! It wasn't like that, but thanks for dishing out more trash to the gossipmongers!"

She laughs. "You got some explaining to do."

I filled her in on The Big Talk, the list of rules on the door, and about Cody's big "L word" declaration. That about put her over the edge with glee. She shared highlights of her and Marco—some of the details I could have lived without knowing.

Who would have ever thought I'd be sitting in a school cafeteria swapping boy stories?

Life's pretty good. I love my job, school's not too bad, and I've got a lot of great people around me—not to mention I'm ridiculously in love. The only thing missing in this montage of happy is my mother. I'd give anything to be sitting at our little table in our tiny, crappy apartment, filling her in on my life.

I'm laughing to myself at Mila's uncharacteristically sappy and detailed description of her and Marco's last date, when I spot Josh walking up the stairwell toward me. My face falls at his venomous expression. I plan on ignoring him and walking quickly past, but he steps in my way.

"You think you're special now that you're with Cody?" he asks, with a twisted laugh. I try to step around him again, but he won't let me pass. "You're nothing," he says, looking me up and down. "I'm not even sure why I bothered. You're far from attractive, and you kiss like crap." He leans back slightly, appraising me. "And personally . . . I like a girl with a little"—he stares at my chest—"more."

"I thought you wanted to be friends," I say, the words dripping with sarcasm.

He steps up to the stair I'm standing on, then advances toward me, backing me against the wall. He positions his face directly in front of mine, deflating my bravado as quick as a lightening strike. I look around—there's no one.

"You know, you're right. I tried to be nice, show you a good time—even said I was sorry—but *nooo*, you thought you were too good for me. Then your asshole boyfriend gets me kicked off the team."

"*Be nice?* That's what you call it, attacking me at the party?"

"Don't be such a baby. Deep down, you know you liked it. All the girls do."

"You are totally sick!" I regret the outburst as soon as it's out.

He grabs me by the jaw and slams my head against the cement wall.

"You know what I think?" He leans in close, his lips brushing up my neck. I try to turn my head away, but his grip holds firm. "I think Cody just wanted you all along and needed to get me out of the way so he could get it."

"That's fine," he says matter-of-factly, releasing me. "It's what I would have done, but watch your back little girl, you never know when I might change my mind. You do have an appeal." He looks me up and down, making my skin crawl.

The door opens below. I push past him and run down the stairs, passing someone on their way up. When I get to the bottom, I bend over, placing my hands on my knees as I try to get my breath.

I hear someone come in. "Are you okay?" they ask as I stand up, fighting dizziness. Their voice sounds hollow, like I'm in a tunnel. All I can do is nod my head. "Are you sure?"

I recognize him as one of the guys from Cody's basketball team. He looks concerned. "I should get Cody."

He starts to walk back out the door, but I grip his arm, stopping him. "No. I'm okay. I just got lightheaded for a second." He looks like he doesn't believe me. "No, really," I say, trying to paint on a smile. "It's all good. I forgot to eat breakfast and ran down the stairs too fast—that's all."

"Okay. Maybe go to the office, they always have snacks if you need them."

"Yeah. Okay. I'll do that."

He walks up the stairs, and I push through the door. Being out of the stairwell helps and I'm finally able to breathe normally.

I manage to get to class but it's all a blur of faces and conversations—I can't focus on any of it. The flight or fight adrenalin is wearing off, leaving me exhausted, and my head is pounding from it hitting the wall.

As soon as the day is done, I rush out of school—I can't be here anymore. And I don't want to see Mila or Cody—they'll know something's up. I just can't deal with them freaking out right now.

When the thing with Josh happened at the beach, it was terrifying, but when some time passed, I just sort of downplayed it. I told myself that maybe Josh temporarily lost his mind, or maybe I led him on without realizing it. It was easier to internalize it that way than hold on to the fear or deal with the emotional scar it left. Now that I see the extent of his instability—what he's capable of—I'm terrified. My god, if he found me alone, outside of school.

A horn blaring jolts me from my racing thoughts. I wave apologetically and continue across the street at a run. I don't stop until I reach the restaurant.

"It's about time!" Anna yells as soon as I walk in the door. "You're late!"

"No, I'm not." I look over at Tony who rolls his eyes.

"Leave her alone, Anna!"

"I just finished school. I even ran," I say, forcing a smile.

"Well, you are slow as a snail," she says, leaning up and kissing both my cheeks. "I missed you! I don't see you the whole weekend." she yells. "What's wrong with you. You look pale. You're not eating! Tony get her a slice of pizza!"

"I don't want food. I'm just not feeling all that great."

She goes behind the counter. "Tony, move over. I've got to make Mamma's remedy!"

I raise my hands in defense. "No! I'm not that kind of sick. I just have a bad headache." I look at Tony for support, but he's focused on kneading the pizza dough. He has a funny grin on his face.

She eyes me suspiciously, then yells, "Marco!"

He runs from the back. "I'm coming. Jeez! You know you don't have to yell."

"Who's yelling!" She shakes her head like it's the dumbest statement she's ever heard. "Take Cassie home."

"Are you sick?" Marco asks, eyes twinkling.

I roll my eyes at him. "No, just a raging headache, and I have lots of homework."

"Yeah. Sure. I can take you."

On the way, he thanks me for introducing him to Mila. Hearing her name makes me realize she's who I need right now. I text her to come over, that it's important.

"What are you doing home so early?" Roxanne asks as I pass by the kitchen. "Are you having dinner with us for a change?"

"Yeah, maybe. Mila's coming over so we can study for our exam," I lie. "It was dead at the restaurant. Is Cody here?"

"No, he's still at practice. Is everything okay?"

"Yep. Can you send Mila back when she gets here?" I attempt to sound calm, but feel anything but.

"Sure."

I get to my room and I don't know what to do with myself. I attempt homework, but I can't focus. I try YouTube videos, but it doesn't help. I pace the floor a bit, go get a drink from the bathroom, then come back and stare out the window.

"What's up?" Mila says, scaring me. I didn't hear her come in. "All you said was get here ASAP."

I'm not going to cry, I'm not going to cry. But I tear up anyway.

"Shit, Cassie! What's the matter?"

I shut the door behind her. "I'm so glad you're here. It's

Josh. He cornered me in the stairwell at school. I swear . . . the look in his eyes." I start to shake.

"Wait, what? Cassie, are you okay? Oh my god. What happened? Here, come sit down." She walks me over to the bed and we sit down, side by side.

I fill her in on the details. She shakes her head in disgust. "I knew—at least I thought I knew—what he was capable of, but I never imagined he could be this warped. What are you going to do?"

"Nothing? What *can* I do? You know Cody and his family will freak out if I tell them. But I'm scared, Mila—really scared."

"What about Shandler? Maybe you should talk to her."

"No way."

"*Cassie*, she's not the same."

"She's not going to talk to me. And what do you mean she's not the same?"

"She slinks around, like she's trying not to be seen, her head is always down, and I haven't seen her talk to anyone. Cassie, she's the queen of darkness—evil to the core, but now she's like hollowed out—lobotomized. You haven't seen her?"

"No, I haven't."

"Look. I hate the bitch, but seeing her like that, a shell of herself? It's scary. I don't know, I was just thinking that if you talk to her—especially now with what he did to you recently—if, you both talked to someone." I shake my head at her. "But it's different now, and if you had Shandler . . ."

"No."

"Okay. Then *you'll* go to the police."

I look at her sideways. "With what? Yeah, uh, officer, I'd like to file a report of a guy that was mean to me?"

She throws her hands up. "Fine! Then, from now on, you're never alone . . . *anywhere*. Even outside of school."

"No arguments there."

"But if anything else happens, I'm gonna *drag your ass* to the station myself. I mean it, Cassie. You think I'm tough? You haven't felt the impact of my Latino blood at full strength."

Seeing her standing there, all fiery and protective. . . I'm not sure how I got so lucky. "Okay." I smile at her. "Fair enough."

"I want to hurt him *sooo* bad!" She raises a clenched fist.

"Hey," Cody says opening the door. "Who is Mila going after *now*?"

"Oh, just some dumb jock who's a little too sure of himself," she covers.

"What's up? Do you need any help?" he asks.

"No, just girl talk," Mila says, trying to sound humorous.

"Oh, god!" He covers his ears, letting go only long enough to shut the door behind him.

I snort. "What a nob."

"Yeah, but an incredibly cute one." The change in conversation feels good—back to something normal. "Look, I gotta go. If you're okay?" she clarifies. "I have a shit-ton of homework."

"I'm sorry."

"For what?"

"Pulling you away."

"*Pfff!* Don't be an idiot. It's schoolwork. Friends come before all else. Well, maybe not before a really hot boyfriend, but even *that's* debatable."

"Thanks," I say, hugging her. "I'm so glad I met you."

"You *should* be. You need someone who's got your back. Speaking of which, I really think you should tell Cody."

I shake my head. "No. I don't want him getting hurt or in trouble over this."

"You know he's going to be pissed if he finds out."

"I know."

"I'll see you at school. By the way, Tiffany is having a party this Friday."

"Not going."

"Come on, go. There's no way Josh will be there. She hates him. Besides, he'd never come. These aren't his people."

"Can I bring Cody?"

"Having one of the hottest guys showing up at your party? I don't think that will be a problem."

"I don't know."

"If for some reason Josh does show up, we'll just leave. Come on, it'll be fun."

"Let me think about it."

"Fair enough." She opens the door. "See you tomorrow?"

"Yup."

"Come in here," Cody calls to me from his room after Mila leaves. I cross the hall feeling incredibly drained. He's sitting up in bed reading his biology book and looking sexy as hell. He motions me over. "Come and hang out with me."

I sit on the side of his bed, fighting the need to fuse my body with his. "What's up?"

He reaches forward and slides the backs of his fingers along my jawline. "I missed you."

I stretch my body toward him and kiss him on the lips. "I missed you too."

Yeah . . . I needed this.

He pulls me onto his lap, returning his lips to mine in a slow, easy kiss. I melt into the security of his closeness, but before I have a chance to process . . . things heat up and an inferno erupts.

I pull away. "*Okay*." I feel like I need to fan myself. Needs aside, I have no idea where his parents are.

He grins. "Didn't you hear them leave?"

"Who?"

"Mom and Dad. They went to their book club."

"Really?" I croak out, suddenly feeling nervous. I clear my throat. "They're in a book club?"

"*Mmm-hmm*," he says, nuzzling my neck. "Surprising, huh?"

"Yeah. Uh, *Sooo*," I say, resisting the urge to purr. "Mila told me about a party on Friday."

He pulls back and frowns at me. "I thought we were having a moment."

"*That's* why I'm changing the subject. Ripping your clothes off could set off a chain reaction, and *I'm* a rule follower—we'd be breaking two, four, *and* six." It's a bullshit statement, and nerves aside, I'm not in the right state of mind for what he has in mind. I don't want those images of today in my head when I'm making love for the first time.

"You want to rip my clothes off?" A devilish grin is plastered on his face. "You know . . . rules are made to be broken. Besides, the word sex is a generalized term *with* varying degrees of interpretation." With the ease of a collegiate wrestler, he flips me over, positioning his upper body just above mine, the lower half between my legs. "I mean, what exactly are they referring to. Is it this?" He gently brushes his lips over mine. "Or this?" He plants feathery soft kisses from my neck down to the top of my breast. "Or maybe this." He lifts my shirt up and kisses a trail down my stomach just above the button to my jeans. He stops, looks up at me, wiggling his eyebrows, then lifts the buttoned waist up and kisses a tender spot underneath.

"*Yep!*" I squeal as I push his head away. "I'm pretty sure that is what they meant. So, do you want to go with me or not?" He sighs and drops his head on my stomach. "*Oof.*" His heavy head feels like a punch.

"You know I have a game, right?" His voice is muffled against my stomach.

I grab a handful of his hair and lift his head so he's looking at me. "Yes. Mila and I will be there, but I thought we could wait for you after—we could all go together. Marco will probably meet us there after work."

"Okay, fine, if that's what you want." He rolls to the side, then playfully shoves me off the bed, making me tumble to the floor. "Now, get out," he teases as I stand up. "I have homework and you trying to seduce me is incredibly distracting."

I roll my eyes at him.

"Cassie?" I hear Roxanne call from somewhere in the house. "Come here! *Now*, please."

"Shit! I thought you said they were at book club?"

"Well, they usually are on Tuesdays."

"It's Monday, you idiot! Do you think she heard us?"

"I doubt it. She sounds like she's on the other side of the house."

I look at him doubtfully.

"It's a big house, Cassie."

"Where are you?" I call out as I walk down the hall toward the kitchen, Cody in tow.

How do I deal with this? Okay, so we bent the rules. She can't expect us to be perfect all the time, right? We're teenagers . . . with hormones and urges. And why did she just call my name and not Cody's?

"The front door," she calls back.

I look at Cody in confusion. He shrugs his shoulders. When we reach the main room, Roxanne is standing at the front door, holding it open. She's talking to someone. When we get close enough, I see Harold standing in front of her.

"Harold, what are you doing here?" I ask. He's not supposed to pick me up today.

He looks nervous. "Hi, Miss Cassie."

"Oh my god! Is my father okay?" My gut clenches with fear.

"Yes, Ma'am. He just wanted me to drop this off for you."

He stands to the side. The only thing around is a white Volkswagen Golf and a massive Hummer.

"What? I don't understand. What am I supposed to be looking at?"

"It's your new car."

"My new what?" I stare at him dumfounded. "What are you talking about?"

He grips his hands together nervously. "Um . . . your dad bought you a car."

I continue to stare at him like he has two heads. *A car?*

"He wanted you to be able to get around." I open my mouth to protest, but he cuts me off. "*So* you could come see him anytime you want."

He hands me a key fob with a Volkswagen symbol on it, then quickly steps to the side. What does he think I'm going to do, hurt him?

"Your father bought you a car?" Cody asks from behind me. "That's a pretty extreme jump from a phone."

"No kidding." I abruptly turn back to Harold. "Why didn't he come himself?"

He gives me a crooked smile. "He was afraid you'd throw the keys in his face."

"*Pfff*. So he sent you?"

He shrugs his shoulders.

"Sorry you had to make the trip, but I can't accept it." I hand him back the key fob.

"Nope." He lifts his hands high. "Sorry, Miss Cassie, one way delivery."

"Figures," I mutter to myself.

"Miss Cassie?" Cody teases.

"Shut it!" I nod in Harold's direction. "Harold is a true gentleman." Harold's cheeks immediately flush red. Oh my god, this big-ass-giant of a man is blushing?

"Yes, Cody," Roxanne interjects. "You should take notes."

He scoffs at her.

"Harold, this is Cody and his mother Roxanne." Harold politely shakes both of their hands. "Harold drives for my father."

"It's nice to meet you." Roxanne says.

"You as well. I need to be getting back," Harold says, stepping away. "I'm sorry I won't get to see you again."

"Why won't you?"

"You won't need a driver."

Roxanne excuses herself to go get Jeff.

"Yes, I will. There is no way I'm keeping this car. He can't buy his way into my life."

Harold lowers his voice. "Cassie, that's not what he's doing."

"How do you figure? Because it sure looks that way to me."

"I understand. But that's not the kind of person he is—he would never think of it that way. He sees a need and gives, no matter who it is. And I mean that literally. So, before you blast him and throw the gift back in his face, hear him out and think about what I said." He turns and heads down the steps. I notice a man in the passenger seat of the Hummer. He fills out the entire right side of the vehicle.

"Oh, come on, Harold, you hardly needed backup," I tease, eyeing his passenger.

He bursts out laughing. Such a deep, rich sound. "I'm *really* going to miss you," he says, continuing to his ride. "I'll see you around."

"How does he know I can drive?" I call to him.

He stops suddenly, looking concerned. "I, we just assumed. Can you?"

I sigh. "Yes."

He looks relieved. He waves and gets into the beast of a vehicle and drives away.

With resignation, I turn to Cody. "Want to go for a drive?"

"You're not mad?" Cody looks amazed.

"It's a mixed bag of feelings—not sure."

"Okay. Do you have a license?"

"Yeah . . . from New York. I'll need to get a California one—I think. That's if I decide to keep it." Cody doesn't look convinced. "What? *I took* Driver's Ed."

"Yeah, but when was the last time you drove?"

"Driver's Ed."

"Crap." He shakes his head. "I love you, but I'm not sure I'm ready to put my life in your hands."

I punch him in the chest. "Don't be such a wuss." I turn and walk to the car.

Roxanne and Jeff come to the door. "You going for a drive?"

"Yes," I say.

"You kids be safe," Roxanne calls after us. "Dinner will be ready when you get back." She heads into the house, but turns. "Maybe just drive around the block . . . slowly."

"You have a license, right?" Jeff asks.

"*Yes*," I groan. "Man . . . such little faith."

"Faith's got nothing to do with it, I'm thinking more about the legalities."

"Don't worry," I say to Cody as I walk to the driver's side. I push the button on the key fob to unlock the car and we both get in.

He looks at me like, *easy for you to say*. "At least most of the kids are inside eating dinner, so at least they'll be safe."

I stop and stare at him. He's serious. "You are such a jerk!"

"What?" he says helplessly.

Cody wasn't too happy with my driving. He kept gripping the door, the dash, and anything else he could brace himself with. He suggested I get Jeff to drive with me, give me a refresher course.

"That was pretty dirty, sending poor Harold into the fire like that," I tell my father on the phone when he calls in the evening. "You should have come yourself."

"Sorry. I know. But my relationship with Roxanne and Jeff is strained at best, plus I knew you wouldn't hurt Harold. Do you like it?"

I thought a lot about what Harold said about my father

being generous when he felt someone needed it. But I'm not a homeless person that needs a car to make my life easier. It's excessive, however you look at it. "It's really nice, but I don't feel comfortable keeping it at this stage of our relationship."

I didn't throw it back in his face, I gently *handed* it back.

"But it's practical."

"How do you figure? I never thought of extravagant as being practical."

"Well, I need my driver, and you need a trustworthy vehicle when you go off to university."

"You still shouldn't have done it."

"Yes, I should, parents are supposed to buy their kids their first car."

I'm silent. Mom would never have been able to afford it even if she had the chance. I feel my defenses steeling into place.

"I'm sorry, Cassie." I hear the regret in his voice. "That was insensitive. Forgive me?" *Silence.* "Cassie?"

"I'm trying. There are a lot of different layers to work through."

"I understand. How about you just keep it for a while. If you still feel the same way in, let's say . . . a month or so, I'll take it back."

"Okay." But only because I really like Harold and trust him. If he thinks my father is one of the good guys, then I need to give him the opportunity to prove it.

"So, you'll drive out to the set to meet me on Sunday?"

"Jeff is going to give me a few driving lessons first . . . just refreshers."

"Oh, I never thought of that. I could hire a driving instructor to come to the house."

"No." *Hell, no*. The last thing I need is more extravagance. "I'm sure Jeff is capable, and he already offered."

"All right then, I will have Harold pick you up and bring you to the set."

I call Mila next. My ears are ringing from when I told her the news.

What a crazy-ass day.

32

"EVERYTHING WILL BE FINE," Mila says.

"What will be?"

"The party. I can tell you're nervous."

We're waiting for Cody outside the locker room. I can't get rid of the fear that keeps making me feel woozy. "I just feel like it's better that I'm not out in public any more than I have to be," I tell Mila.

"What are you going to do, hide forever? It's been a week, maybe he's over it, he hasn't bothered you right?" I shake my head, no. "Besides, life goes on. Just be smart and don't let him catch you alone."

I feel calmer the moment I see Cody. He wraps an arm around my shoulders. "Hi, Mila." He looks at me. "You ready?"

"Yup." He squeezes me to his side and kisses the top of my head.

Several teammates come out the dressing room. They tell Cody, "Later," and some say, "Hi," to Mila and me.

Cody and I aren't an oddity at school anymore. Once the

initial shock wore off, we weren't a topic anymore. There are a lot of disappointed girls, though. I see their expressions of longing as we pass. It's pathetic.

"Great game," Mila says.

"Thanks. You drove tonight, right?" Cody looks at her hopefully.

I pinch his side "Prick!"

"Scag."

"Toad."

"Toad?"

"Interesting relationship," Mila says, her eyes darting back and forth between the two of us.

I laugh. "Mila's driving. I'm getting better, though. Jeff says so."

"From what I've heard, he's just being nice."

I drill him in the arm. "Asshole!"

The party is in full swing when we arrive. Marco is waiting at the entrance for us. There's a contrasting couple—he's really tall, she's super short; he's quiet and reserved, she's loud as hell.

I'm actually enjoying myself. Mila was right. Everyone is super nice. The conversations are wide-ranging and interesting—way different from the stupid parties I went to with Josh.

Mila starts doing the pee dance. "Cassie."

"I know. Me too."

We're in the middle of a shoving match for first dibs to the bathroom, when a girl speeds past us crying. She's readjusting her clothes before entering the party, when Mila says, "Hey, you okay? What's the matter?"

"Nothing," she says, wiping the mascara from under her eyes.

"Something's obviously wrong," Mila insists.

"*No!* It's fine. Just leave me alone, okay?" She smooths down her hair, then quickly disappears into the crowd.

"You should mind your own business," a voice says from behind us.

An icy chill runs down my spine. Josh is leaning against the entrance to a bedroom looking smug as he zips and buttons his jeans.

I stand frozen . . . sick at the image of him—his expression. Why is he here? He's not supposed to be here.

Mila flies at him in a rage, shoving him hard, but her impact only has him taking an amused step backward. "We're going to the police, you twisted fuck!" she screams at him.

He jabs his finger in the middle of her chest, pushing her away from him like an annoying pest. "Nobody is going to believe you." He nods his head in the direction of the girl who ran off. "She'll never say anything. I didn't force her into that bedroom. She came in with her hands all over me. I just gave her what she wanted."

"Was that before or after she said *no*!" Mila takes a swing at his head, but Josh easily catches her wrist and yanks her up against him.

"If I'd known you were into the rough stuff, I wouldn't have let you go so easily. Besides, how does that saying go? 'No usually means yes'—something like that."

"Let her go." Josh looks at me a moment before releasing her with a look of disgust. He makes a move to leave, but Mila steps in his way.

"Seriously?" he says, looking bored. He watches a couple as

they pass, then turns back to Mila. "What are you going to do . . . beat me up, little girl?"

I quickly take a firm hold on Mila's arm, pulling her to my side. She looks at me as I shake my head at her.

As if satisfied that everything's been resolved, he says, "Ladies," then dismisses us with a warm, friendly expression—not a trace of the disturbing confrontation that just took place.

Mila starts to go after him again. "Stop!" I yell. "Can't you see he's insane? Please!"

"Why should I?" she snaps.

"Because you antagonizing him is only going to make it worse. I don't want to see my best friend hurt, and I can't get enough air."

She rests her hand on my shoulder. "You're shaking. Cassie, look at me. Just breathe."

I bend over, letting my head fall. Mila gently rubs my back. "Breathe," she says in a soothing voice.

As the control returns, I straighten up. "I'm ready to go to the police, but we need to find that girl. Do you know her?"

"I think I've seen her around school, but I can't say for sure. She's pretty young, maybe a freshman, a sophomore—I don't know. What an idiot! She probably thought she could boost her popularity by hooking up with him."

"Hopefully she didn't leave. Maybe we can get her to come with us," I say.

"Do we tell Cody and Marco, or what?"

"And have them get thrown in jail for assault? No way. Let's just find her. We'll make an excuse to the guys then skip out with her."

"Okay," Mila agrees.

"But let's stay together. I can't handle running into him alone."

"Sure."

We weave our way through the crowd. The thought of running into Josh again makes my stomach twist up tighter than it already is. I know I've got to be stronger than this, but it's easier said than done at the moment.

After looking everywhere for the girl, we head back to find Cody and Marco.

"Did you fall in?" Cody jokes. "You and Mila have been gone forever."

I force a laugh, "No, there was a long line."

Cody lifts my chin. "Are you okay?" He inspects me closer. "Did something happen? You look really pale."

"Actually, I feel like I might be getting sick."

Mila jumps in. "I'm not feeling well either." She glares at me. "If you gave me the flu, you're dead."

"We should get you home," Cody says.

"I can take her," Mila quickly interjects. "Same car, same germs, you know?" She starts pulling me toward the exit. "Marco, you can take Cody to his car, right?" Before anyone can respond we rush out.

"We're heading to the police, right?" Mila asks.

"*Hell*, yeah!"

"Can I help you?" a female officer asks.

"We would like to report a rape," Mila says. "Well, a possible rape," she clarifies.

The officer doesn't react, but her expression hardens. "I'll direct you to Officer Banks, he handles situations of this nature. Just a moment and I'll get him."

She walks over to an officer who's busy typing on a computer. He looks up at us, then slowly hefts himself out of his chair and motions for us to follow him. He opens a door to a room with a long table and several chairs around it. "I thought you girls might want to talk in here where it's a little more private." He leaves the door open slightly.

We all sit. The officer places a laptop in front of him. He starts typing then looks up. "Okay. Tell me what this is all about. Starting with your names."

Maybe it's his tone, but I already feel like *we* are the criminals. I look at Mila, giving her the go ahead. We had planned ahead of time that she would do most of the talking.

While the officer takes notes, she explains what we saw at the party and the details of how Josh attacked each of us.

Officer Banks looks up at us when Mila finishes. "So, what's the name of the girl you thought *might* have been raped tonight?"

"We're not sure. We tried to find her at the party to get her to come with us, but we couldn't."

"*Mmm-hmm.* Okay. Let's back up a bit." He readies his fingers over the keyboard. "What is the address of the party? Were there any adults in attendance?"

Shit. I don't like where this is heading.

"What's that got to do with anything?" Mila snaps.

"They are relevant questions," the officer retorts.

Mila looks at me and I know she's concerned about getting her friend in trouble. "No, they're not!" she states defiantly.

"Fine. We'll get back to that. What school does the girl go to?"

"Jefferson, I think."

He leans back and stretches. "So, the only information you can give me is that you saw a girl you don't know coming out of a bedroom crying and a boy zipping up his pants."

Mila and I look at each other. My expression says, *I told you so*, hers says, *what a useless asshole*. Although, when he reiterates the facts, they do sound flimsy.

"I'm sorry, girls. But without a name, what can I do? Maybe if you could find her at school and get her to come in and make a statement. Now, once again . . . what is the address where the party was held?"

"But, what about what happened to me, and to Cassie?"

"Neither of you filed a report when it happened. Mila, it's been over a year. Are you sure this isn't a jealously thing? Could it be possible that seeing Josh with this new girl sparked a need for revenge? We see that happen quite a bit."

Mila slams a hand on the table, making both me and the officer jump. "Are you fucking kidding me?" she explodes. "Did you not hear what I said? He tried to rape me . . . *and* Cassie. If someone hadn't stopped him, he would have succeeded, and may have with that girl tonight. It's not just us, there are rumors around school about other girls."

He leans forward, narrowing his eyes at her. "Now, calm down, young lady. It was just a question."

"Well, it was a stupid one," Mila retorts.

"That is quite enough," he sputters, looking indignant.

Mila crosses her arms over her chest and glares furiously at him.

The officer turns to me. "Cassie, you've been pretty quiet. Do you have anything to add?"

No. It's not worth it. It all pretty much played out like I expected.

"Not really."

"It's okay. You can talk to me." I look at the table and shake my head. "Can I have a glass of water?"

"Sure." He gets up and leaves the room.

"Mila, this is a waste of time."

"You're right, let's go."

We get up just as the officer walks in holding a paper cup.

"Where are you going?" he asks.

"Leaving. It's not as if you're going to do anything," Mila lashes out.

"It's okay," I say, acting as peacemaker. "We didn't mean to take up your time. As you said, there's nothing you can do without a name and the past is the past." *And* it's not worth getting Mila's friend in trouble, when he clearly isn't going to be able to help.

"Listen, both of you," he lectures. "It's important that you come forward right away with these things. It makes it hard for us to prove anything when it's been several months, or in your case—he directs a disapproving gaze at Mila—a year. Witnesses don't remember clearly, or things get diminished or embellished. Maybe you *could* have got him on assault, especially if there were witnesses that would have corroborated your statement. But as it stands . . . I'm sorry. I wish I could be more help." He sighs. "We'll file a report. It's not much, but at least it will be on record. If you find that other girl, get her in here. Maybe with all three of your testimonies, we could at least bring him in for questioning."

"Thanks for your time, Officer." I reach for Mila's arms, but she moves out of reach.

"I thought you people were here to serve and protect. I *don't* feel protected and definitely no justice will be served. You know what? Cassie was right. She told me you people wouldn't do anything, but I didn't believe her."

"I'm sorry, girls. Next time you'll know—"

"Do you *hear* yourself!" Mila's voice booms. "Next time? Are you fucking kidding me? *Next time* someone could get *seriously* hurt. *Next time?*"

I want out of here. I feel violated all over again. "Mila, he's right, come on. Let's just go."

"Thanks, Officer," Mila says, leering at him. "I'm sorry if we disturbed your donut break!"

"That's uncalled for!" he snaps.

"Sorry, about that," I say to him, pulling her out the door with me. "*Enough*, Mila. I want to go home."

"Can you *believe* that crap?" Mila says on the way to the car.

"We just need to find that girl."

"And if we don't?"

"I don't know. Come up with a plan? Maybe a way to catch him?"

She rubs her hands together, in sadistic glee. "Now you're talking my language. I like the way you think."

"Mila. You seriously scare me sometimes. You're like a miniature pitbull, you don't know when to back down."

"No, Josh is the one who should be scared. I'm going to nail that son-of-a-bitch to the wall. And no, I won't back down. I did before, but never again."

"Cassie. What took you so long?" Cody asks, concerned. "I thought you'd be home before me."

"I know. Mila and I stopped to get some Pepto, and then had to pull over a couple of times so she could throw up. She ended up worse than me." I hate lying to him, but there is no way of explaining this that comes out favorable for him or me.

"That sucks."

"Yeah, but I'm doing a lot better. I'm going to go to sleep, though . . . in case the nausea comes back."

"Yeah, sure." He hugs me and kisses my cheek. "Want me to tuck you in?"

I laugh. "No. That's okay. I'll see you in the morning."

"If you're sure . . ." He places my hand over his heart, giving me sad puppy dog eyes.

"I'm mostly sure. Now go to your room. We've got rules to follow, remember?"

"Okay." He slumps his shoulders and shuffles away.

"Oh my god! What a baby." I run and jump on his back, kissing his cheek over and over, making loud sloppy noises.

He carries me to his bed and dumps me on it, then climbs next to me, pulling me into his arms.

"Hold on a second." He sits up and pulls his shirt over his head, then lies back down, settling me into the crook of his arm.

I feel the rhythm of his heart against my cheek. I slide my arm over his bare stomach, resting it there. His bare skin touching mine is intoxicating, and I can't keep my hand still. I brush my fingers up the side of his ribs, then over his chest, and begin to follow a line of hair moving downward.

He groans and turns on his side, facing me. "I don't think you're well enough to want to see this through, so hands to yourself."

I laugh. "I suppose not." But I do need him close. I turn

over and he pulls me in, spooning me. I can feel his hardness against my backside. This has got to be difficult for him, but he doesn't pressure me and I appreciate it.

I hear his deep breathing and know that he is asleep. I wish I could fall asleep that fast.

I stare out into the dark and remember the look on the girl's face. If I would have been braver, maybe she wouldn't have been in that situation. How did he even end up at the party? Maybe the young girl invited him? House parties are unpredictable. You tell a couple of people and before long the whole school is at your house. I'm not sure why Mila thought it would be safe.

I'll only stay a bit longer, just need to absorb a bit more of Cody, and then I'll go to my room. I don't want to risk Roxanne's wrath if she finds us together.

I know everyone says, "Why me?" But seriously . . . why me? I hate this vulnerable, helpless feeling. I focus on Cody's breathing, trying to keep my mind clear of all the negative thoughts. I know that thinking like this isn't going to solve anything. I match my breathing with his.

33

I WAKE up to another day of blinding sun after a crappy sleep. I didn't mean to fall asleep in Cody's bed. Luckily, I woke up before the sun and moved over to my room.

I should stay in bed today—I'm grumpy as hell—but everyone will want to know what is wrong. I could continue with the stomach flu excuse, but I can smell the bacon, and it's got my stomach growling. I throw on a sweatshirt over my girlie boxers and drag my feet to the table.

I plop my butt down next to Cody. "Nice hair," he teases.

"*Bite me.*"

"Morning," Roxanne says from the kitchen.

"Morning," I mumble.

Cody leans in. "Did someone wake up on the wrong side of the bed?"

"You could say that."

"Can I get you anything?"

"No."

"Still feeling sick?"

“Not really.”

He waves a plate of fresh blueberry pancakes under my nose. “Does this help?”

“A little.” I smile inwardly, stabbing a few with my fork and adding them to my plate.

“How about this?” He places a couple of strips of bacon next to the pancakes.

“That doesn’t hurt.” I feel myself start to unclench.

“And this?” He leans over and kisses my cheek.

“*That* definitely helps.” I smile over at him.

“I like your shorts.” He brushes his fingertips up my thigh. I smack his hand away, laughing.

“She’s back! Hallelujah.”

“Prick.”

“Ass-hat.”

Roxanne comes out of the kitchen, giving us the hairy eyeball. She places the eggs on the table, returns to the kitchen, then says something to Jeff who looks over at us and shrugs.

I give her a weak smile. Cody ignores her.

He leans over and whispers, “Did you sleep in my bed last night or was that just an amazing dream?”

“I don’t know what you’re talking about,” I tease. “I was in my bed all night.”

“So, what are you kids up to today?” Jeff asks, sitting at the table.

“Brent, invited me to visit him on the set of his latest movie,” I say. “Harold is picking me up since, *apparently*,” I look pointedly at Cody then at Jeff, “I still need driving lessons.”

“Hey, we’ve only been at it two days, a couple more and you’ll be good to go. Let’s practice again this evening. I’ve got some time. Oh wait . . . you're seeing your dad. Tomorrow then."

"Okay." *I'm not that bad.*

"Long time no see," I say to Harold as he opens the car door for me.

"A welcomed surprise." He beams as he takes his position behind the wheel.

"Harold?"

He starts the car. "*Hmm?*"

"Can I sit in the front with you? I feel stupid back here."

"Uh . . ."

Not waiting for a reply, I open the door. Harold starts to get out. "*Harold!* I can open my own door."

"Miss Cassie," he says when I settle in the seat next to him, "you're making it hard for me to do my job."

"Chill your dill. No one will know."

"Excuse me? My what?" He coughs out a laugh.

"Never mind. I'll tell you what. If we have to make a formal appearance at let's say . . . the Grammys or something"—I pause for effect—"then I will for sure sit in the back."

He pulls away from the curb. "You are one of a kind."

"I like to think so. And you don't have to call me Ma'am and Miss, just Cassie is fine."

He looks over at me as if to say, *don't push your luck.*

"Please don't take it as an insult against your profession, but I'm not some princess from Beverly Hills. I'm from the Bronx, so the whole proper etiquette thing is pretty much lost on me."

"Where I'm from, it has nothing to do with etiquette, it's a sign of respect. So you'll continue to get the Miss and the Ma'am whether you like it or not."

"I really do like you, Harold."

"And I you, Miss."

"Can I ask you a question?"

"Mmm-hmm."

"There is this guy at school that's done some really bad things to some of the girls. He catches them off guard and sexually abuses them."

I notice his knuckles turn white as he grips the steering wheel. "Okay."

"Um, so that's it. Never mind. I'm not even sure why I brought it up—a squirrel moment, I guess."

What was I thinking? That I would get Harold to go beat him up? So stupid.

"Has this guy touched you?" I look at him with the plan to remain indifferent, but he looks ferocious, and I'm struck speechless. "If he has, I'll find out who he is and break his fucking legs."

"No, no. *Uhh* . . . nothing like that." The king of manners just said The F-Word.

"Sorry, Miss Cassie. It's a sensitive subject with me."

Harold pulls into the movie studio's main gate, shows the guard his credentials, and is waved through. There are warehouse buildings everywhere with people milling around—some in costume, golf carts zipping this way and that. It's awesome. He pulls up alongside a building that looks like it has offices in it.

"Don't even think about getting out to open my door," I tease. "I got this."

"Just give your name to the receptionist inside, he's

expecting you." He sounds distracted. "Miss Cassie?" Harold asks as I step out of the car.

I lean down so I can see him. "Yeah?"

"If he touches you again, you *will* tell me," he demands.

I feel my cheeks flush and shut the door quickly behind me. Shit! I shouldn't have mentioned it.

"I want to show you something," my father says, as I follow him down a long corridor. "This is a screening room." He holds a door open for me. "Just have a seat anywhere you like."

The room isn't very large. There are maybe twenty seats in front of a large screen. I sit in the back row. Brent joins me a minute or so later with a remote in his hand. "I hope this isn't a mistake," he says and presses a button, lighting up the screen.

My mouth drops open when Mom steps into the frame. "Oh my god," I gasp. "What . . . I—I." I give up finding the word and stare.

She walks up to a surfboard, tucks it under her arm, and delivers her line to another female character.

I inhale sharply at the sound of her voice. I never thought I'd hear it again. All I have are my memories and a few photographs—we never had a video camera. But seeing her large as life in front of me . . . she looks so young and vibrant. There's not one shred of the life that robbed her of her youth.

I can see my father watching me. I'm sure he's waiting for me to say something, but I can't—I don't have the words. I lean forward to get a little distance. Resting my elbows on the chair in front of me, I cover my mouth with my hands.

"She was only supposed to have a small role, but the lead

was difficult to work with and your mom . . . well, her personality was so vibrant, she blew them away."

I lean back in my seat, still void of coherent thoughts.

"Do you want me to turn it off?" he asks gently.

I shake my head. I can't let her go. I know this is only a role she's playing, but I can't help feeling this was the real her. I find myself grasping for pieces of it, wanting so much to know who she was before all the hardship.

The movie ends and the lights come on. "It never made it to the theatres," he says. "I was devastated—thought it was my big break—when really it was the beginning of my downfall."

"I understand what you risked showing me this," I say after a moment. "It could have gone either way. It's been hard to get a grip on this other life of hers. I was so angry that she'd kept it from me—finding out why, made it easier to forgive. But then you were real, not just a story from the past to explain why we were alone, but a living, breathing reason for our struggles. You became the object of my hate, a face to place the pain. But I'm starting to accept that you're more than that. You're a person with your own painful past. Luckily for you, I have friends that insisted you deserved a second chance. There's a lot I'm still sorting out."

"At least you're trying. I appreciate that. I live with the consequences of my actions every day. The fact that you're letting me into your life—slowly, I know—lessens the burden of that guilt, but more importantly, reconnects me with a missing piece of my life. You are a gift, Cassie, and I'm so sorry I didn't realize it until it was too late. I'm hoping that you let me make it up to you somehow."

"By buying me a car?"

He looks angry. "Cassie, I don't give a *damn* about the car, drive it into the ocean for all I care. I was looking at it from a practicality standpoint, nothing more."

I process this information. "Okay."

"Okay, what?"

"I'll keep the car, on loan."

"Good, now I can have Harold to myself again."

I laugh. "He's awesome."

"He's become quite attached to you as well."

"So, were you in any other movies?"

"Just small roles here and there. Like I said before, after your mom left, things got pretty bad. When I got my life back together, I started working on sets, learning all aspects of the business, and little by little, took on roles with more responsibility. Coping with alcoholism is ongoing. It took me a long time to get my confidence back, and trust that I could handle stressful situations without feeling like I needed to revert back."

"Well, you've done very well for yourself."

"I suppose I have. I wish I could take the credit for my transformation, but I can't."

"Why's that?"

"It was actually Harold that saved me."

"Really?"

"He found me passed out by some garbage cans. He could tell by my clothes that I wasn't homeless. He discovered my address from my driver's license and got me home, sober, and cleaned up. Over coffee we talked, and he got me to my first AA meeting, even became my sponsor. He helped me get my life back."

It's hard to picture my father that way, seeing him now. Oh my god . . . and Harold. "Harold was an alcoholic?"

"Yes. Iraq really messed him up. When he came back from his final tour, he couldn't hold on to a job because of the drinking. When he finally started going to the AA meetings, he was living on the streets, but I didn't know that until much later."

"That's awful. How did you find out?"

"It was at one of our AA meetings, I asked him if I could buy him dinner to thank him for all that he'd done. I was working again and doing well. When we were talking, he said something that alerted me to his situation. It was hard to confirm if my suspicions were correct without insulting him, but I had to take that risk. I still remember the humiliation in his eyes. It was unthinkable to see a war veteran reduced to such desolation and poverty. I offered him a job and a place to live immediately. That's how he became my driver. But he's more than that, he's my best friend."

"I hate to even *think* of him like that."

"He wouldn't want you to. We helped each other come back from a living hell."

Bonus points to my father for giving him an opportunity to regain his dignity.

"Cassie?"

"*Hmm.*" I respond, lost in thought.

"I want to say one more thing. I'd give anything to take it all back—go back in time, smack some sense into myself so I could have watched you grow up. I missed so much, Cassie."

"Yes. You did. But there's no going back. As Mila says, we can't be the person we are if we weren't who we were."

He laughs. "Oddly put, but that's is my philosophy as well."

"It sounded better when she said it."

"Doesn't matter. The message is clear. It's the challenges we face that help define who we are. And I think you've become someone pretty special."

"Yeah. You're not so bad yourself," I tease. "So, can I meet Channing Tatum?"

He lets out a surprised laugh. "Sure. Let's see if he's around."

34

"GET UP! We are going to the beach," Cody announces, waking me from my peaceful slumber.

I growl at him.

"Wake up!" He jumps up on my bed. Straddling me, he jumps up and down, jumbling me all over.

I smack his leg. "Quit!"

"Fine." He maneuvers himself so he's snuggled up next to me. "Get up. We're leaving in an hour."

"News to me," I grumble. I hate being woken up.

"Executive decision." He kisses my neck. "Morning."

"Morning. You know, that was a sucky way to wake me up?"

"I got a better way. Want me to show you?" He pumps his eyebrows suggestively.

"Sex junkie."

"Yeah, give me my fix, *woman*." He rolls on top of me, making obnoxious pucker noises with lips.

I push his face away. "*Ew*. Get off."

"Come on," he says, getting up off the bed. "There's nothing better than a sunny day to cheer you up."

"I *am* cheery!"

"Good, carpe diem!"

"I'll seize the day all right . . . and smack you up side your head."

"I dare you to try." He pushes me over and smacks my butt. I jump off the bed and chase him into the family room.

Roxanne looks up from her computer, startled. "What's going on!"

I stop chasing him. "Cody woke me up." I follow him into the kitchen and grab a bowl of cereal and sit down opposite of Roxanne. Cody sits next to me, elbowing me for no reason, so I smack him back.

"And you guys are how old?" Roxanne says in a dry tone.

"What's that got to do with anything?" Cody asks. "It's important to stay young at heart and all that crap."

She smiles. "*You*, my son, are a piece of work."

"You made me."

"Hey, is it okay if I invite Mila and Marco along?"

"Yeah, sure, no problem."

"Where are you two off to?"

"Beach," Cody says around a mouthful of cereal.

"Cody. Don't talk with your mouth full." Roxanne admonishes.

"*Mmm-mm*." Milk dribbles out of his mouth.

She rolls her eyes at me.

Back in my room, I check on my phone for the weather—a

perfect eighty-two degrees—beats the damp cold and slushy Spring in New York.

There's a knock on my door. Cody enters before I can say anything. "Excuse me. I could have been getting dressed."

"*That's* what I was hoping for."

"You have a one-track mind, Cody. *Seriously*."

"I'm a healthy teenage male. It's hormonal—can't help it. You ready or what?"

"Yep." I grab my bag with the beach essentials and follow him through the house.

"You want to drive?" he asks.

I recently got my new drivers license. "You feeling brave?"

"I have faith."

"Sucker." I shove him to the side and take the lead. I open the front door, then stop short. Cody bumps into me. The word "Bitch" is spray-painted on the passenger side. "Oh my god, Cody." I reach behind me for support, my eyes still fixed on the damage.

"What's the matter?" He grips my shoulders. "Shit." He yells into the house. "Mom, Dad, come here! Hurry!"

I plop down on the front step and stare in shock.

"It's going to be okay." He sits beside me, sliding his hand up and down my back. "It's only words. It can be repainted."

"It's brand new," I choke out.

"What's wrong?" Roxanne and Jeff come rushing out. I turn. Roxanne puts a hand to her mouth. "Oh, my."

"Who would do such a thing?" Jeff asks.

Josh . . .

"I'm calling the cops!" Jeff heads back into the house.

"Cassie, are you okay, honey? Here, let me go get you some water."

"Thanks."

She disappears into the house as Jeff comes back out. "The police are on their way."

"Here you go, baby." Roxanne quickly returns, handing me a bottle of water. "I'm so sorry. This kind of stuff doesn't usually happen in our neighborhood."

Roxanne and Jeff walk down to the car. I get up and follow with Cody. So much for being independently mobile.

It's not just the passenger side. It says "slut" all the way across the trunk, and "whore" on the driver's side. It has to be Josh . . . or Shandler. Maybe she found out that it was me and Mila who sprayed her car. No one would write this stuff randomly. This is vicious intent. I pull my phone out of my bag and take pictures, sending them to my father. It can't be Shandler, not with how she's been acting lately.

"Do you want to wait out here or inside for the police?" Cody asks.

"I'd rather stay outside. I need the air."

Cody pulls me into him, wrapping his arms around me. I tuck my head under his chin. "I'm so sorry, Cassie."

"Don't worry, Cassie," Jeff says. "We'll get it repainted in no time."

I know, but I can't afford to repaint it. Effing prick! He must have seen me driving it. It's got to be him.

Ping!

Brent: Are you okay? Did you call the police? Is Roxanne and Jeff there? Just in the middle of a shoot. I will call you as soon as I get a break.

Me: Yes to all, and okay talk to you later.

. . .

The police show up. I give a statement, they take photos, and then ask if I have any idea who might have done it. Of course I answered no. After they left, Roxanne and Jeff returned inside.

"You should text Mila and tell her we can't make it," Cody says as we walk back to the house.

"No way. I already—"

A car comes screeching to a dead stop in front of the house. Harold jumps out with a gargantuan-sized man in tow. He reaches me in two seconds flat and takes hold of my arms. "Are you okay?" He looks me over, then scans the area like a professional who knows how to assess and command in volatile situations. I would have hated to be on the opposing side of him in the military.

"I'm fine," I chuckle as he breathes a heavy sigh of relief. "It's okay, Harold. How did you get here so fast?"

"I wasn't too far away. My son had a baseball game. I came as soon as your dad called me."

Harold has a kid? I feel awful for not asking.

"My father shouldn't have pulled you away. You left your son there?"

He pulls me to his chest and squeezes the air out of me. "His mother's with him, and he didn't tell me to come. I was worried."

"Harold," I cough. "I can't breathe."

He sets me back. "Sorry. When your dad called me, I guess . . . I—I overreacted a bit. But he was panicking, and he didn't have any information just photos, which he texted me. But it's okay now? Have the cops been here?"

"Yes. Come and gone."

I nod in the direction of the overly large, stone-faced man looking over my car. "Who's the muscle?"

He smiles. "That's my younger brother George. His daughter plays on the same team. George," he calls out. George comes over. "Miss Cassie, George—George, Cassie."

George holds out a huge hand. "Nice to meet you."

"And you remember Cody, my boyfriend."

"You left the 'boyfriend' part out the last time you introduced us." Harold gives Cody a stern look.

Cody smiles back at him, unaffected. "It was unofficial at the time."

"I'm so sorry you two missed the game," I say, changing the subject.

"It's okay. I had to make sure you were okay. Besides, the game was almost over."

George returns to my car.

"This won't be a problem," George hollers to us. "I can get it taken care of in less than a week."

I look at Harold, questioningly.

"George owns a body shop. Tow truck should be here any minute."

"You rock!" I say loud enough for George to hear.

He grins proudly and gives me a thumbs up.

I lean over to Harold. "Will he let me pay over time? I'm not sure if I'll have enough money to cover it."

"I'm sure we can work something out." His grin says I won't have to worry about a thing.

"Don't look at me like that. This is my responsibility. I'm only borrowing the car, so I need to pay for the damages."

"I understand how you feel . . ." He takes me by the arm and pulls me away from Cody and quietly asks, "Does this have anything to do with that guy that's been victimizing girls at school? The one you were asking me about?"

I tense, and know he can feel it, but I lie anyway. "No. My friend and I plastic wrapped a girl's car and spray-painted mean comments on it as payback for bullying a girl at school. She must have found out I was involved. This was probably payback —she just didn't use the plastic wrap."

He looks me square in the eyes and waits.

"What? We did. I know it was wrong, but at the time it felt so right."

The tow truck pulls up, and he breaks eye contact. I have to control myself from sagging. His scrutiny was intense.

I follow him toward my car.

"Does your dad know about that?" He jerks his head in Cody's direction, while giving him a murderous look.

"Hey, now," I say, pulling on his arm to get his attention back. "He's really nice."

"He better be, or we'll have a situation."

The protectiveness make my heart gush. "A situation?" I laugh.

"Yes, Ma'am."

I truly love this man.

"What do you mean her car was graffitied," Mila screams and punches the back of Cody's shoulder from the backseat.

I cringe at the pitch of her voice.

"Ow!" Cody yells. "I'm driving!"

She zeroes in on me. "What the *hell*?"

"I'll explain later, okay?" I don't want her tipping Cody off that it was probably Josh.

"No! Tell me now!"

I glare her a look like, *let it go.* "Later. Why ruin such an amazing day."

"You're right," Mila concedes, taking the hint.

Cody turns to me with a suspicious look. He knows Mila isn't one to back down from anything. I smile innocently in return.

Lying on my back with my knees bent, I slide my feet back and forth rhythmically through the sand. The sun feels amazing.

I try my best to block out the morning's events by focusing on the sound of the waves, when someone kicks my foot, jarring my peace. My eyes fly open, ready to skewer the evil entity.

"Let's go for a walk," Mila says, reaching for my hand and yanking me up.

I growl at her.

She smiles at the guys in a way that says we're going to swap girly secrets, then drags me down to the water.

"We are *so* going to get him back for this!" Mila says when we're out of hearing range.

"There's no friggin' way I am going on another one of your *revenge missions*. Besides, it could have been Shandler."

She gives me a knowing look.

I stop. "Okay, fine. It was probably Josh, but still, no way am I going after him."

"Why not?"

"I'm not interested in poking a poisonous snake—*that's* why!"

"*Come on!*" She shakes my arm, looking for a different

response. I return the gesture with a blank stare. She lets go and huffs out a breath.

"It's really nice out." I continue our way down the beach.

"I'm not talking about simple revenge." She matches my stride, ignoring my attempt at changing the subject. "I'm talking about monumental payback!"

I drop my head back, groaning loudly. "Let it go. *Seriously*."

She plants herself in front of me and throws her hands in the air—her usual dramatic style. "I can't! We have to catch his sorry-ass."

"Mila. *No*."

"We could film him or something, or maybe you could wear a wire, get him to confess. You know how pompous he is. He'd never suspect anything, and he'd brag and threaten and say all kinds of nasty things."

"Mila! This isn't some TV show—this is my life. I'm not sure you realize how demented he is."

"Fine! Then we're going to the police again and telling them what happened to your car."

"They already came. I didn't tell them because there's no proof."

"We can't just let him get away with this. Come on . . . tell me you know that!"

"If you're so gung-ho, *you* wear the wire or whatever."

"I'm not the one he's mad at."

"I said *no*."

"Listen, we could maybe ambush him outside of his house. You know . . . before he gets into his car. He parks on the street. He's not going to do anything major where people could witness it. You could have your cell phone on and record everything he says, and I could video it from across the street."

"Isn't that like entrapment or something? Besides, he'll see you." Damn, she's sucking me in. "I mean, no."

She grins like she knows she's got me. "No, he won't. I'll crouch behind a car. I'll be the last thing he'll be paying attention to."

"Mila, this is crazy."

"Do you want to stop him or not!"

I want to make him pay, but I don't want to involve myself any more than I already am. His anger at me seems to be getting worse and staying away from him is the most intelligent thing to do.

But, Mila is right. We have to do something.

So I put myself at risk to do it?

I focus on the waves for a moment, running scenarios through my mind, weighing the pros and cons. Mila stays quiet. Probably hoping I'll come around.

It would be in a neighborhood in broad daylight. What could he do? And if we get his arrogant, vile admissions, we might be able to get the police to take us seriously.

"When do you want to do it?"

She narrows her eyes at me, the corner of her mouth lifting. "How's next Saturday?"

Reality jabs me with a burst of adrenalin. It's one thing to fantasize about revenge, another to plan on it. "Frick!" I stare at her, wide-eyed. I clasp my hands on top of my head, turn in a circle, stop, inhale deeply, blow it out loudly, then place the back of my hand on my forehead. "Oh god! This is crazy, Mila—even by *your* standards. How the hell will we know when he's leaving?" I place my hands on my hips, bend over, trying not to hyperventilate, then stand up straight. "Shit!"

"Calm down. It'll be okay."

"Calm down? Seriously?"

"Okay, let's think about this. How can we get him out to his car?" She taps her finger on her lips like she's trying to think of a cool place to go eat.

"*Ahhh!*" I groan in frustration.

"Got it! I'll call him and play like I made a mistake and realize how hot I am for him, or some bullshit story like that. I'll tell him to pick me up. He's so arrogant, he won't think twice. As soon as he comes out to his car, you can approach him, accuse him of graffitiing your car. No one will be around and he'll probably brag about it, then comment about the beach."

"He's not that stupid. He'll know something is up."

"No, he won't. His brain is in his dick. It's very small."

I choke out a laugh. "Did anyone ever tell you that you should be in law enforcement?"

"No, but the FBI is where I'd like to end up someday."

"No way!"

She looks embarrassed. "Or something like that, I don't know for sure."

I've never seen her embarrassed. Who knew it was possible? "I think it's great. I guess we never talked about our futures much."

"I've never told anybody before."

"Thanks for telling me."

She smiles and we head back.

The rest of the day was tough. I tried hard not to think about our scheming. Cody asked me several times if I was okay. I did my best to appease him, but I'm pretty sure he knew something was up. When we got home, I showered off the sand and saltwater while contemplating the sheer stupidity of Mila's plan.

Wrapping a towel around my head, I hear my phone ringing and run to my room to get it. It's my father.

"I'm so sorry I couldn't get away. We were right in the middle of a shoot, and I am now just getting a break."

"It's okay. Harold showed up, guns blazing."

He laughs. "I bet."

I smile to myself with images of his ready-to-do-battle expression. "I'm glad he came."

"Me too. Do you know who might have done this? Is there anyone at school you're not getting along with?"

"Who knows? There are always mean kids at school." My stomach clenches when I think of Josh and our plan.

"How about I come and get you. Take you to dinner."

"Actually, it's been a crazy day and I'm kind of wiped out."

"That's okay. How about this weekend? We have a break from shooting."

"Sure. It will have to be Sunday though. I have plans Saturday." Ugh! Hopefully everything goes okay.

"Sure, that works. Pick you up at six?"

"You or Harold?"

"Just me."

I snort. "You mean you can actually drive yourself?"

"Ha, ha, young lady. I'll have you know, I get a lot of work done while being driven. You know how traffic is in Los Angeles. I'd be missing several hours a day just driving. Hey, Harold says you and Cody are dating. I don't like the sound of that." *Thanks, Harold.* "You live in the same house. Maybe you should come and live with me?"

"We are not there yet, and I'm not moving. Besides, Cody's a gentleman."

"Well, I don't like it. I can't think that Roxanne and Jeff are okay with this."

"Not much they can do. Roxanne watches us like a hawk, though."

"Good for her."

"We can talk more about it at dinner."

"Okay, but we *will* talk about it."

I want to scoff at the whole parental protectiveness thing, but I hold back.

Cody knocks on the doorframe as I disconnect the call.

"What's up?" I ask.

"You and your dad getting together?"

"He's not my dad, he's my father?"

"What's the difference?"

"A dad raises you, a father does not. Anyway, he's taking me to dinner Sunday, why?"

"No reason. Just wondering. I'm glad you're trying to work it out." He walks over and wraps his arms around my waist, pulling me close.

"Yeah, I guess I am too. I know we have a long way to go. Things aren't just going to be *okay*, but it's a start."

He kisses me on the forehead. "I'm proud of you. You could have held a grudge for the rest of your life, but you didn't—you took a chance—that's pretty amazing."

"Thanks." I smile up at him. His compliment feels good.

"You and Mila were gone for quite a while. You aren't planning anything stupid, are you?"

Since I suck at lying, it's time for evasive tactics. Reaching up, I slide the tips of my fingers up the side of his neck and into his hair. Gripping tightly, I slowly draw his lips to mine. His groan makes me smile.

Playing the aggressor is kind of fun. And my plan of diversion is keeping me from thinking about Mila's stupid plan. *Uh*, now it's in my head again. I feel lightheaded. I just need to focus on Cody—his full lips, the feel of his muscles under my hands.

A little piece of heaven.

35

Monday:

Josh comes up beside me as I walk to my next class. He grips my arm roughly and smiles like he adores me. “I’m *so* sorry to hear about your car. I wonder who would do such a thing? You have a great day now.” He releases me and walks in the opposite direction.

Wednesday:

“It’s all set,” Mila says at lunch. “He’s leaving to pick me up at seven. I figured it’s a good time. It’s after supper, people will be out and about, and it’s not too dark. I’ll be able to see better with my camera that way.”

“He actually fell for it? What did you say? Never mind.” I hold up a hand stopping her. “I’m sure whatever it was, was disgusting.” I already feel sick. “This is crazy. I’m scared shitless.”

“Don’t be. I’ll be there with you the whole time.”

I look at her like, *easy for you to say.* "What if he sees you?"

"Once he sees you, he won't notice anything else."

Thursday:

I can barely eat or sleep.

Friday:

Mila and I go to Cody's game. I can't function normally.

Saturday:

We park down the street from Josh's house. Mila camps out behind a tree across the street while I wait at a couple of houses down, crouched behind a shrub. My insides are going crazy—nervous sweats, heart racing, my stomach twisted into knots—I feel like I'm going to puke.

This is so stupid! I'm just about to run over and tell Mila I'm done, that I don't want to do it, when I see Josh walking to his car.

Ahhh, Shit! Okay. I breathe deeply as I rub my hands on the tops of my legs. I should just let him go. I stand up anyway, my feet carrying me toward him against my will. I've already turned my phone on record.

"Josh," I smile nervously. "Hey."

"What the hell are you doing here?" He eyes me with distaste. "Oh wait, let me guess . . . you came to apologize." His words reek of sarcasm.

"Something like that," I laugh nervously. "I feel really bad about you getting kicked off the team. It wasn't right." That wasn't my planed script—it just came out. He doesn't respond, just looks at me suspiciously. "No. I'm serious. This whole thing got blown way out of proportion."

"You got *that* right."

"And that girl Mila and I saw you with at the party—"

"You didn't see shit."

"Well, she was crying."

"Stupid bitch was a tease, but I taught her a lesson. Don't offer if you're not willing to give, and since she offered, I took."

"Makes sense," I respond, even though his words make me sick. How can anyone talk like that and believe what they're saying.

"Interesting that you're here, being that I'm on my way to hook up with your best friend." He tilts his head and regards me curiously. "Didn't she tell you?" I try for a shocked expression, as I shake my head no. He dismisses my reaction with a wave of his hand. "Doesn't surprise me, girls are always backstabbing each other." A grin spreads across his face. "I have to say, I was excited when she called, especially now that I know how feisty she is. I *do* like it rough—but then you already know that." He shrugs his shoulders indifferently as he unlocks his car with the key fob. "Too bad. I was really looking forward to getting her underneath me, but since you're here . . ."

It takes a split second for his hand to snake out and grip my arm then slam me against the car, pinning me there with his hip while he opens the passenger door.

"Mila!" I scream as he shoves me into the passenger seat.

Next thing I know she's on his back, pounding on him, screaming for him to let me go. I make a move to get up, but he steps on me, using his weight to keep me in place while he fights her off.

"Go, Cassie, run!" Mila yells, not realizing I'm pinned.

Josh suddenly stumbles backward. Mila has her arm around his neck and pulling backward. Exploding in anger, he throws her to the ground. I watch in horror as her head snaps back, hitting the pavement.

"Mila!" I make a rush for her, but he grabs me and shoves me back. I land halfway in the car. "I have to see if she's all right!" I kick and punch at him wildly as he fights to get me all the way in the car. "She's not moving! Help!" I scream, hoping someone will hear.

Intense pain followed by shards of light explode through my head from the impact of something hard. I'm momentarily stunned, which allows him to shut me in completely. The next thing I hear is the sound of locks clicking into place. I look toward Mila, who's still on the ground, not moving. I frantically pull on the door handle, but it won't open.

"Got to love those childproof locks," he jokes.

I look at him in horror.

"Shall we?" he says excitedly, as if we're going on an adventure.

I start pounding on him, but he shoves me back against my seat and raises his fist, his expression fierce. "If you want me to deck you again, I will." He pauses, his eyes piercing mine, waiting for the fight to leave and the fear to return. When I stop struggling, he nods his head. Visibly satisfied, he continues. "It would be a shame to damage that beautiful face any more than I have to—the rest of your body?" He tilts his head and raises his eyebrows. "We'll see about that later."

He starts up the car. I crank my neck as far as it will go, watching Mila's lifeless body as we drive away. The tears begin to fall as I sit back, defeated.

"I knew the moment Mila called something was off, but I figured what the hell, and made my plans for the evening anyway. I never imagined you two would gang up on me." He looks over, impressed. "I'm not sure what your plan was—"

"I'm sorry!" I interrupt. He has to take me back. "It was dumb of us to underestimate you. I knew you were smart—"

"Damn right I am!"

"I just thought we could get you back for what you did to my car—it was totally stupid of us. Look, you made your point. Just take me back and we'll forget the whole thing."

He pretends to mull it over. "*Mmm* . . . no. We're going to have some fun. I told you, I made plans. You'll like it," he says, as if we're lovers.

I watch as the houses become more spread out, until there's nothing but grassy hills. Suddenly, he slams his hand against the steering wheel, making me jump. "Do you know what my father did when he found out I got kicked off the team! He broke two of my ribs!" He hits the steering wheel again.

No one knows where I am. My mind races as I try and figure out what to do next. I remember my phone in my back pocket. It's getting dark now. If I take it out, he'll see the lit screen. I'll have to leave it for now.

"You'd never know . . ." he says wistfully, his mood changing again. "All those times, I just let everyone believe they were sports injuries. It was so easy—the lies. Mom got tired of them, I think that's why she left—well, and the fact she couldn't handle the beatings. She was weak, though."

I look around as we turn onto a bumpy, dirt road.

"She deserved every beating she got. You know that?" He glances at me for confirmation. I just stare at him. "Dad said she was an ungrateful whore and was always flaunting herself. As if she could do better," he says as an afterthought. "You women are all alike—you don't know a good thing when you see it."

We pull up to a barn or maybe it's an old garage. A large door is hanging halfway off its hinges.

"It's pretty cool, isn't it?" He smiles at me, excited. "I found it when I was driving around. I do that to release my anger, you know. It's an emotion that needs to be kept contained to get what you want in life. I learned that from my father." He sounds envious. "It's the anger that drives me to be the best." He turns the car off. "Come on." He smiles brightly as he opens his door. "You'll see. I'm going to make you feel *so* good, you'll be *begging* me to take you back."

As soon as he gets out of the car, I whip out my phone, my fingers struggle as I quickly dial 911.

Josh yanks the door open and rips the phone out of my hands, throwing it as hard as he can. "You bitch!" He grabs me by the hair and drags me out of the car. My head hits the doorframe and everything goes black for a second. I stumble along behind him as he continues to pull me in the direction of the building. I grip his wrist to release some of the tension on my hair. "Josh! *Please*," I beg. "Stop!"

He changes his hold to my arm. I dig my heels into the ground. "Let me *go*!" He jerks hard, and I fall forward onto my hands and knees.

He stops and stares down at me as he releases a loud exasperated breath. "I'm sorry I hurt you. I didn't want to. Really, I didn't." He carefully pulls me to my feet and then caresses the side of my cheek with the back of his hand. I'm too stunned to move. He smooths my hair out of my face. "But you deserved it. I can't have you acting like that and expecting to get away with it. It's your own fault."

My head is pounding, making it hard to think clearly. He leans forward, pressing his lips gently to mine. "I want you so bad," he whispers. "Don't you know that?"

I shove hard against his chest. He growls and grabs my wrists, forcing them behind my back, then lifting them high, making me cry out. I'm pinned against his body. I struggle to get away. "Stop! I'm sorry."

"God, you feel good. You're making me so hard."

I freeze. "Please," I plead, tears falling. "Don't."

"You don't have to be scared. It might hurt at first, but after, you'll be *begging* for more. They all do." He relaxes his hold but keeps his grip on one wrist as he yanks me forward. I try to shake my hand loose while screaming as loud as I can.

"Scream all you want. No one will hear you. Actually, I kind of like it," he laughs. "This is going to be *awesome*!"

He gets me through the door. There's a filthy, half-torn mattress on the floor. "Oh my god. How many girls have you brought here?" I cry out.

"None, actually. Although, I wish I'd thought of it sooner. Mila was going to be the first, but this is much better. You are who I wanted anyway—wanted all along. Shandler was the one that made me see it. She knows me well, knew how much I would enjoy your company. Even told me I could have her anyway I wanted if I went after you. How could I pass up two-for-one? But then the dumb bitch said no. She thought she could play me." He backhands me. "You're all a bunch of liars." I put my hand to my mouth in shock. "*Shhh*—shhh. It's okay." He comes close, soothing. "I ended up having her anyway—just like she said, 'anyway I wanted.'" He licks his lips. "She was a hell-cat. I think I *still* have scratch marks." He laughs maniacally.

"Let me go!" I pull my hand loose from his grasp and run for the door, but he catches me quickly. Gripping me around the waist, he carries me kicking and screaming toward the mattress. Reaching it, he slams me down, then jumps on top of me, pinning my arms with his knees. I struggle against him, trying to gain my freedom.

"Keep it coming, baby," he taunts. "I like the fight. *Damn*. I should have brought a video camera."

"You are so sick!" I strain against his hold to scream in his face, all while tears stream down my face.

He clamps a hand around my throat, squeezing tight. I pull at his fingers, trying to loosen his hold so I can get air. Oh god! I can't pass out.

He leans down and brushes his lips over mine, releasing his grip slightly. I fight for a full breath, but before I can get it, he covers my mouth completely with his and forces his tongue inside.

"Please stop!" I beg, the words muffled against his mouth

He pulls back to look at me. "Stop?" He sounds incredulous. "I'm just getting started." He positions himself between my legs "You know you want it." He thrusts his hips into me. "Tell me how much you want it."

"Why are you doing this?" I cry.

"Because I can." He lifts his hips just enough so he can jam his hand down the front of my jeans—his fingers probing. I cry out in pain.

"Yeah. That's it. *Mmmm*. Can you feel how much I want you?" he says, grinding into me again.

I try to buck him off. "*Whoo-hoo*, you go, girl! I like a wild ride."

"Get off!" I shriek. Suddenly, the weight of him is gone.

"Cassie, oh my god, are you okay?" I feel a hand on my arm.

I punch and kick. "Don't touch me," I scream.

"Get back!" a voice yells.

"Cassie!" The voice pleads. It sounds so familiar, but disappears. "Mila?" I croak out. It sounds like Mila, but it can't be.

"My name is Officer James. You're safe now." A woman's face comes into view. She's kneeling next to me.

"Oh my god!" I wrap my arms around her as I cry out hysterically, then it all come back. "Please, we have to go!" I struggle against her to get up. "He might come back."

"It's okay. He's retrained. My partner has him. Just stay down."

I hear sirens.

"Cassie!"

"Mila? Is Mila here? Mila!" I scream.

"Cassie!" I feel her arms envelope me. "This is all my fault. Are you okay? Answer me!"

"Young lady! I told you to stay in the car."

I feel Mila being pulled away from me. "No!" I scream, gripping her with all the strength I have left.

"I'm so sorry," she says into my hair.

Racking sobs overtake me. I can't stop shaking. I'm so cold and I feel sick. I look around. "Oh my god! Get me off this mattress!"

Mila and the officer help me up. "It's okay, we've got you," the officer says. "Take it slow."

"I have to get out of here." I think I'm going to be sick. I take deep breaths trying to hold it off.

"I understand. Just stay with us," the officer says as she leads me outside. When we're out, I collapse, taking Mila with me. "Are you hurt?" The officer crouches down next to me. "Cassie, can you tell me? Are you hurt?" I can't stop crying long enough to answer. The sirens are loud now. "Listen. Do you hear? The ambulance is on its way, okay? You are in shock. I need you to be still until they get here." I feel a blanket being wrapped around me. "Just hang in there a moment and we'll get you to a hospital."

I look over just as a man is shoving Josh into the police car. I bury my head in Mila's shoulder. "I was so scared." I grip at her frantically. "Don't leave me. Please don't leave me."

"I won't." She's crying now too.

The EMT people bring a stretcher alongside me. One of them shines a light in my eyes while another person checks my pulse. There's a nice lady. She's talking to me. She has a kind smile. It's the last thing I see before everything goes black.

36

My head is pounding—everything hurts. I open my eyes, trying to orient myself to where I am. Mila is curled up in a chair next to me, Roxanne's talking to a nurse outside the door, Cody's asleep, holding my hand against his face, and my dad is standing by the window, staring out into the night.

"Dad?" my voice is barely audible.

"Cassie!" Mila yells.

Suddenly, there's a huge commotion—Cody is hugging me hard and yelling at me, Roxanne is crying and planting kisses all over my head and face, Mila has wrapped herself around my waist, squeezing the air out of me, and Jeff, who appears out of nowhere, is leaning over Cody looking at me with fearful concern. Through the assault, I see my dad at the end of the bed looking terrified.

"Hey! What are you doing?" A nurse yells, pulling everyone off of me. "All of you . . . get out. Now! I *need* to see how my patient is doing."

A major argument ensues from everyone except my father, who remains at the foot of my bed, staring at me.

"Dad?" No response. "I'm okay," I say cautiously. He looks so fragile, like he could shatter at any moment.

"Dad," I say again.

He covers his mouth and chokes out a sob. Everyone is still fighting with the nurse as she shoos them out the door.

Harold appears at his side. "She's going to be fine." He pats Dad on the back. "*And you*, Miss Cassie." His voice is stern, but his eyes show the deep affection. "I'll deal with you later."

I nod once as his words grip my heart.

"Come on." Harold tries to direct Dad toward the door, but he won't budge. "The nurse needs some time alone with her, then she's allowing everyone to take turns visiting. Cassie's going to be fine," he reassures him.

"Why didn't you tell me?" he says at last, looking devastated. "I could have helped."

"Come on, gentlemen," the nurse says impatiently as she tries to usher Dad and Harold out. "It's time to go."

Harold places his giant arm around the nurse's shoulders, escorting her out instead. "Cassie just needs a moment with her father." I hear him say as she stares up at him looking outraged. He looks over his shoulder at me and winks. I try to smile back, but it's too painful. I turn my focus back to my dad.

He comes over, sits gently on the side of my bed, and picks up my hand, cradling it gently. "If things were better between us," he chokes on the words, "you might have felt comfortable enough to talk to me."

"It wasn't that. Mila and I had already talked to the police, and they said they couldn't do anything without proof. Then he vandalized my car. Mila came up with the idea of taping a confession so we could give it to the police." Dad starts to object, but I cut him off. "I know . . . it was a bad idea—you don't even have to say it, but it made sense at the time."

The terrifying experience starts to replay in my mind. "Then it all went wrong!" I sob, the hysteria threatening to drown me. "Oh my god, Mila!" I sit up abruptly, trying to get out of bed. "He threw her to the ground, and she wasn't moving!"

"It's okay." Dad stops me, taking me into his arms. "You're safe. Mila is all right. Remember? You just saw her."

He rocks me gently as I cry. I grip him hard. "I was so scared."

"I know, baby." He strokes my hair. "It's going to be okay. You're strong. It's just going to take some time."

I hear the door open. "I'm sorry, Mr. Carson," the nurse says in a gentle voice, her bluster gone, "but I need some time with Cassie."

"You need to rest," he says getting up. I reluctantly let him go. "I'll just be outside."

He shuts the door behind me as the nurse changes my IV. "Do you have to go to the bathroom?" she asks. "You will be very lightheaded for a while and will need help."

"No, I'm okay."

"The Doctor has asked me to give you something to help you sleep." She injects a fluid into my IV. "I have a boy outside that says he's your boyfriend. He's getting out of control, fighting everyone to see you. Your father says it's okay to let him in. Do you want to see him now?"

"Yes, please."

The moment she opens the door and nods her head, Cody rushes in almost knocking the nurse over. She grumbles at him as she smiles.

"Cassie." He wraps his arms around me, squeezing tight.

"I'm so sorry." Fresh tears roll down my face.

He leans back, wiping them away. "I've never been so scared in my life. Why would you do something so stupid?" He doesn't let me answer. "When this panic finally leaves, I'm really going to be pissed at you." Tears well up in his eyes. "When Mila called, I couldn't understand her. I thought the worst. I thought I'd lost you." He wipes at the tears.

"No. It's okay. I'm here." I place a hand on his cheek. "What happened? Everything went black."

"The doctor said it was partially from the concussion you sustained, but also from shock. You look so beat up."

I touch my face—it's swollen and painful. "How did they find me?"

"I'm not a hundred percent sure, Mila talks so fast. But from what I understand, a neighbor called the police when they heard the yelling and a squad car was nearby. They found Mila just as she was standing up. They tracked your location from her phone, I think." Cody's eyes suddenly blaze with anger. "They heard you screaming, Cassie." He drops his head in his hand and breaths deep, then looks at me. "I swear, if he gets out for any reason, I will beat him within an inch of his life."

"I know. Let's hope it never happens." I'm so sleepy.

"Cassie," Cody shakes me gently, "are you okay?"

One eye manages to open. "The nurse gave me something to sleep." My words are slurred. "Don't leave me."

"I won't." Feeling safe with him next to me, a peaceful sleep takes over.

EPILOGUE

CODY and I are heading off to New York in a couple of weeks. He received a scholarship to a school in Brooklyn, and believe it or not, I made it into Pratt. My dad said he had nothing to do with it, but I'm not sure I believe him.

I won't be staying with Luigi and Maria, because my school is too far of a commute—it's near Cody's. It took a lot of arguing to get them to understand why it would be easier for me to live in the dorms. Eventually, they gave up the fight, but I had to promise to visit them three times a week. I'm not sure I can hold up to that, but I'll try. I can't wait to see them and introduce them to Cody.

After I recovered from my injuries, Harold took me and Mila to his gym and taught us self-defense techniques. He said there was no way he was letting me go to New York without knowing how to, as he put it, "Seriously defend myself."

Mila was a natural bad-ass and absorbed the training easily. Me . . . I needed a lot more practice. But in the end, I had Harold lying on the mat a couple of times. The man is ex-

Special Forces, so I know they were bogus takedowns, but it felt good anyway.

After our training was completed to his satisfaction, he decided to hold regular classes, free of charge, to anyone who wanted to learn. Harold's brother, George, who happened to be a black belt in jiu jitsu, got in on it as well.

Mila wouldn't stop beating herself up over what happened to me. I explained that I am my own person and make my own decisions. It was a stupid thing to do, but she did not *make* me go after Josh. I went of my own free will. She was accepted to the University of California and will work toward a double major in forensic science and psychology, with the hopes of getting accepted into the FBI training program. I think the whole thing with Josh cemented her desire to join the Force.

Since Josh was eighteen, he was tried and prosecuted as an adult. And it wasn't just from my testimony that sealed his fate, but testimonies from several other girls. The most surprising was Shandler. Going through the trial process was rough, but having so many friends and loved ones by my side, made it a lot easier.

My dad was upset that I was moving away so soon after he found me, so he bought a small apartment in Manhattan. That way we can visit between films. We still have a long way to go in building a relationship, but at least we've started. I've completely let go of my anger toward him. I figured there was no point hanging on to it. It doesn't serve a purpose, and besides, it would only hinder our attempt at moving forward. He is not the man he was.

I can't presume to know why my mom continued to hide from him. She must have seen from the media that he was successful and known it would be next to impossible to still be an abusive drunk and be that accomplished. I suppose she let her fear dominate her and for whatever reason, never allowed herself to accept the possibility he could change—that it might be safe enough to reconnect. Maybe when it comes to protecting a child, there's no chance worth the risk. I still feel she should have told me when I was older. And I struggle with everything she left out of our relationship—her past, all her memories and experiences. I would have liked to have been a part of those. But again, what's the point of hanging on to the resentment? It will only make me bitter, and I don't want to have those negative thoughts when I think of her. So I try to focus on how much she loved me and the moments we shared. That's all that should matter anyway.

Dad is working on a documentary about sexual abuse in high schools and universities—how easily it happens, the frequency, how the police and judicial system have their hands tied with ineffective laws, and how women can protect themselves. He also created a website with loads of information along with a link to Harold's self-defense classes, and a 24 hour national hotline for victims of rape or physical abuse. The best is his grassroots organization, funded by all the Bigs in Hollywood to help victims get the emotional support they need, as well as free legal advice and court representation when needed.

I'm beyond proud.

Me, I'm excited to continue doing what I love most . . . art. The thought of going back to New York is a bit scary—everything is so different—I'm different. And being faced with all those old memories will be hard, but I'll have Cody with me, as well as Maria and Luigi. I won't have to deal with it alone.

The trauma I experienced still comes back occasionally,

mostly from triggers—things I associated with the attack. I'm lucky, though. I have people around me that help when I need it. A lot of victims don't have that kind of a support system and have to cope with the horrors alone. I hope the work my dad is doing will help them.

I know now that I should never have stayed quiet about what Josh did to me. It's hard standing up and fighting for yourself when you feel victimized. It's easier to hide or blame yourself for what happened, but then the ones that hurt you are free to continue.

No one has a right to violate you—No one—Ever!

THE DREAM

Everything I Knew to be True is based on a dream I had. After finishing the novel, I thought it might be interesting for the reader to see how it all started.

I have very detailed dreams. When I had this one, I knew it was something more. As soon as I woke up, I wrote as much as I could remember on my computer. Obviously, it's in rough shape, but I thought I should present it in its raw form.

I had to go live with a family. I think my mother died or something. I am a teenager. The family has a son named Cody and his room is across the hall from mine. He is good-looking and I feel awkward around him because I'm so attracted to him. I grew up playing with him, his mom and mine were always together—they were best friends. I don't know about my father. The family I'm living with has a pool. I'm sitting outside and hear Cody's father fighting with another guy. Cody's dad is a builder or a contractor or something. They are yelling at each other. The man threatened to kill Cody's father. Something about the mob trying to extort money from him. I tell Cody and we try to help his father without him knowing. I have strong feeling for Cody and it hurts to be around him. We hide at his father's construction site one night to see if we can catch the bad guys, Cody kisses me, but were interrupted by a loud noise. I see the guy that was fighting with Cody's dad. I wake up.

Made in the USA
Coppell, TX
12 June 2023

17994764R00204